Captcha

Captcha Thief

by
Rosie Claverton

Captcha Thief © Rosie Claverton

ISBN 978-0-9933815-0-8
eISBN 978-0-9933815-1-5

Published in 2016 by Crime Scene Books

The right of Rosie Claverton to be identified as the author
of this work has been asserted by her in accordance with the
Copyright, Designs and Patents Act 1988.

A CIP record of this book is available from the British Library.

Printed in the UK by TJ International, Padstow.

For Huw – with you, I am home.

Acknowledgements

I cannot thank Deb Nemeth enough for her work as my editor and novel midwife, continuing to believe in this book and my writing when I was close to giving up. She elevates my writing to a different level and I am so very privileged to work with her.

Thank you to Sarah Williams and all at Crime Scene Books for giving Amy and Jason a future together on the page.

Because of these excellent people, this book is much richer: Professor Ken Pye, for his expert knowledge of beaches; Dyfed-Powys Police, for details of their emergency response and radio protocol; Lisa Gray, for being Jason's guide to Glasgow; and the Holyhead Coastguard, for helping me commit the perfect crime in their waters.

And thank you to the National Museum of Wales, a magnificent arts institution in the heart of Cardiff, and undeserving of the terrible crime I have placed at its door.

Chapter 1

A mere impression

Night after night, he returned to that one place.

If he listened very carefully, he could hear the water lapping against the gondola. His body seemed to sway with the gentle motion of the little boat, and the air held the cloying mist of a Venice evening, the rich aroma of ripe, roasting tomatoes drifting across the canals. The last rays of sunlight played warm across his face, before the great orb finally dipped below the horizon.

In that beautiful half-light, the vivid pinks and oranges of a Mediterranean sunset, the glorious San Giorgio Monastery loomed before him. With the sun behind the tower, he couldn't see the detail of it, only shadows in grey and greyer and black. It was breathtaking. It was priceless.

But the real beauty lay in the reflection. The building stretched out over the water, rippling with every wave, the boat moving with the monastery. No clear, still reflecting pool this. The ever-shifting waters tossed the light this way and that, until the magnificent tower was no more than an uncertain shadow on the water. An absence of colour.

Chink!

The sharp noise broke his reverie and Paul Roberts was back in Cardiff.

Angry at the disturbance, he moved his flashlight towards the sound. It was probably just the old building settling, shifting some of the workmen's tools. The museum renovations were taking bloody months – Mike from the day shift said the builders were more often holding mugs of tea than hammers and saws.

Paul returned to the picture, but Venice was gone, the illusion faded with that rude awakening. He was alone in the

1

chilled gallery, his ill-fitting uniform chafing against his skin. He scratched at the reddened skin where the waistband of his trousers dug into flesh. He had put on weight again.

He lumbered across the gallery, the last vestiges of Italy falling away behind him, as he headed for the pokey little security office and his instant noodles. He might stream the NFL kick off game – working night shifts had given him a taste for American sport. As a Welshman, his first loyalty was to the rugby, but American football had its charms. Even if those boys were sissies for needing all that padding just to run about a field.

Shhhhhck!

The ripping sound cut right through him and Paul turned on his heel, flashlight raised like a baton. 'Who's there?'

Between the little puddles of light around the artworks, the black was absolute, only made deeper by the brightness of the lights. Paul squinted into the black spaces, his heart beating up into his throat as the seconds stretched into millennia in his panic. Who was lurking in the darkness and what did they want? His boss was never going to forgive him – neglecting his duties, mooning at paintings. If something was lost, could he forgive himself?

He heard a whisper of movement to his right. Despite the screaming of his nerves, Paul ran through the archway into the adjacent gallery, looking left and right for the intruder.

Then he saw her.

The cruel rend was jagged, uneven across the background – more like a lumberjack's hack than a surgeon's precision. The top of the canvas had flopped over like a dog-ear, obscuring face and gloves and bustle. All that remained visible were her perfect skirts, fold upon fold of cerulean, azure and sapphire, and that cheeky inch of scandalous toe protruding beneath them.

The bastard had cut 'The Blue Lady'.

Paul could weep for her. His hand stuttered forward, to restore her beauty, but then he jerked back. He must not damage her. Talia and Soo-jin and Noah – they would know what to do for the best. They would save her.

2

He should call them right away, before the cops. They had to preserve her – the weight of the canvas threatened to tear her further, rip her open like one of Jack the Ripper's whores. Split open for the vultures—

Thud!

Paul's head collided with the painting and he slid, stunned, to the ground. He tried to get up, face his attacker, but his arms were strangely heavy, his legs uncooperative. His body was a sack of stones, beyond his control, a ghost of something like pain spreading over the back of his head.

He gasped for air that would not come and, as he looked up at the encroaching darkness, his vision was filled with the most perfect blue.

And a splatter of red.

Chapter 2

The mausoleum on the corner

The museum was lit up like a carnival, the flashing blue lights reflecting off the white marble façade as if a waterfall had suddenly sprouted from above the colonnade.

Jason parked his vintage Harley beside Detective Inspector Bryn Hesketh's unmistakeable unmarked car. While many ageing cops had back seats covered in dog hair, Bryn's was matted with the fallen strands from the heads of his brunette daughters. Jason had yet to discover either of their names, as Bryn had made it clear that he was risking his manhood by even asking.

Two uniformed coppers nodded as they let him through the cordon, no questions asked despite his shaved head and leather jacket. The pair were young enough to only remember Jason as the hacker's assistant and not from his prison record or handcuffing him for swinging a punch down St Mary Street on match day.

The imposing wooden doors stood open, midmorning light flooding the beautiful atrium. Jason hadn't visited the National Museum of Wales for years, not since he was a boy running among the dinosaurs, but time hadn't taken away from the awe he felt in the space. The vast marble ceiling stretched above him, dark red banners jutting out from the walls to contrast with the white. A statue sat at one end, frowning down at the horde of law enforcement officers that had taken up temporary residence.

Another uniform directed him up the right-hand sweeping staircase, past a tense, middle-aged woman wearing a bright, flowery blouse. She was frantically talking into her mobile phone in a language he didn't recognise, her striking eyebrows threatening to hit her hairline. Jason's knowledge of Welsh consisted of one to ten and a handful of stock phrases – 'I like

5

coffee', 'fish and chips, please' – but this sounded like something more European. Spanish, perhaps, which made sense with the light brown tint to her skin. The woman nervously wiped her forehead with a handkerchief, beads of sweat immediately replacing those removed. 'Bad day at the office' didn't even begin to cover it.

At the top of the stairs, Jason rounded the balcony and looked down into the hall below. It was huge, beautiful staircases at each end, and framed by a circular gallery at the top. The statue suddenly seemed small, barely more than an ornament on a stark mantelpiece.

Behind him, someone cleared their throat. Jason turned and recognised the sour-faced crime scene attendant waving a pair of white overalls and little booties at him. He donned them without much fuss – an old pro at this crime scene malarkey – and signed his name on the clipboard: *Jason Carr. Assistant to Amy Lane, Independent Police Consultant.*

He ducked the crime scene tape and stepped into an art gallery. Even with his Neanderthal tastes, Jason could tell this was pricey stuff, a collection of the best paintings in Wales. Some of the pictures looked vaguely familiar. It was a pretty impressive collection if he recognised the paintings.

However, as he couldn't see a crime scene, he walked on before hearing voices from the right-hand gallery. As he entered, he was struck by the famous flowers on water painting by that French bloke. Lily pads? Something like that.

'From the stellate shape of the wound, I think we're looking at a garden-variety hammer.'

Indira Bharani's voice carried easily in the small space and Jason's eyes were drawn to the pathologist. She was kneeling beside the body of a security guard with a bloody mess where the back of his head should be. She nodded to Jason as he entered, and he was glad for her calm, considered presence over her more intolerant colleagues. The police department still held plenty of animosity towards outsiders hanging with their pack, especially when those outsiders were ex-cons.

Behind Indira and the body, DI Bryn Hesketh examined a seemingly-empty picture frame. It was massive, stretching from Bryn's ankles to just above his head. It took Jason a moment to realise this wasn't some piece of modern art, but a painting with a large hole in it.

'Robbery gone wrong?' he asked, gaining Bryn's attention.

'Looks like,' Bryn said. His suit's creases had creases, and his greying hair had several tufts out of place – he'd obviously been roused from his bed by the case, called in on his day off. The privilege of being the most senior detective in the department, one of only a few left after a recent shake-up.

He beckoned Jason closer. 'But see here, how this bit of blood has a tear through it?'

'He killed him and then he finished removing the painting.'

Jason expected to feel revulsion, the turn of his stomach, but he was surprisingly unmoved. Maybe he was getting used to murder.

'He was stone cold about it. I think we're dealing with a professional.'

Bryn's gloved fingers dipped into his pocket for his ever-present leather notebook.

'Though he wasn't expecting trouble,' Indira interjected, her dark eyes flashing between her cap and mask. 'A hammer is a poor murder weapon.'

'What did he steal?' Jason asked.

The remaining canvas was a wash of pale blues, pinks and greys and could've belonged to anything, no trace of its main subject visible in what remained.

'Only the most famous piece in the museum.'

Jason grinned at the newcomer, clapping Detective Sergeant Owain Jenkins on the shoulder so that his floppy fringe bounced.

'Owain! When did you start back?'

Owain's return smile was a touch off his usual easy expression. 'Two weeks or so. First time they've let me away from my desk.'

Jason regretted bringing it up now. He didn't want to think about the visits to Owain's hospital bed or the weeks after, when he was too pale and too tremulous to even hold a spoon. A gunshot wound had almost stolen him away, the resulting fallout from the botched investigation sending an earthquake through the department. From what Jason had heard, the detective superintendent had lost his job and they were down two full-time detectives. No wonder Bryn had bags under his eyes.

Owain quickly reported to Bryn, as if he was also eager to shrug off the past few months. 'Security logs confirm that there was no break-in. The robber-slash-killer used one of the staff's swipe cards – uniforms are with her now. Her car was broken into last night.'

'Professional outfit. I knew it.' Bryn turned to Jason. 'That's where you come in, boy.'

Jason was jotting down notes in his own notebook, near identical to the ones in Bryn's and Owain's hands.

'Sure. I'll tell Amy the bones of it. She'll want to see the security logs, of course, and the CCTV footage.'

Bryn hesitated. 'That's not … This one's not for Amy.'

Jason looked at him blankly. 'But you called me.'

'You. I called you. I was hoping you had a few old street contacts who might know who's dealing in art over coke these days.'

Jason laughed. 'I was never in that kind of gang. We were more into chucking stones at expensive cars and—'

'Robbing the gold exchange.'

Jason's expression was stone. 'Nothing to do with me, that one.'

The oft-repeated lie came smoothly and Bryn obviously didn't believe a word of it. They maintained the polite fiction that Jason had paid his public dues for all his crimes and that Bryn didn't know the truth about how Jason ended up in prison.

'Well, see what you can dig up.'

Bryn turned back to the painting and Jason felt like he'd been dismissed, even though the whole thing sat uneasily in his gut. How could he go back to Amy and tell her that he had a case but she didn't?

'So … you're not after Amy at all? You're really gonna leave her out of a murder?'

He caught the look between Bryn and Owain. It was a look full of secrecy – and doubt. If no answers were forthcoming, Jason would work on the younger cop down the pub after they finished for the day.

'She's got a lot on her plate, hasn't she? Between those private cases and this new-found love of the great outdoors?'

'I wouldn't go that far,' Jason said.

He had seized on Amy's ability to make it into his car with only one or two pills as a crutch, just taking the edge off her crippling agoraphobia, enough for her to make that giant leap without descending into panic. He could persuade her outside the house for short excursions, sitting in car parks at the edges of natural beauty spots and gazing at them through glass.

'Well, whatever she's up to, it'll do her good to have a break, won't it?'

Bryn wouldn't meet his eyes. What was going on here?

The uneasy feeling intensified and Jason decided to play on his friends' soft hearts.

'Listen, she's bored to tears. She needs something to focus on, something nice and legal that we can all approve of.'

'*Legal* isn't the word I'd have used,' Owain muttered.

'What you don't know can't hurt you,' Jason said. 'Please, Bryn – she's driving me crazy. Do us a favour, will you?'

'All right, all right.' Bryn held up his hands in surrender. 'She can look at the CCTV. But I don't want her sticking her nose into art trafficking. That's big business for the gangs, bigger than drugs. She'd be tempting all sorts of trouble down on her.'

'I'll tell her to be careful.' But Jason knew there was a fat chance of that once Amy heard the painting's story. International paper trails were her favourite type of hunting.

'Make sure you do. Can't lose our pet hacker now, can we?'

Jason grinned. She might struggle to step outside the front door, but Amy always dived in head first where a murder was concerned. He would never be able to keep her away from a chase like this.

And, when the fire filled her eyes, the thrill of investigation animating her body, Jason couldn't see why he'd ever want to.

Chapter 3

Oil and water

Amy checked her email for the tenth time that morning – nothing. Zip, nada, nowt.

The investigation front had been quiet for weeks, aside from the usual cheaters and petty thefts. Her brain itched for activity, the need to solve a puzzle, put together the connections that would lead to a victory, an arrest, justice.

After weeks of enforced hiatus, while Amy recovered from her injuries and Jason waited for the criminal justice system to come to its senses, she wanted to leap out of the gate and straight into a case. Instead, they had bumbled along without much to entertain them except Netflix and Jason's culinary attempts to interest Amy in vegetables.

And they had Jason's sudden desire to explore the wilder, greener side to Cardiff and its surrounds. It was a fervour Amy could've done without, but Jason loved being out and about and she liked the way he smiled at her when he was driving her to somewhere new, sharing his Cardiff with her.

Her phone buzzed and she picked it up without looking. 'Jason?'

'I have a case for us.'

Amy vaguely recalled Jason saying something about Bryn that morning, but she'd been in the middle of a Creeper attack on Minecraft and thought it safe to ignore him.

'Robbery? Murder?'

'How about both? I'm bringing some CCTV home and I'll fill you in then.'

As he disconnected, Amy felt a burst of warmth at the way he said 'home'. Most of his stuff was here now, not at his mother's, and Amy sometimes liked to pretend that if she stopped paying him, he would still stay. They were friends. He was her best friend.

Amy had never had a best friend before. She had retreated into the house during her early teen years and never really left. She had friends in every corner of the globe, connected to them via various different threads of communication, but nobody who knew her. Not like Jason knew her.

It was for him that she had agreed to venture beyond the front door. If she had a couple of diazepam, she could just manage it. Not claw the car door apart or start screaming incoherently. She had coped before, she told herself – it would get easier. The car doors were still intact, at least.

She brought up the BBC News website to see if she could work out their case from the local headlines. But she didn't have to go further than the front page, the robbery and murder at the National Museum of Wales the top story after some agitation in Eastern Europe. A dead security guard and a missing masterpiece had earned Cardiff a spot on the national stage, although the city was probably sick of murder-tinged publicity.

She felt the thrum of curiosity in her blood, her mind already leaping away to all the possibilities, the theories. Her fingers danced of their own accord, the data singing to her as she threw herself out into the streams.

By the time Jason came home – *home* – she would know 'The Blue Lady' inside out. He was always so impressed by the way she found things out, how her mind deciphered all the pieces of the puzzle until they formed a cohesive whole.

He inspired her to be better. She wanted so desperately to be better for him.

Jason headed down to the security office with Owain and took the CCTV footage into his custody. He left Owain to ask some follow-up questions and was heading back down the corridor to the front entrance when he heard a woman crying.

He stepped through an open doorway into a workshop with various works of art dotted around the benches. Everything from canvas to pottery to jewellery was included in the collection, in different states of restoration or cleaning. Some works were protected from prying eyes, shrouded in heavy dust covers against the walls. Beneath an elegant scabbard from which an antique sword handle protruded, the crying woman sat at a desk, sobbing into her handkerchief. Her bobbed black hair covered one half of her face entirely, but from what he could see, she looked East Asian, in her late-twenties, and wore a white smock covered in smudges of paint.

'You all right, love?' he asked, which was a stupid question, because clearly she wasn't.

She jerked upright and waved the handkerchief in front of her face. 'I'm fine. It's nothing.'

He perched on the bench beside her. 'Doesn't look like nothing to me. Did you … did you know him?'

She started crying again and scrubbed at her eyes desperately. 'You will think me so heartless. I didn't know him.'

Jason didn't know what to make of that – until he recognised the painting behind her as another of those particular oil paintings, the ones with the splodges that looked like the artist was in a hurry. Like *Water Lilies* and the missing blue lady, around which this woman's world was built.

'Don't worry,' he said. 'We'll find the picture.'

She looked painfully grateful for his understanding. 'Thank you, sir.'

'Soo-jin! No visitors allowed in the workshop.'

The owner of the voice had a tumble of dark curls, loosely tied close to her neck, and darker eyes. She had one hand on her hip, the picture of indignation in a paint-stained white coverall, and was shadowed by a skinny man with an artful three-day stubble and a smock similar to Soo-jin's.

Jason stood up to greet them properly. 'I'm with the police.'

The woman snorted like a hog. 'The police? Don't be absurd. Get out before I have you arrested.'

'I'm a police consultant,' he tried to explain, even though it was a little white lie.

But she wasn't buying it. 'You're a hack, don't deny it. Playing on Soo-jin's naïveté.'

'Talia!' Soo-jin protested, but it fell on deaf ears.

'I am counting to ten. If you're not gone by then, I will scream and bring all those nice uniformed officers down on you.'

Jason drew a business card out of his pocket and handed it to Soo-jin. 'If you need anything,' he said, before walking past the angry Talia and back out into the museum.

He bumped into Owain in the atrium and they silently walked out together towards the Harley.

'Right odd lot, they are,' Jason said. 'One woman crying over a picture and another paranoid that I'm a journo.'

'That's the price of being a genius. Just look at Amy.'

Jason thought Amy's oddities were more tied to her volatile anxiety than her oversized brain, but he didn't correct Owain. He spent most of his waking hours with Amy – she took time to decode, and he wasn't surprised that most others didn't have her figured out.

'Give my love to Cerys,' Owain said, as he opened his car door.

Jason paused before putting on his helmet. 'You're seeing her tomorrow, aren't you?'

'Can't now, can I? Not with a case like this on the books.'

Jason had seen precious little of his sister since she'd started police training, and the weekends she wasn't studying were more likely to be devoted to Owain than anyone else. Jason didn't mind the cop dating Cerys because he was a good bloke, but he didn't like her being messed around.

Owain shrugged helplessly and got in the car. Jason watched him drive off, bemused. For him, family always came first. If his mam or sister needed him, he would drop everything in a heartbeat.

But then he also worked for his best friend and she would always need more looking after than Gwen and Cerys combined. Other people had jobs they left at the door, but acting as Amy's live-in assistant demanded everything from him. Friday was technically his day off, but he'd chosen to answer Bryn's call. Chose work over hanging out with his mate Dylan at his garage, tinkering with dodgy motors and dodgier parts, or going out for a few pints. Maybe that meant he was finally growing up.

Or maybe he had caught the mystery bug and couldn't walk away.

Chapter 4

Mad skillz

By the time Jason arrived home, Amy knew everything about *La Parisienne*.

The artist was a renowned Impressionist painter – so famous even Amy had heard of him – and the model a theatre actress. Demure and ladylike by today's standards, she had been a sexual provocateur in her time. And now she had been stolen.

'How did you find that?' Jason asked.

'I turned on the news.'

Amy suppressed a thrill at the pleasant surprise in his voice. She liked to surprise him.

'Here's the CCTV.' He offloaded a couple of CDs on the desk. 'Indira's going to email you her report when she's done.'

'This is going to be a very different murder.'

'Why'd you say that?' His voice carried from the kitchen and Amy could hear the kettle rising to the boil.

'The victim wasn't chosen. He was unlucky. The crime worth investigating is the theft.' Amy paused, her imagination kicking into gear. 'Unless the killer stole the painting to cover up the murder. Maybe Paul had made enemies among the museum staff and they plotted together to kill him in the night, make it look like a robbery.'

'The security card was stolen.' Jason placed a mug of tea at her elbow, traditional chocolate digestive balanced on the rim. 'And it's a lot of trouble to go to just to kill a guy.'

'There are simpler explanations.' Amy tapped the digestive against the side of the mug, leaving a chocolaty smudge. 'I should do a social media check just in case.'

'What do you want from me?' Jason asked.

It was a dangerous question, when he was looking at her like that in the reflection of her blank third monitor. But Amy knew the way he meant it – the only way he meant it.

'Do you know anyone who deals in fine art?'

Jason burst out laughing, which was unexpected and unnerving. Amy felt a prickle of heat on her neck and shoulders, anxiety rising.

'What? What's so funny?'

'You and Bryn have strange ideas about Cardiff street life.'

Amy's fear died away. 'What about Lewis?'

Jason's childhood friend was currently locked up in Swansea Prison, which was where Jason would be – if he'd made it to the gold heist. His best friend Lewis had been resentful for a long time and it had taken a family tragedy to bring them back together, brothers once more. Amy was pleased that Jason had friends, even if they were notorious felons.

'I can ask him,' Jason said. 'I'm heading over tomorrow anyway.'

'I'll search from this side.'

Finding the secret dealers of priceless artefacts would be more than difficult. When your client had enough money to splash out on a liberated museum piece, he had enough money to hire bad guys to come after you if it all went pear-shaped. Security was the highest priority, and anonymity the next.

'Bryn says be careful.'

Amy made a vague humming noise, only half listening as she clicked on another link about Henriette Henriot, the actress in the missing painting.

Jason kept talking. 'Guess you don't just type "missing Renoir for sale" into Google.'

'That was almost funny. Have you been practising?'

Her remote connection to Bryn's desktop at Central Police Station registered a new glut of evidence, which she greedily downloaded. She scanned the preliminary crime scene report and then reached out to smack Jason on the arm.

'You didn't tell me Owain was back.'

'Owain's back.'

'How does he … look?'

Her right leg twinged as she asked, a phantom pain that was all in her head. Like so many things that ailed her. She and

Owain had barely escaped their last major case with their lives, and the memories lingered even if the scars were fading.

She could've reached out to him, let him know that the nightmares were normal and soon he would feel able to face life again. Except that had never been true for her, and this latest haunting was no better or worse than those that had preceded it. From a simple childhood embarrassment that had crippled her to fighting for her life, the result was always the same: more anxiety, more nightmares, retreating into the darkness beneath her duvet.

But she had Jason now. And the work, the mysteries that made it worth getting out of bed and facing her fears. Most days.

'All right,' Jason said, giving nothing away before changing the subject. 'Cerys is free this weekend. Might have her over for dinner one night.'

Amy noticed how he had given up asking her to join them at Gwen's house, knowing she would always say no. She couldn't handle the anxiety of even thinking about entering a place so foreign and remaining trapped there all evening, away from her sanctuary.

She reviewed the rest of Bryn's evidence – a few crime scene photos, but fingerprints and DNA still processing – before digging out her old DVD drive to transfer the CCTV to her server downstairs. After the police had poked around in it, she had spent the whole summer refitting it with Jason's assistance. It was hot work, even with the air conditioning working at full power, and Jason had removed his shirt on a few occasions.

She needed to find an outlet for this tension before it became unprofessional. It might be time to review the Ann Summers catalogue for the fifth time since Jason had started working for her.

Amy had always considered herself focussed and dedicated, when her depression was bearable. But her attention was waning, more intent on watching her assistant than keeping an eye on the evidence. Though he was an attractive man, it went deeper than that – she depended on him. He was vital to her.

17

'You all right?'

Jason's voice brought her back and she realised she was holding the CD over the open drive, staring off into space.

'Tired.'

It was her default excuse. The one that would prevent further questions from him. Stop him guessing the real cause of her absent-mindedness.

Processing the discs took a few minutes, so she looked over the crime scene photos, forcing herself to look, really look. But nothing was going in and Jason leaning over her shoulder in his customary position wasn't helping.

'It's a funny choice of weapon,' he said.

'Maybe it's all he had.'

'For a pro? Your backup plan for a job gone wrong isn't a hammer to the head when a gun pressed against his back would do the job, or even something gun-shaped if you can't get hold of the real deal. Why risk the time for GBH or murder when the threat works better anyway?'

At moments like these, Amy was abruptly reminded of Jason's past. She didn't ask exactly what he would choose, or whether his experience was practical. Some things were better left in the dark.

AEON, her loyal computer, beeped to let her know the CCTV transfer was complete, and Amy cast a look over the files.

'Only the past twenty-four hours. I'll need at least a week to look for the reconnaissance men.'

'I'll get you the rest tomorrow.'

To Amy's ears, he sounded bored, distracted. She glanced back at him and saw the phone in his hand.

'Text?'

'It's nothing,' he said and put the phone away.

Keeping secrets. Probably another woman, as per usual. Amy had lost count, though she kept the background checks saved in a private corner of her server. He was her assistant and it was in her interest to protect him. Or so she told herself.

Amy pushed her thoughts to one side and opened up the CCTV. She chose to examine the murder window first. The first disappointment was that the footage was in greyscale, silent, and not infrared-enabled. However, they had placed a camera directly on their masterpiece.

'There he is.'

Jason had returned his attention to the monitor, as a person dressed all in black and wearing a balaclava entered the room. He made a beeline straight for the painting – and did nothing. He seemed in awe of it, taking in every inch of the picture. He then examined the frame, looking but not touching, patient and thorough.

'What's he doing?' Jason voiced both their thoughts as Amy tried to detect the method in his madness.

'He's looking for the alarm triggers?' Amy hazarded a guess, but she had no idea.

After this continued for several minutes, he withdrew something from his pocket and started tapping tentatively at the frame.

And then he dropped it.

He froze, listening. Slowly crouching, he tucked his gloved fingers under the hammer and attached it to a belt. Returning to the picture, he withdrew something else from the belt and suddenly slashed along the top of the frame. He started drawing the knife down the right-hand side – and stopped.

He moved away from the picture, out of frame, and a few moments later, another man ran into the shot. He approached the painting and stared.

'The security guard,' Jason said.

The attack was swift. The man in the balaclava leapt in and knocked Paul Roberts over the head.

'He's short. Look at how he hit him overhead like that. A whole head shorter than the guard.'

Jason's commentary broke the spell of the gruesome film, the victim falling forward to head-butt the canvas. His legs collapsed beneath him and he fell on his face in front of the painting.

The body's legs twitched and then lay still. The man in the balaclava stood over him for a long moment before reaching down and removing the hammer from his head. He wiped it on his own trousers and returned it to his belt, before standing over the security guard's body and continuing to cut.

'Fuck, that's cold.'

'He wiped the hammer on his clothes,' Amy wondered, stuck on that detail. 'Specific evidence that links him directly to the crime. How could he be so stupid?'

'He killed him instantly. Must be a professional.'

'On his trousers! Surely an amateur.'

They looked at each other, Amy not quite meeting Jason's eyes. She was torn between demurring to him, placating him, and standing her ground, acting like his boss. Instead, she said nothing.

The footage played on. The thief and murderer cut free 'The Blue Lady', reaching above his head to finish the left-hand side, and rolled her up. He walked away with the painting tucked under his arm, leaving the dead man in his wake and never looking back.

'We have an unshakeable witness to this murder and yet we have no idea who did it.' Frustration burned in Amy's veins. The evidence was forensically perfect, yet next to useless.

'We have the weapon, the motive and the opportunity,' Jason said, his voice echoing her quiet fury. 'But the suspect list could be infinite. That painting must be worth millions.'

'Forty million. And hundreds of private collectors willing to pay at least that to possess her.'

'Her?' Jason sounded amused. 'It's a picture of a lady, not a real one.'

She was real once. Amy held her tongue, because she knew how ridiculous that sounded. She didn't know why the theft of a picture should affect her like this. It was a lifeless thing.

But it wasn't, was it? The unspeakable blues of that dress paled in comparison to her flawless skin, the sparkle of mischief in her eyes, the knowing smile. To Amy, she was a missing woman akin to a kidnap victim.

Amy cycled through the feeds and noticed a conspicuous absence. 'That's strange. The laboratory area has no cameras.'

'Makes sense – cover the expensive stuff with the best money can buy, but leave the back rooms with nothing.'

'Not if you want to uncover a thief's exit strategy.'

Amy picked up the feeds from the external cameras, each guarding one of three exits from the museum, and waited. After fifteen minutes, she set the footage to fast forward, speeding through the minutes and hours until the image lightened with the dawn. As the time stamp rolled over to 08:30, a female security guard approached the side door and opened it with her swipe card.

'Where is he?' Jason asked.

Amy continued to watch the door, as a number of museum staff filtered in. Then, the police came crashing in through the front door and the museum was locked down, a few staff members milling around outside as those inside presumably remained in the CCTV black spot until the police could interview them.

The footage cut out at exactly nine o'clock – the end of twenty-four hours of footage. The rest of the day was still recording at the museum.

'I need that CCTV,' Amy said. 'Because, going by the evidence we have—'

'The thief never left the museum.'

Chapter 5

Me and my shadow

When Jason reached the museum, the mass of police officers had been reduced to a couple of plods reluctantly keeping watch in front of yards and yards of crime scene tape.

While Amy searched for old city maps and blueprints of the museum building, Jason played errand boy by fetching the rest of the day's CCTV along with the preceding week to check out anyone looking shady. When Amy latched on to a theory, she was like a dog with a bone and everyone else servants to her master plan.

Jason didn't recognise either copper on the door, so he felt around in his jacket pockets for the ID Bryn had given him. Nothing.

The Carr charm was probably not going to cut it, as both officers would be up for disciplinary action if they let in a reporter by mistake. Besides, one of the lads already looked nervous at his presence. They were more likely to arrest him than call Bryn to see if he checked out.

'Skulking around crime scenes? Anyone would think you're a criminal.'

Jason scowled at his smart-arse sister, as Cerys strode over to him. Her probationary constable uniform was immaculate, though tufts of peroxide blonde hair escaped the confines of her pristine cap.

'What you doing here?'

'Lead didn't work out.'

Jason knew he wasn't the smartest bloke, but he also knew Cerys wasn't allowed on cases yet and Central Police Station was just across the way. He was going to have words with Owain when he saw him.

'Uh-huh. Fancy helping Amy out for a bit?'

Without further instruction, Cerys marched up to the cordon and beamed at the two officers, all eager eyes and bouncing on her toes.

'Y'alright? DI Hesketh sent me over to fetch some evidence. Pretty exciting stuff, isn't it? I've never worked a murder before!'

The officers rolled their eyes and lifted the cordon, as Jason sidled up beside her.

'And I'm—'

'The evidence courier. Have a good evening, now.'

Cerys yanked on Jason's arm and dragged him into the museum.

'Oi! I'm not the courier!' His protest echoed around the great marble hall.

'You want to tell them you're an ex-convict and maybe they'd seen your face all over the news a few months ago? Why was that again?'

'Shut up,' he muttered.

'Can I help you?'

Jason registered the vivid colours of the blouse before he recognised the Spanish-speaking woman from earlier, though her accent was definitely American.

'Afternoon,' Cerys said, before Jason could answer. 'I'm Probationary Constable Cerys Carr and we're here to collect some...'

She glanced at Jason and he realised he'd never actually told her why they were there.

'CCTV footage.'

'I'm the curator – Lucila Paniagua.' She reached out to shake Cerys' hand. 'Any news of our lady?'

Cerys shook her head, and genuine sorrow filled the woman's face. It was almost as if she'd lost a relative, regarding 'The Blue Lady' as a person just like Amy had. Though Lucila had probably seen the picture every day, while Amy had only had her first glance an hour ago. She continued to mystify Jason, even after nearly a year of working for her.

Lucila escorted them personally to the security office, where the security guard confessed that they only had four days of footage.

'We only have so many discs,' she said. 'But you'll catch him, won't you? For Paul?'

'We'll do what we can,' Cerys said, a second before Jason wanted to promise her they would. 'When the museum reopens tomorrow, keep an eye out for anyone suspicious. Especially in the galleries.'

The guard nodded seriously, as if the instruction was being burned into her brain, before Lucila walked them to the side door down a bland staircase.

'Security are taking it hardest,' the curator said. 'The rest of us didn't know Paul well – Christmas parties, things like that. He only worked night shifts. He loved the time alone in the galleries.'

'Why was that?' Jason asked.

'He had a passion for the Impressionists, more than some of our technicians. He'd spend hours with … what was it? *San Maggiore*? The cleaners have to go over that spot of floor every morning, because of the scuffs from him staring.' A sad light entered Lucila's eyes. 'But not anymore, I suppose.'

When they reached the door, Jason noted the second police cordon and a plastic evidence bag taped over the external card readers and keypad.

'This where he got in?'

'You know better than me.'

Jason glanced back up the stairs, remembering their route. 'And how many cameras on this stretch?'

'Only one outside the door and one at the end of the laboratory corridor. We had some tools go missing last year. Our senior technician Talia insisted we monitor the staff.'

'I bet she did.' Jason remembered well the wounds from her tongue-lashing.

Lucila smiled. 'I see you've met. She's broken-hearted over the painting. We all are.'

Jason decided to just throw his wackier line of questioning out there. 'And this is one of only three doors, right? No other … hidden exits or secret passageways?'

Lucila started to laugh, the sound threatening to take over her entire body, before she brought her mirth under control.

'If there are, no one's told me.'

Lucila left them at the door, Jason tucking the discs inside his jacket as they passed the cordon. A dense Cardiff drizzle was falling, the overcast sky turning afternoon to premature evening.

'You staying round Mam's tonight?' Jason asked.

Cerys rounded on him. 'Why do you say that?' She was sharper than him, always had been, and she jabbed a manicured finger into his chest. 'You knew Owain was blowing me off this weekend.'

'What you and Owain get up to—'

'Fuck off! You knew, didn't you?'

Jason strode back towards the Harley at the front of the museum, forcing Cerys to trot to keep up. 'It's the case, Cerys. Nothing personal.'

'I get to decide whether it's personal, not you! You could've warned me.'

'No way am I your go-between. I run enough errands for Amy and Bryn.'

She sulked silently until they got back to the bike, the rain falling in heavy droplets now, beating a rhythm on his uncovered head.

'Want a lift down Butetown?' he asked, grudgingly.

'Yeah, all right.'

He gave up his helmet to her, as she climbed on the pillion and he kick-started the bike. Nothing. The engine didn't even splutter, the nothingness of a failed start.

He tried again with the same result. Frustrated, he climbed off and looked it over, hoping to spot something obvious he could tidy up and be on his way.

'You need to stop relying on rust buckets,' Cerys said.

'This is a genuine 1940s Harley Davidson,' Jason said with feeling.

'Yeah, yeah, Cap's bike – I remember. Better make my own way while you haul that into Dylan's garage.'

She was off before he could stop her, but she had a point. He couldn't strip down the engine in the centre of Cardiff, and definitely not in the rain. He made a quick call to Dylan, who chastised him for dropping out of their drinks date by text before arranging to pick up the bike round the back of the university's creatively named Main Building. The students weren't back yet and they'd have some room to manoeuvre both the bike and the old truck.

Jason walked the Harley round the other side of the museum, ignoring the amused laughter from the police on guard. He, at least, would soon be out of the rain, whereas their shift lasted hours. The mean-spirited glee warmed him as he passed the closed museum car park on his right and the memorial park on the left. The roads around Park Place were lined with cars, cheap parking near the city centre hard to come by, but he saw only a few people, on their way to somewhere else.

He found a spot for the Harley outside Main Building, a name more befitting an anonymous concrete monster than the elegant marble affair with a flourishing garden. It was tempting to seek shelter in the foyer, but without the hubbub of students and considering the recent crime on their doorstep, security would be twitchy around strangers.

Speaking of strangers... A striking blonde across the street caught his eye. She was maybe early thirties with a shining head of golden hair, a more natural shade than Cerys' platinum blonde, turning bronze under the rain. Her coat was expensive, the kind they sold knock-offs of down the market, and beneath it she wore a pinstripe trouser suit with high-heeled boots.

And she was standing next to a posh Mercedes 4x4 without getting in it.

Jason looked for any explanation for her standing in the rain, but she didn't check a watch or phone, wasn't smoking a cigarette. Thinking about cigarettes stirred something in his veins, but he forced it down. After a stubborn chest infection that just wouldn't shift, Amy had cajoled him into quitting – ninety-three days and counting. Felt like a decade.

The woman could just be lost. Or waiting for someone. But maybe she was an art thief returning to the scene of the crime, trying to discover how much the police knew about her.

They'd assumed the person on the video was a man, but Jason couldn't swear to it. Without her heels, she might be about the right height, judging by the roof of the 4x4. Maybe she had seen him emerge from the museum and thought he knew something, because who else could she be watching?

Jason nonchalantly pulled his phone from his pocket, fired off a text to Amy, and walked off down the road. If he was wrong, no harm done. If he was right, though ... this would be the breakthrough they needed to feed this case and reclaim the painting. It would be nice to see his name on some positive news stories for a change.

He walked past the Main Building and right up a ramp to the made-over Biomedical Sciences building. The nauseating smell of formaldehyde oozed from the basement windows, the signature scent of the preserved human bodies the medical students dissected here.

At the ramp, he turned left and flattened himself against the wall. Looping his Bluetooth headset over his ear, he heard Amy's voice as clearly as if she stood next to him.

'Main Building camera too far for a face, but she's definitely on the move. Stand by.'

He could tell when Amy had been watching too much crime drama because her phone calls were styled after police radio. He forced his shoulders to relax, a stance of readiness not rigid tension. He wasn't looking for a fight, but one always seemed to find him anyway.

'On the ramp. ETA twenty seconds.'

He was cutting off her supply of *Homeland*. It was the only solution.

The woman rounded the corner and Jason moved, crowding her against the wall without laying a finger on her.

'You my secret admirer?'

She arched an eyebrow. 'What's to admire, Mr Carr?'

The tension flooded back, setting his teeth on edge. 'Who says?'

She withdrew a leather cardholder from her pocket and Jason internally groaned before she even flipped it open.

'Frieda Haas, National Crime Agency. What's a notorious thief doing at the scene of an art heist, hmm?'

'I work for Amy Lane, Police Consultant. I was there on official business.'

However long he spent out of jail, he would never shake the label of *thief*. No matter how many cases he solved with Amy, the past wouldn't leave him alone.

'Your private investigator licence, please.' She held out her hand, but in a way that meant she knew he had nothing to show.

'I'm her assistant. I fetch and carry, run errands.'

Jason had no idea whether Amy had a licence, but he suspected the answer was no. She could probably find one at short notice, however. The advantage of knowing the back doors of so many government departments.

'The legislation doesn't come into force until next year.' Amy's voice returned to his ear.

Shit, he'd been played.

'Is that badge legit?' Amy continued. 'I'll check the National Crime Command database.'

'Can your employer verify—?'

'Have you met Bryn yet?' Jason asked. One sure-fire way of checking her out.

'Bryn?' she said blankly, setting off all sorts of warning alarms in his head. But then the mist lifted. 'You mean DI Hesketh? I've not yet had the pleasure.'

'You often start snooping around before letting the city cops know you're here?'

'You know a lot about cops, don't you? Comes from staring at them from across the interrogation table.'

'Why don't you come down the station and learn with me? I'm sure Bryn would love to interrogate you.'

'Are you arresting me?' Her voice was mocking, almost teasing. 'Or did you leave your handcuffs at home?'

Something about her gnawed at him, like an itch that needed to be scratched. She was hot, no denying it, but her cool blue eyes gave away absolutely nothing. He wondered what it would take for her to show her hand.

'Don't trust her.' Amy again. 'Don't go anywhere with her alone.'

Jason slipped the headset from his ear. 'I'm sure you'll come quietly.'

'Oh, I wouldn't be so sure of that.'

Her smirk would stay with him, he knew, as she walked away down the ramp and Jason followed. He couldn't have stopped himself if he tried, and he wasn't sure he wanted to.

Chapter 6

This land is my land

Bryn watched Owain out of the corner of his eye, as the young detective put together the murder board.

The detectives' office at Central Police Station was open-plan, the walls lined with vast windows to look out onto Park Place. On the other side of Cathays Park and the Wales National War Memorial was their crime scene, the noble building in white marble a stark contrast to the ugly concrete the police force called home.

The museum was completely shut down for the day, the staff falling over themselves to give the police every chance of returning their precious painting. But art theft wasn't exactly Bryn's area of expertise – hell, even murder was a rare event in the Welsh capital. He had phoned for assistance from the National Crime Agency and they'd promised to send someone down within the week.

But by the end of the day, the painting could've left the country. It wasn't like airport scanners and coastguards were set up to hunt down masterpieces shoved down the side of a suitcase. They didn't have a sniffer dog for that.

Bryn clicked on the folder in the corner of his desktop, called simply 'updates'. A dozen CCTV stills and a file full of notes appeared, which he moved to a different folder – creatively named 'old updates' – and printed for Owain's board.

He hadn't wanted Amy involved in this case, but Jason had pushed him and, like a fool, he'd relented. The acting detective superintendent wanted to fend off any hint of irregularity after the scandal that had hit the department earlier in the year, and Amy was definitely an irregularity.

He handed the pictures to Owain, who pinned the series of CCTV images around the crime scene photos. 'These images fit with Indira's preliminary report, though she hadn't realised the hammer was … lodged like that. He was dead within a minute, she reckons.'

A few curious onlookers came over to gawp, but they retreated at Bryn's glare.

'Anything else?'

'Prints and DNA still processing, but he's gloved and masked, so not much chance of transfer. I've asked Catriona to compare this to European art heists from the past five years to see if the MO matches.'

Catriona Aitken was only a detective constable so Owain technically outranked her, but as lead investigator, Bryn should be giving the orders. Maybe Owain was trying on the rank of inspector, seeing how it fitted. Because the rumour mill had it that the new detective superintendent would be coming from within the ranks, leaving a vacant detective inspector post for the taking.

And all eyes were on Bryn.

Of course, he should be ranked detective chief inspector to apply for the post, but their last DCI had retired three years ago and the higher-ups had never got round to appointing another. Interview phases would come and go, but it worked out better for the budget if the existing inspectors shouldered the extra responsibility.

The chief constable had come sniffing round the office once or twice, but Bryn had hidden in the stationery cupboard until he'd gone. If he was asked to apply for the job by the big boss, he'd have no choice but to say yes. And be confined to a desk for the rest of his days.

But if he didn't apply, what then? He was getting on in years and how would the department look with a complete stranger running it? The acting super was from North Wales, which was bad enough, but what if an Englishman took the helm? It didn't bear thinking about. Maybe he owed it to his boys – and girls – to become their super.

'Bryn? Bryn, are you listening?'

Owain's words brought him back to the task at hand and he gestured at the board.

'Good thinking, the MOs. Let me know if she finds something.'

Owain smiled half a smile, forced to put on a happy face. But Bryn was well acquainted with liars.

'If something's bothering you—'

'Bryn!'

The office was silenced by Jason's shout – or possibly by the tall blonde at his side. She strode up to Bryn without waiting for an invitation.

'I'm Frieda Haas from the National Crime Agency.'

Bryn blinked at her. 'Bloody hell, you're quick. I wasn't expecting you 'til at least Monday.'

'And yet here I am. I will expect your full cooperation with my investigation and will be deputising your officers as required.'

Bryn tried not to swear. She had a tinge to her accent that, combined with her name and Aryan poster-girl looks, made him think German. He could add cold efficiency to his equation now.

'This is a South Wales Police investigation—'

'Not anymore. Do you understand the diplomatic significance of this painting, Mr Hesketh?'

Bryn ground his teeth. Robbing him of his title was a cheap psychological trick, but he couldn't help the way it grated on him. 'Enlighten me.'

'The French tolerate British possession of Impressionist paintings because we guarantee their safety and security. Now one of them is missing, presumed stolen. What would happen to the National Museum of Wales if France demanded the repatriation of all French paintings?'

'It would financially collapse,' Owain said. His eyes were fixed on the newcomer like an eager puppy dog. It only took a whiff of the Big City to impress the boy with big ambitions.

'And Welsh tourism would take a hit it can't afford. If other museums received similar demands, the financial recovery could stutter. This is about so much more than a stolen painting.'

Chapter 7

Smooth operator

Amy was seething. How dare he hang up on her! While flirting with that moronic NCA officer!

She threw her phone on the floor, the casing bursting open and the battery lying exposed on the floor. She left it there out of spite. If Jason wanted to get hold of her, he could come home.

Staring at the broken phone, Amy realised that had been a particularly stupid thing to do. But she couldn't quite muster the effort to put it back together, so it remained as a symbol of her anger – towards Jason and NCA agents who blatantly wanted to sleep with him.

Amy knew Jason was a hit with women, but she rarely witnessed these encounters. Somehow, it made the reality more solid, the churning in her gut justified. Of course, this was professional interest. While she'd like to say his tail chasing had never compromised him professionally, she remembered all too well the witness he took to bed and the ill-fated date to a body dump.

She swallowed a couple of little blue pills, to quiet her anger, and returned to her research. The original design and blueprints for the National Museum of Wales were locked away in an archive somewhere, and the historical map data was sadly lacking – at least, in an online-accessible format. From what she could tell, however, there had been a number of architectural landmarks nearby, including an old convent, numerous canals and, of course, Cardiff Castle. The museum had been built in what had been Cathays Park, the only remnant a small patch of grass in the centre of the civic buildings which boasted the city's war memorial.

It was therefore feasible that there was some underground way out of the museum that the thief could've exploited. Amy would need to access experts in historical architecture to confirm it, and the most likely candidates worked at said museum. Which argued for an inside job.

She would need external verification of possible locations before sending Jason in to investigate. It would be too easy for one of the museum staff to misdirect them, if they didn't know what they were looking for.

Amy set AEON to finding a list of names who might be able to help and switched her focus to investigating art heists. She was surprised by the sheer number of missing paintings, expensive ones, never found. She concentrated on Impressionist works, but the high-profile thefts involved brazen raids by men with guns.

One theft caught her eye – the targeted removal of a Cézanne piece from Oxford during the millennium celebrations. The entry was stealthy, but that was the only similarity. Thieves used scaffolding to get in and set off smoke canisters to cause confusion, whereas their thief had used a stolen key card and a brutal hammer blow.

However, Oxfordshire Police believed the painting had been targeted for theft. Perhaps that was the case here? From what Amy could see, it was the most famous piece at the museum. She interrogated the museum's website for nineteenth century paintings of comparable value – and stopped dead.

One picture in particular had caught her eye, the most spectacular beauty filling her screen. A woman with startling red hair, like DC Aitken's carrot top, painted by Dante Gabriel Rossetti. Amy was captivated by the colours, the vibrancy of it all. She had never realised art could be alive like this, as if she could reach out and touch it – as if she were out among these things, in the real world, feeling the sun and tasting the fresh air.

The door buzzer sounded and Amy saved the painting for later, the colours still burning bright in her mind.

'Yes?'

'Amy, it's Owain.'

She buzzed him up. Should she reinstate Bryn and Owain's access privileges to the flat? She had shut them out after the police investigation into Jason earlier in the year, but they had all kissed and made up since then. Yet she liked having more control over her space, with only Jason able to come and go as he pleased. It made her safe space safer, secured her territory. She had increased the trip sensors around the perimeter, added more barbed wire and cameras. It was her fortress.

The lift doors opened and she turned to see him for the first time in weeks, the first time since … before. He was thinner and his eyes were pained, the same look she saw in the mirror every day. But he was whole and alive, and sometimes that was enough.

It was unlike him to visit her alone for an investigation, usually tagging along with Bryn and staying in the background. It was unusual, but Amy wasn't quite sure what it meant yet.

'Welcome back,' she said, pushing her curiosity to the side for the moment.

He smiled half a smile and said nothing. He shifted his laptop bag off his shoulder onto the sofa, tactfully ignored the disembowelled phone decorating the floor, and handed her an encrypted memory stick.

She opened up the files – in quarantine, of course – and scanned through the lines of code. She wasn't familiar with security systems outside her own, but she recognised a log when she saw one.

'Who owned the stolen card?'

'Talia Yeltsova. Senior Oil Painting Conservationist. Her car was broken into last night but, as the radio was obviously missing, she didn't check to see if anything else was stolen.'

'Where was her car parked?'

'Outside the museum.'

Amy drummed her fingers on the edge of the keyboard. 'Why was her access card in the car if she was at work?'

Owain pointed at the code on her screen, careful not to touch her precious monitor. 'Looking at the log, you need a card to get in but not to leave. Security signs everyone in and out on paper and she arrived at nine-fifteen. The museum was already open, so she probably came in through the front door.'

Amy pulled a face at the paper records. Why anyone would store important information on something so fragile was beyond her.

Owain, however, was one step ahead. 'I scanned and uploaded it to police evidence. It should be on the stick.'

Amy opened the hi-res scan and scrolled down the list. 'Out at twenty-five past eight. Did she report the theft?'

'No police log. We're checking with the insurance company.'

'Sunset was at...' her fingers drew the data to her, like a spider flexing the strands of her web, '...nineteen fifty-three. That's half an hour of darkness. Where exactly was she parked?'

She opened Google Earth and Owain pointed out the row of parked cars right in front of the museum's main entrance, a small park up against them and the main road a stone's throw away.

'How did no one see him?'

Amy found the time window and camera angle on the CCTV footage she had stored. The image frame concentrated on the main entrance and quality was poor, but a few cars were visible in the background.

'Show me the exact position,' Amy said.

Owain pointed at the leftmost car. 'That one. Volkswagen Golf. Red, not that you can tell on this.'

She scrolled through the footage, but only a few people passed by, not one stopping near the car. 'He pulled this off in daylight.'

She started again from nine in the morning, the car parking up after a minute and the day zipping past in a haze of people and cars. It was just after two o'clock when she saw him, wearing a baseball cap with an oversized hoodie drawn over it. He walked up to the car, his back to the camera, and reached for the window. He withdrew his hand and then returned it a moment later, seemingly passing through solid glass to delve inside. Within a minute, he was walking away across the park and it was all over.

'Professional,' Owain said.

He sounded slightly awed but trying not to be. Most criminals in Cardiff tended to be gifted amateurs at best.

'Inside information.' Amy rewound the footage and captured the segment. 'He knew exactly where she kept the key card.'

'If she left it out, it would be easy. Or he looked the day before.'

'We need to find out what he did to the car. Is it impounded?'

'She already took it to a garage. We sent a couple of uniforms over there, but they're a same-day service. The evidence is gone.'

'The technique alone may be telling. We need to figure out his MO.'

Owain's hand settled on her shoulder. 'There's a lot of 'we' in this case suddenly.'

It was odd, his hand being there. Only Jason touched her like that, but she didn't move or shy away. He was warm and the smile on his face had grown more real.

'Where's your bloody – oh. Owain.'

Owain's hand fell from her shoulder but Amy did not look at Jason, her cheeks red with unnamed shame.

'Just bringing over some evidence,' Owain said, his voice too even, like a man calming a bull.

'When she didn't answer her phone, I thought...' Jason trailed off.

Guilt flooded her. She always answered her phone – and when she didn't, she was immersed in a deep depression or a serial killer had broken into the house.

But then she remembered she was angry with him. 'How's your NCA friend?'

'At her hotel. You should've told me you had something for Amy – I could've brought it.'

Jason's voice was accusing, but he had no right to be angry. She burned with questions – how did he know Frieda was at her hotel? Had he escorted her there? Had he ... lingered?

'It came after you left,' Owain said.

But that didn't add up. They would've checked the security logs early in the day and, besides, a personal delivery wasn't required. He could've added them to Bryn's evidence folder and called her.

Which made her think he had come over to see her. But why?

'You'd better be getting back to work,' Jason said. 'Because there's so much to do, isn't there?'

Suddenly, she understood the hostility, though Owain's actions now puzzled her further. If he had blown off Cerys for the case, why had he made time to see her?

Owain moved away from her, past Jason and into the corridor beyond. She still didn't look at Jason, even as she heard him plucking up the pieces of her phone from the floor.

'He's messing her around,' he said.

He had no idea she was annoyed. It was hard to stay angry with someone who was completely oblivious to it.

'You need to be more careful with your phone,' he continued. 'Or answer the landline.'

She'd left the telemarketing software running again, comparing voice imprints to a series of harassing phone calls received by a local businesswoman. She'd have to put her private work on hold if she was taking on the museum case, of course. Murders tended to consume her entirely.

Except, this time, it wasn't the dead man's face that haunted her, but the delicate features of a woman who'd died a century earlier.

Chapter 8

Memento mori

'The Blue Lady' was staring at Truth.

She rested on an easel against the wall, out of direct sunlight and shrouded in netting. She couldn't stay furled in a couple of old bin liners, despite how much Truth itched to stuff her back into the darkness. Instead, she looked at her captor through her veil of white lace. She didn't accuse or judge, but her blank eyes were worse than any condemnation. She was vapid, empty. She thought nothing, knew nothing. What a worthless subject.

What had Renoir seen in her? What did so many morons see in her?

Perhaps it was their reflection staring back that fascinated them. They saw something of themselves in the nothingness of her face, her soul. They came every day in droves to coo and cluck over her, pretending to know something of Impressionism, claiming they loved 'The Blue Lady' to complete strangers and then forgetting about her for another year.

Maybe that was why *La Parisienne* repulsed Truth, who was nothing like the sheep who crowded those marble spaces with wide eyes and slack jaws. Beneath a quiet veneer, Truth was so full of thoughts, ideas, opinions, colour and contrast. But no one saw that.

They saw this hollow girl painted in brightest blue and assumed she had colour. They saw her and failed to see Truth.

But now they had to look. She had wagered freedom to finally be seen, to stop disappointing. Not in some gallery among so many other so-called masterpieces, but standing alone. The robbery was already in all the newspapers, a nation-wide sensation – but that did not thrill her the way it might some. Only one person's opinion mattered, a good opinion that could never quite be gained.

But that security guard – why was he there? Why had he come running? Why couldn't he have stayed away? She was now stained with his blood, a black spot that could not be removed, like Shakespeare's haunted woman.

Yet Truth was no further down the road to salvation. Trapped in limbo, only the waiting remained, draining life and colour as it eked out from hour to hour. She could wait a lifetime, but not with the harlot's eyes burning a hole through the thin shield of the netting.

At least the dappling of red on those bluest of blue skirts made something interesting of her. Until it was painstakingly expunged from the oils, the whore restored to her former vacuous vanity. How easily the physical stain could disappear, yet the guilt beneath wore on.

Until that time, Truth was forced to look on the silly little girl in the portrait. But it would be worth it in the end – to finally be recognised, respected.

Visiting Swansea Prison felt like stepping back in time, retreading the steps of his past but rewriting the ending.

Jason had been banged up here twice before and he'd more than learned his lesson the first time. Being beaten to within an inch of your life tended to condition a person against risking a repeat experience. The second time was also his fault, but only in near-fatal stupidity rather than criminality. It had all come out in the wash for him, but he saw the scars their misadventure had left on Amy, on Owain.

Every time he visited Lewis, it was as if a shadow fell over him, a heavy cloak of dismay and failure. *You're back*, the walls whispered. *You will never really leave us. Once a thief, always a thief.* Only when he escaped could he truly breathe again.

A few guards recognised him but he didn't acknowledge their smiles or scowls. Lewis waved at him from his seat, Jason's mirror in height, build and shaved head. They even shared the same tattoo, a fierce Welsh Dragon curled up on their right shoulders.

'Jay Bird,' Lewis said, clasping his arm before letting Jason take his seat. 'How's tricks?'

'Still walking on the right side,' Jason said, grinning. 'Still rotten through and through?'

'Chaplain tells me I'm a reformed sinner.'

Lewis matched Jason's broad smile, but he suddenly looked much older, as if a forgotten weight had fallen again on his shoulders. The loss of Lewis' little brother Damage tormented them both. Jason dealt with it by thinking about it as little as possible, and drinking whisky when he couldn't bury the pain anymore. Lewis had instead tried to make sense of it as best he could. He'd seen counsellors and men of God, tried meditation and hard work, and shunned anyone in Swansea Prison even remotely connected to drugs. Which didn't leave him with a lot of friends.

However, he had started hanging out with a better class of criminal and working towards his transfer to Cardiff Prison. That brought him into contact with exactly the kind of people that Bryn wanted to know about – the fraudsters and smugglers and gentlemen crooks.

Jason got straight to the point of his visit, respecting Lewis too much to lie about his reasons. Lewis listened attentively but silently, giving nothing away. Jason knew that none of this information was new to him. The prison grapevine often had the details of a police investigation before the papers.

'And the police want to know who might be into a thing like that.'

Lewis sat back in his chair. 'Obviously, the blokes I know have been banged up in here this whole time. And I'm not a grass.'

Jason snorted. 'I know. You didn't speak to me for two weeks when I told my mam about what you were growing in the back garden. I'm not asking for names. More like … what kind of blokes are they? Local boys? Out-of-towners?'

Lewis folded his arms. 'What's in it for me, Jay?'

His mate had always been mercenary. That was how they'd ended up planning a gold exchange robbery and not knocking over the corner shop.

'Bryn's already writing you a letter for the transfer board. Because he's a good bloke and I asked him. You know I've got nothing else for you.'

Lewis' face was impassive, stony. 'My mam likes One Direction.'

Jason blinked. 'Right.'

'There's a concert coming up. She needs tickets and an escort.'

Their eyes met. And they burst out laughing, startling everyone else in the room.

'Oi, Jonesy!' A guard called across the visiting room, a soft face that Jason recognised. 'You too, Carr. No need to be rowdy now.'

Jason threw him a sloppy salute before turning back to Lewis.

'Deal. But I'm sending my mam. I love Auntie Elin, but not enough to sit through that shit.'

Lewis leaned forward, eyes sparking with amusement but voice pitched much lower. 'The word in here is that the crew can't be locals – no one round here has the connections or the balls. Something similar went down in Oxford about fifteen years ago, but one of my boys knows the guys what did that and says it's not them. They wouldn't have killed the guard, no way. The gangs who are into moving art get into it because they don't want the hassle of drugs, guns, and girls anymore. And they work big.'

'How big are we talking?'

'Jay, come on. We robbed the gold exchange and that was the crime of the year. These guys just made off with a painting worth millions. One fucking painting! But it's high risk at both ends, y'know. What if the buyer don't like it? What if you're going international and his boys take against your boys? My friends who know about these things tell me it's all Arabs and Chinamen. Who wants to get involved in that shit?'

'So, they shove it in a suitcase and fly it out to Dubai?'

Lewis chuckled, quieter so they didn't draw too many eyes. 'Nah, butt. The Oxford boys made for Liverpool. Same way the drugs go – in and out on the boats.'

'Good job we're a landlocked country in the middle of Europe,' Jason quipped. 'Any idea where to start?'

Lewis subtly glanced left and right, checking out their immediate neighbours.

'The boy in the know? He's a Gog.'

Jason didn't ask further, though he wanted to interrogate Lewis about which part of North Wales he was from and where along that vast coast to begin. But they had been talking in hushed tones for too long and the last thing Jason needed was to be suspected of a conspiracy or for Lewis to be fingered as a snitch.

They chatted about the Autumn Internationals, their mutual friends on the inside and out in the world, and how Cerys had mutated into a sensible proto-cop with a copper boyfriend. When their time was up, they embraced with a slap on the back and the promise to email.

And the old guilt burned in Jason again, the knowledge that the clouds hanging over his head would soon dissipate to reveal blue skies but Lewis had yet more time to serve under the cosh. Time they should be sharing, together.

He should've been at the gold exchange that day, standing beside his best mate as they robbed an old man blind. But he had been arrested one week before for stealing their getaway car. For years, Lewis hadn't been able to forgive him for that abandonment, the reason their plan had fallen apart. If he'd been there that day, maybe they'd still be leading a life of crime, or retired rich somewhere hot and sunny. Instead of Jason visiting his mate in prison.

He went out the gates and it started to rain, a typical Welsh absolution, the chains dissolving into the puddles, and Jason walked away, free in body if not in mind.

45

Chapter 9

Knucklebrained

Her unvented anger had exhausted her and Amy slept late, her bed more inviting than the case. She drifted in and out of broken sleep, repeatedly sucked back into obscure dreams of shadows and a hundred false awakenings.

When she finally rose, it was gone midday and the house was empty. Amy recalled Jason saying something about visiting Lewis this weekend – perhaps he had made an early start. She made some toast and tea in her dressing gown, before gravitating towards AEON to check for overnight developments.

Indira had uploaded her preliminary autopsy report, including possible connections and disparities from the evidence collected by the scene of crime officers. One report compared trace found all around the body to that recovered from the deceased's clothes and shoes. One entry stood out: 'silica and particulate organic matter consistent with natural beach sand'. No such sand was found on Paul Roberts' shoes, which meant the killer probably brought it with him. Like breadcrumbs, the trail of sand would also give a cunning Scene of Crime Officer confirmation of the entry and exit points that the killer used. Amy put another mark in the amateur column.

She checked the results of Paul's social media search. The results were sparse, a forgotten Facebook profile amongst a slew of older, mothballed networks that hadn't seen use in years. Who still had a Friends Reunited account?

She would need access to his home computer or his work account to get a better picture of his browsing history, his interests, his connections. She fired off a quick email to Bryn with her modest requests, before looking for a distraction while waiting for new information. Why hadn't they thought of this before now? How was she supposed to work without data?

Bryn had been getting sloppy about evidence provision recently. She'd had to ask on more than one occasion for the files and access she needed since returning to work after the accident. At first, she'd thought Bryn didn't want to overburden her after her injuries but she'd been recovered for weeks now. He had no excuse for his continued laxity, in her mind.

Part of her was aware she was being unfair and knew that Bryn had a lot on his plate, but if he wanted her help in these crimes, he had to give her something to work with. She could only get so far working from unofficial sources – social media, remote access, supposedly secure government databases.

The lift doors opened, startling her. 'Honey, I'm home!'

Jason thought he was being funny again, that was all. But Amy smiled all the same.

'Good day at the prison, dear?'

'Same old, same old. Didn't fancy hanging about this time.' He came up behind her and flipped open his notebook. 'Ready?'

Amy found that she wasn't angry anymore. Relieved, she opened her notes and assumed her typing position. 'Ready.'

'"Lewis" unnamed sources reckon this is part of an organised crime network operating on and off boats, like the drug supply. Definitely not the same blokes who robbed Oxford. And he thinks we're looking at a North Walean connection.'

Amy nodded as she typed: *CI HMPS gangs boats Oxford X N Wales.* 'Anything else?'

'I've got to buy tickets to One Direction.'

'If that's how you're spending your salary, I might need to reconsider my generosity.'

'Oh, give over.' Jason gently shoved at her shoulder and she didn't flinch. She was getting better at that. 'Tea?'

'Please.' She finished the dregs of her last mug before handing it off to him. 'This intel fits the evidence perfectly. The SOCOs found beach sand tracked in by the killer.'

'They can do tests on that, can't they? Find out if it's from North Wales' beaches?' Jason called from the kitchen.

'Mm.' Amy scanned the report again. 'They've sent it to some national lab for analysis, but it could take a few days. You're turning into a proper detective, aren't you?'

'I just know my limits. I bring you second-hand gossip and you turn it into evidence that would stand up in court.'

'That's Bryn's job. I just shore up your gossip with my own, before handing it over to the real police.'

Jason laughed. 'Modesty? From you? You're a genius at this and you know it.'

Amy blushed and tried to cool her cheeks with her palms before Jason came back in. 'I'm all right,' she said, noncommittal.

But she knew that Bryn needed her and she liked that feeling. Cardiff Police didn't have access to computer forensics and that meant she was it. It was a huge responsibility, but she didn't mind. She liked to be needed. She sent the scant details of Jason's prison intelligence to Bryn via email, flagging up the connection to the sand. Playing her part.

Jason returned with her tea and she took a break from the computer, sitting beside him on the sofa as they drank in companionable silence.

'Did you find anything out while I was gone?'

Amy filled him in on her lack of information from Paul's social media, at which he nodded in all the right places. She had him well trained.

'So, what's next?' he asked.

'I have hours of CCTV to review.'

She felt Jason's eyes on the side of her face, boring a hole. 'And me?'

Amy hesitated. She didn't have anything that needed fetching, no suspects to be interrogated. Bryn hadn't responded to her request for Paul's data and devices, so she had no need for Jason's particular skillset.

'How are we for bread?'

'Seriously? We're looking at a murder and you want me to pop to the shops?'

Amy flustered. 'I have nothing for you to do.'

'I can look at CCTV just as well as you can. We've got the tablet or my laptop.'

She hesitated, a moment too long.

Jason huffed and got up off the sofa. 'Fine. I'll check the cupboards for Cerys coming over tonight. Let me know if you think of some "one-brain-cell" tasks, yeah?'

'Jason, I didn't mean it like that,' Amy protested.

Jason towered above her, all six feet of him radiating barely contained frustration. 'Look, I know computers aren't my thing. But you could teach me some stuff, enough to help you out. I'm not only good for my feet and fists.'

'I know. I do know.' Amy had no idea how they'd got into the bizarre situation of her giving Jason reassurance. It was a strange place to be.

'I'm just saying I can do a lot more if you let me.'

He retreated into the kitchen, leaving Amy staring after him. Maybe she hadn't been fair. But what if he missed something? She had years of practice looking at CCTV and she knew she could comb every frame perfectly. It would be difficult to let go.

But she trusted him with her evidence, with witnesses and dangerous situations. Amy trusted Jason with her life. Was trusting him with AEON really that different?

Amy headed for the shower, her mind still churning over this new development. The hot water would clear her head and give her the opportunity to think it through, away from the distraction of Jason's earnest eyes and how much she wanted to please him.

She had to make this decision with her head, and not her unreliable heart.

Jason unloaded the dishwasher with jerky movements, frustration bleeding into his household chores. Other people had jobs that gave them weekends off and bosses who trusted them with more than just playing errand boy.

Sure, he hadn't done much with himself in school, preferring to bunk off and shake down younger kids for their lunch money, case the best corner shops for a bit of thieving, or find who could score an eighth or two for a session down by the river. That had been his education, learning how to please himself and his mates, and intimidate anyone who got in their way.

But he thought he was better than that now. He wasn't just some thug who got answers with a bruising. He was doing honest work, for Amy and the police. Why wouldn't she let him prove that he could do more than just fetch, carry and clean?

The doorbell rang. They weren't expecting Cerys until later, so who was paying them a visit? When the bell rang again, Jason crossed into the living room to find it empty and the sound of the shower running coming from down the corridor.

With AEON locked down, Jason moved towards the intercom and pressed the button the old-fashioned way. 'Yeah?'

'Jason, it's Owain.'

'Oh. Hi.' What the hell was Owain doing here two days in a row?

'Hi. Can I ... come up?'

'Yeah, sure.' Jason buzzed him up and waited in the corridor. Something weird was going on here and he intended to find out what.

The lift doors opened and Owain strode out, dressed down with his laptop bag on his shoulder. 'Where's Amy?'

'She's in the shower. You need something?'

'Mind if I disturb her?' Owain tried to peer around him, as if doubting he believed Jason at all.

Jason decided he was getting to the bottom of this. 'Why are you here? I thought you were working.'

Owain tapped the laptop bag. 'This is work.'

Jason moved across the corridor to block Owain's path to Amy. 'I'm all ears.'

Owain's hand gripped the bag strap until his knuckles turned white. 'The CCTV—'

'Yeah, we've got it.' Jason wasn't budging an inch.

'I'm here to help. Her analysis.'

Jason's mouth went dry. After she'd turned him down... 'Since when does Amy need help with computers?'

'Jason, please—'

'Since when?' he shouted, getting in Owain's face.

Owain tensed, his whole body rigid and his eyes squeezed shut. As if bracing for a blow.

Jason deflated immediately. 'Fuck, mate, I'm not gonna hit you.'

Owain released a shaky breath and slowly opened his eyes, as if he was afraid of what he might see. 'Sorry. Just … jumpy.'

Jason had seen this kind of jumpy before. Amy startled like a rabbit in the face of a 4x4. But he'd never seen Owain wear it, like a heavy cloak weighing him down. But a brush with death altered a person, didn't it?

Jason had seen the evidence of Amy's nightmares, dark circles under her eyes and savagely bitten fingernails, and heard the stifled cries through the floorboards. He'd kept an eye on her, but he hadn't ventured past her bedroom door. Some lines shouldn't be crossed in your boss's house, and entering Amy's room for more than a wake-up call and a cup of tea was out of the question.

'How about I put the kettle on while we wait for Amy?' he said gently.

Owain nodded, still pale and trembling. Jason shepherded him towards the living room and made the tea, adding an extra spoonful of real sugar to Owain's. He took it silently and stuffed a chocolate digestive in his mouth, like a small child at his nan's house.

Jason watched him, his own hands unable to keep still in his lap. Because for all his protests to Amy, despite everything he thought he could make of himself, he still led with his temper, choosing the physical over the mental to solve a problem.

No wonder Amy couldn't trust him with peanuts. Jason wasn't even sure if he could trust himself.

Chapter 10

Two pairs of eyes

Amy washed the sweat from her skin, trying to be rational about Jason and his effect on her. She was used to struggling on with a head full of cotton wool, from the depression or the panic, lack of caffeine or a little too much red wine. But for another person to put her in a spin like this … The last person to have that kind of hold over her had been her mother, that raging hatred that had consumed her teenage years until she had finally escaped from her.

Stealing from her parents was the best day's hacking she'd ever done and she refused to regret it. The insurance company had coughed up, her father had changed his passwords to another predictable set of cricketing highlights, and they had all moved on with their lives. Except Amy and her sister were five million pounds richer.

Their parents had never found out who stole the money. Just as they had failed to notice Grandma's fading memory, leaving the old woman to raise two young girls. Leaving Amy and Lizzie to bury their grandmother. It was only when Lizzie had reached out to them earlier in the year that they even knew what had happened to their daughters. Their father had assumed it was being 'taken care of', like so many little things. His mother's memory. Lizzie's education. Amy's fragile mental health.

Rinsing the bitter taste from her mouth, Amy pushed the past away and boxed it up inside her. It would keep. Back in her room, she threw on whatever was to hand and headed for the living room.

She stopped short at the sight of Owain on the sofa. He was staring into his mug, looking both lost and hopeful that the tea would somehow hold the answers.

'Owain's brought his laptop,' Jason said, from the kitchen doorway. 'To help with the CCTV.'

She heard the hesitancy in his voice, with an edge of anger. He wanted her to intervene, to drag Owain back from wherever he had fled. But, if she let Owain in, she would be admitting that she could share her work – just not with Jason.

Amy was torn. Jason was her assistant, her best friend. But Owain needed a purpose, needed to keep moving in case he realised that in stopping the world had changed irrevocably. She recognised that look from the mirror. Maybe she could fix him in a way she had never managed for herself?

But before she could answer, Owain was unpacking his laptop and he'd lost some of the shadows from his face, his eyes. He almost looked like himself again. Amy knew exactly how much the work was therapy. Could she deny him that?

'What about me?' Jason asked.

She tried not to hear the hurt in his words. 'You were going shopping. For Cerys.'

Owain slumped, head bent over his laptop though she knew he was listening intently. Whatever was off between Owain and Cerys, it wasn't due to a lack of feeling on either side.

With an aggressive glare at Owain, Jason picked up some bags from the cupboard and made for the door. 'I'll just be shopping then.'

She knew she'd offended him, but he would survive. She couldn't leave Owain to fend for himself, as she'd been left. It was worth Jason's flare of temper to provide the crutch for once, instead of being the one dependent on it.

Amy picked up the set of CCTV discs and fanned them out for Owain.

'Pick a card.'

Seething at being ordered to pick up the groceries like he was some kind of fifties housewife, Jason dumped the empty shopping bags in the boot of his Micra and decided he was going to check on the Harley.

Dylan hadn't called, so she wasn't ready to ride, but maybe they could spend a couple of hours figuring it out together.

Jason missed his long hours at the garage, tinkering with cars and bikes, but Dylan's tendency to work with cheap parts of dubious origins meant he had to keep his distance. Jason's criminal record and Dylan's dodgy parts were too well known for either of them to prosper from that arrangement.

And the bloody shopping could wait. He had suspected Amy was blowing him off, but now he had confirmation. It wasn't about guarding her domain from all-comers – it was about keeping Jason out. The anger faded now, replaced by sadness and a sense of loss. He wasn't Amy's only assistant, the one person she could completely rely on. Other people could take his place in an instant, and in some cases, do things that he would never be permitted to touch. As if he were a naughty five-year-old who couldn't be trusted with the remote control.

As Jason drove between the Students' Union and the museum, he glanced across at the entrances. Still cordoned off and guarded. Not only had the place lost its most iconic work of art, but it must be haemorrhaging money from the lack of tourists. The mystery nagged at him. He wanted to be part of it. He couldn't bear to be shut out like this.

He drove past the castle before leaving the town centre, crossing the bridge into Canton. The shabby end of town was a mishmash of young professionals, new immigrants, and old Cardiffians, where a polski sklep stood next to an ancient greasy café, both frequented by hipsters.

As he turned into Dylan's road, he spotted a familiar Mercedes 4x4 parked outside. Jason loathed posh 4x4s, the province of rich middle-class parents who wanted something to drive their children to school in and didn't care about the hit to their pockets. But take one of those cars down a proper dirt track in the country and it would never survive the bumps, ditches, and ice-marked lanes it was supposedly built for.

He parked and marched up to the forecourt, where Dylan and Miss National Crime Agency were peering into a covered trailer attached to the Chelsea Tractor. He might hate the car, but this was his chance to get inside information on the investigation. Prove his worth to Amy and get back into the crime solving that had united them.

But any cunning plan died when he saw what was inside the trailer. The Harley Davidson touring bike was all black seduction, the newest model with an eye-watering price tag that Jason couldn't hope to afford even with Amy's generous salary. He felt sick with envy, yet the beautiful machine also added a touch of gloss to his impression of Frieda.

'Now I'm the one with the admirer. Though not so secret.'

Jason realised he was staring, at both her and the bike. Her cool amusement should've rankled, but it just added to her confident air. He couldn't deny her whole attitude was attractive, tantalising.

'I figured you for a BMW girl,' he said, trying to cover his naked admiration of more than just the bike.

'Time for a change. I tire easily.'

'Miss Haas was looking at your Captain America bike,' Dylan chipped in.

She glanced back at his bike, in pride of place in the centre of Dylan's space. 'A loving restoration. You must be a proud parent.'

Jason shrugged, unwilling to admit his beloved bike wouldn't even start on a mild day in autumn.

'If only she would turn over, eh, Jason?'

Dylan, however, never knew when to keep his mouth shut.

'I can take a look, if you like?' Frieda offered.

'I think we've got it,' Jason said, too quickly.

But her expression didn't flicker. Why wouldn't she give anything away? She was another mystery to solve, and he was fascinated by her refusal to react. Professional veneer or personal protection? He longed to know the truth of her.

'Dylan was just giving my tourer the once-over before I take her on a trip.' Frieda reached out to caress the leather seat of her bike. 'Sometimes it takes a professional eye to get the job done.'

'Leaving Cardiff already? Case closed – or just not enough excitement for you?'

His tone was biting, but that professional comment had riled him. She was needling Amy and him, and he wasn't going to stand for that.

'Wales' beaches won't inspect themselves.'

'You're following the sand lead?'

Jason was aware of Dylan in his peripheral vision, dithering about giving them some space to talk or eavesdropping on the murder investigation some more. He shot his mate a look, and Dylan muttered something about brake fluid before making himself scarce.

'The full analysis could take weeks. From the prison intel and the first-pass data, we have enough to narrow down the geography. We have to move fast if we want to stop the painting leaving the country – if it hasn't already.'

'You're going alone?'

An Englishwoman alone in the heart of North Wales was just asking for trouble.

'You want to be my chaperone?'

'If you let me drive.'

The words were out before he'd thought them through, but he immediately liked the idea. Time to play with a beautiful bike, and get to know the beautiful woman who so puzzled him.

'I'll let you try her. I'm leaving in an hour. Where should I pick you up?'

'I'll meet you here,' Jason said.

A woman on a motorbike showing up outside Amy's would likely give her a heart attack.

Amy. Shit.

Jason wasn't a free man. He had responsibilities to Amy. But if Owain was installing himself in their living room, he didn't see why he couldn't follow another lead. The young detective was capable of fetching in the sandwiches and Amy could make her own tea.

'Better let the boss know then,' Frieda said, reading his mind.

'She'll get it,' he said, knowing exactly how big a lie that was.

Chapter 11

Forty thieves

'There's something odd about this girl.'

Amy continued to scan the flickering images on her screen, glancing at Owain's reflection in the blank third monitor. 'Odd?'

Owain waved his index and middle fingers vaguely at the centre of the screen. 'She's walked up and down the Impressionists gallery four times, but she's not looking at the paintings.'

Amy paused her video as Owain tilted the laptop screen towards her. He played the footage at double-time and Amy watched one solitary woman flit around the gallery, inspecting every picture's frame and every statue's base without looking at a single work of art.

'Checking out the security system,' Amy said. 'Can you get a good angle for a still?'

Owain stopped the video and moved to capture it.

'Move it on a little,' Amy nudged, and he obeyed. 'There, stop. She was turning out of that glare. Worse angle, but clearer image.'

'She's probably too short for our thief,' Owain said. 'Look at her against "The Blue Lady" here. She's nowhere near tall enough to cut the top of the frame.'

'He wasn't working alone. Keep looking – there may be others.'

Amy scanned through more footage, the chaos of the main hall causing her temples to ache. Or maybe that was her brain telling her to ease up on the caffeine, a war between the sluggishness of her sleepy brain and the need to quell the anxious fluttering in her chest.

Jason had been gone an awfully long time. She tried not to think about it, but he usually completed a basic two-day shop in under forty-five minutes including travel both ways. One hour and fifteen minutes had passed since he'd left the flat. What if something had happened to him? Her fingers itched to bring up the GPS tracker and locate his phone. Or the small coin-sized tracker she'd slipped into the lining of his favourite leather jacket, the one in the dashboard of the Micra, or the one in the shell of his motorcycle helmet. She liked to be prepared for any eventuality.

She almost missed the girl mounting the stairs two at a time to get into the galleries above. She flicked to the camera footage of the Impressionist gallery, but the girl was nowhere to be seen after ten minutes of scanning. Amy changed to the main art gallery on that floor and spotted her. She entered the gallery and continued her strange routine, checking frames – but only of certain pictures. Amy marked their positions on her gallery outline map, hoping to find some correlation between the pictures she picked. Artist, perhaps? Dollar value? Or maybe just the shopping list of her employer?

When Jason came home, she'd send him round the gallery to mark the positions of all the paintings. The CCTV footage was too poor for identification and he needed something to occupy him.

She had to maintain his interest in the work. Assistant to Amy Lane was only an attractive job title so long as Amy's work was stimulating. Without the police cases, the thorny private investigations, what was there to keep him here? Amy didn't flatter herself that she was enough. It was murder that had drawn him in and it would be murder that kept him close.

The man caught her eye because he was so still. He sat on the bench nearest 'The Blue Lady' and stayed there for forty minutes, looking at something on his phone. Occasionally, he would glance up at the picture, squint for a moment and then return to the phone. As his right hand cradled the phone, his left hand squeezed the edge of the bench, working its way all around the edge.

Eventually, he left his spot – but not before Amy had taken a series of stills. Another potential suspect. Amy noted down the timestamp and the location on her map.

As soon as he left, another man took his place, sitting in the exact same spot for seventeen minutes, before moving on. He also had his phone in hand. 'Filming?' Amy muttered.

'Say again?'

Amy had forgotten Owain was in the room.

'I have a pair of strange men sitting in front of "The Blue Lady" with their phones.'

'I have a middle-aged woman doing the same.'

Amy reviewed the stills. 'But only for a few minutes. It's an unlikely crew.'

'Maybe they've been recruited in? A cell structure – each of them only knowing their part and no one else's.'

The lift doors whispered open and a ball of tension dissolved in Amy's chest.

'Jason. Can you go to the museum and map out—'

'Can't.' He hauled two large shopping bags through the living room and into the kitchen. 'I have to go away for a bit.'

Her heart stopped, a squeezing fist occupying its position in her chest. She couldn't speak, couldn't breathe.

'Something happened?' Owain said, worried. 'Is Cerys—?'

'She's fine. Coming over for dinner. Frieda and I are taking the fight to North Wales. Show them Gogs what's what.'

Frieda. Her anxiety morphed into white-hot anger, not enough diazepam in the world to calm the storm.

'You work for me. Me.'

'It's for your investigation. I'll phone in every day.'

'You're taking off with some London bitch—'

'You don't even know her.' Jason's body was all hard lines, steeled for a fight.

'Neither do you!'

'She's police, Amy. I'm not hanging out with some drug lord.'

'Not this time. Not yet. How can I trust you not to die out there?'

The anxiety and anger spiralled together, until she was spinning in a dizzy haze. When Jason left her protection, bad things happened. Fist fights, gunshots, running for his life. She couldn't ensure his safety on such short notice, not in North Wales with its patchy mobile signal and poor CCTV coverage.

She'd stood up, but she didn't remember when, facing him down like a matador with a bull. Except Jason wasn't charging. His mouth was a grim line, but his eyes were dark and pained. Hurt.

'You don't trust me to go.'

'I don't trust her!'

'I'm going, whether you like it or not.'

'If you go, I'll … I'll…' *Fire you.*

But she wouldn't do that – couldn't even make the threat. He knew he held all the cards. She would never fire him and he could do exactly as he pleased. She was too afraid of losing him, even to protect him.

'I'll be back in a couple of days,' he said.

She could tell it was a lie. He had no idea when he was coming back. How long he was leaving her, placing himself out of her reach and in danger.

'I can take care of things here,' Owain said.

But she didn't want him. She wanted Jason. Jason, who knew all her little idiosyncrasies, her favourite snacks when she was stuck on a problem, and exactly how she took her tea.

She wanted them to be a team again. She wanted him to rely on her, as she depended on him. But she knew she was losing control, losing him, and she had nothing that could stop the car crash occurring in front of her.

'I'm going to pack,' Jason said, and didn't look back as he left her.

Gripping the edge of the desk, Truth fought the urge to run. Every cell in her body urged her to get out, flee far away. She had to get away from here, away from *her*.

She took a deep breath, closed her eyes. Counted to ten.

She wasn't going to leave. She was going to see this through. Even after years of trying and never quite achieving, she had never yet quit.

She wouldn't let that painted stare drive her away.

Waiting for a response was agonising. She didn't even know if the message had been received, if it was being discussed, if someone had called the police. It was the uncertainty that killed her, fuelled her desire for flight.

But where would she go? She had no one who could take her in, and she could not live with herself if she left, nor with the consequences. Not now. All her hopes were pinned on Renoir's infamous whore.

No, Truth had to wait. When the museum reopened, she would check out the lie of the land, see what could be seen. She had spotted the others and she had to ensure they came nowhere near the upper galleries. She hoped they would remain shut, but the museum management were money men who cared only for profit. They would not keep their prize pieces hidden from gormless eyes and grabbing hands.

Art should be reserved for an elite who could appreciate it. The Salon in Paris and the Royal Academy in London knew the truth of it. Those who tried to buck the trend, bring art to the masses, only achieved true greatness in death – where their radical thoughts could be separated from their grand works. When they became, instead of the anarchists, part of the establishment to be rebelled against.

Was Truth an anarchist now, a rebel? She had stolen a painting, killed a man. But theft and murder were sins old as story – nothing radical in sin. They were the price of her devil's deal, the price of the life of a woman who did not love, did not hate, but merely expected her to do her duty.

If this continued, waiting without answer, she would have to take matters into her own hands. The television revealed nothing, but the police might catch her scent at any time. She might have to take care of those in the know, perhaps even those who pursued her. She needed to buy more time, except time was trickling through the glass with every passing day. She was losing with every minute lost.

'The Blue Lady' smiled at her with her nothing eyes.

'Slut,' she said and spat.

The glob of spittle struck the net curtain and gravity tumbled it over the lace to the floor with a splat. Anarchy. *Rebellion*.

Disgusted, she turned her back and ignored the laughing eyes of the bitch.

She only had to wait.

Chapter 12

Over hill and vale

Amy hadn't said goodbye.

Jason had packed his bag and marched into the hallway in his leathers, ready for another fight. But she'd just stood there, fiddling with her fraying hoodie sleeve, watching him. Her eyes were wide, huge dark pupils eclipsing all but a slither of green around the edges, black holes in her drawn, milk-pale face.

He did not speak and she said nothing, and he was gone before he could regret it.

Except now he felt it. He'd known working with Amy would be difficult from the first moment he stepped into her domain, and expecting it to get easier had been foolish. Being Amy's friend was as much hard work as being her cleaner or her assistant. Every time he thought he understood, she demanded more – and he was running out of life to give.

But he also had his faults, no point denying it. He had something about him that stopped her trust being total, keeping parts of the work from him, trusting Owain the copper over Jason the ex-con. And how had he reacted to that? By running off to North Wales with a woman she hated on sight, even if that was totally misguided. What was there to hate about Frieda?

He parked up outside Dylan's, behind Frieda's Mercedes, and waited in the car. The sky was a mixture of oranges, pinks and shadows, and he reckoned they only had an hour or so before they lost the light completely. But the country lanes were better by headlights – you could see a driver coming by the glare off the hedgerows, and only a heavy-duty lorry would have difficulty passing a touring bike on a back road.

If he could forget Amy's face, he could get excited about this trip. Hot bike, hot woman, hot trail of a murderer. An entirely legal buzz in his veins with an acceptable level of danger for his mam and his boss.

Operating under the protection of the National Crime Agency, he could wander where he pleased, piss off the local cops if the investigation called for it. He could have the freedom he'd possessed as a kid running with his best friends through Butetown – then, he hadn't cared about the law, thinking himself invincible. Now, he knew what the weight of the law felt like, but Frieda could give him licence to break the rules.

Of course, she might turn out to be a stickler for rules and a complete killjoy, but she was taking a completely impractical bike over Snowdonia in pursuit of a case. He suspected she had a little rebel in her.

A sudden rapping at the glass made him jump and he wound down the window.

'You're late,' Frieda said.

He locked the car, handed the keys to Dylan and donned his helmet. Frieda held out her hand silently for his pack and stuffed it in the saddlebag. Her leathers were perfectly fitted for a hard ride, no vanity in the cut and a few scuffs on the elbows. She'd clearly put in a lot of riding time but the leather was still expensive, well-maintained.

Jason mostly wore jeans and jacket riding around Cardiff, but he suited up for a long ride, like seeing Lewis in Swansea or taking in the coast. His one-piece was in need of thorough conditioning and he brushed at the flecks of mud dusting the outside of his thighs.

'Stop preening, princess. We have a lot of road to go.'

Jason didn't rise to the bait, didn't comment when she mounted the bike and nodded her head towards the pillion. He was too tall to ride like this for long, but he'd known what he was signing up for. The thrill of the ride would be worth the sore arse.

He mounted the bike and chose the grab rail over her waist, before leaning in a little. 'I'm heavy for a pillion.'

'I've chauffeured men hundreds of times,' she said dismissively. 'My ex was built like a wrestler and we survived the Lake District.'

The engine throbbed through him, a tamed tiger waiting to be unleashed on unsuspecting Welsh roads. She moved without warning, but he had played pillion before to Dylan and his excitable sister, so he knew what to expect from an erratic driver.

After that, though, she was considerate. The traffic in Cardiff was minimal and they headed for the M4, the main artery of South Wales. However, Frieda ignored the turning and continued on the A470, a broad, busy main road that soon dwindled to little more than a lane with some road markings.

Jason had never crossed Mid Wales before, never ventured much outside his Cardiff home. He'd looked up the route on his phone before he'd left Amy's – over four hours, staying on the one road, though that road would change its shape significantly.

Frieda was a law-abiding citizen, it seemed – or else she couldn't go too fast with his fat arse weighing down her bike. They soon left behind town lights for trees and vast bodies of water, the haunted Llwyn-on Reservoir the first they saw but by no means the last. The still waters captured the fading light, glowing in muted red as if a dragon slumbered beneath the surface, witness to danger and tragedy.

The twilight chill settled on them both, and Jason dared to reach out, moving closer to Frieda's warm body. The last time he'd been in the Valleys, he'd have given anything for a motorbike and a woman beside him, but Frieda's body heat was the only warmth she was likely to give him.

Why had she brought him along? National agencies didn't just pick up waifs and strays, bringing them along for the ride. If she needed backup, she could seek out the local cops, not a former gang runner with priors for assault and theft. Maybe, under that icy gaze, she liked him. She wanted to get to know him.

But this was business, work. She must've seen something he could offer her. But he was the first to admit he was dull-witted compared to Amy or one of Cardiff's detectives. He was handy in a fight but she had no way of knowing that. Though she had looked over his criminal record – what could she have seen there to make her think he'd be good for this job?

Of course, Amy had seen something in him, but Amy had been desperate. Thinking about her made him feel uncomfortable, uneasy, and he pushed the thoughts away, out into the night. He was going to enjoy this ride with Frieda, and damn Amy's expectations.

Only a few cars passed them as darkness swallowed the road, scattered lights between the trees marking pubs and houses along the way. Villages popped out of nowhere, with increasingly unpronounceable names, and vanished just as quickly.

He lost track of time just as the road opened out on to a little town the sign proclaimed to be Rhayader. Frieda swung the bike into a deserted car park and killed the engine.

'I'm hungry,' she declared.

'Pub?'

'Not if you want to drive.'

They settled for fish and chips, leaning against a wall, hot grease coating his fingers and lips, dripping onto his boots. Frieda said nothing until her dinner was mere paper and scraps, wiping her fingers on the feeble napkins and stabbing her plastic chip fork into their remains.

'The roads are quiet,' she said. 'We'll be in Bangor before midnight. I've arranged a room there and we'll move on in the morning.'

Jason noted the use of *room*, singular, but said nothing. Was he being brought on this trip as entertainment? Was he okay with that? He'd never been particularly discerning about who he took to bed, but they were working together professionally. Surely that was against the rules?

But the longer the silence lasted, the harder it was to ask. He polished off his cod, removed the worst of the grease with an unsullied corner of the newspaper, and finished his can of Coke.

The bike was designed for the novice and veteran alike and, with some gentle nudging from Frieda, he started her up. The

NCA officer climbed onto the pillion and wrapped her arms around him, snug and warm at his back.

Riding out of Rhayader, not knowing where this journey was leading him, Jason felt like a king.

Cerys turned up just after Jason left and retreated to the kitchen with Owain, where they pointedly did not argue, exchanging the bare minimum of words required to cook dinner.

Amy had struggled to settle after Jason left. She wanted to work, to distract herself, but she kept returning to the GPS tracker that showed him moving farther and farther away from Cardiff. When the mobile signal gave out entirely, she shut down the programme and went to the kitchen, where there was light and people and a different kind of tension.

Cerys made a passable macaroni cheese, even if it was nothing like Jason's, and they ate in tense silence.

'How's the investigation going?' Cerys asked the table, but she looked at Owain.

Owain looked at Amy, but she was not in the mood for chat and stuffed another forkful of pasta into her mouth.

'There's a lot of CCTV to go through,' he said.

Cerys waited for him to elaborate and, when he said nothing more, she tried a different tack. 'If you need any help, I have nothing else to do tomorrow.'

Amy refused to meet Owain's pleading gaze. If he did not want to spend time with Cerys – and Amy had no idea why that might be, apart from the fact that all Carrs were infuriating and irrational and should probably be shot – then he would have to tell her himself. Amy was not a creator of excuses.

'That would be … good. I think there were some things Amy needed at the museum.'

'You should both go,' Amy said. 'Take in the galleries. Make notes.'

'It's not a date,' Owain said quickly.

'We don't need a date,' Cerys said, her voice sharp, acid. 'We've been going out for five months. We live together!'

'I know that,' Owain mumbled to his plate. 'I meant … it's work, isn't it? Not for fun.'

'You can have lunch,' Amy said, magnanimously. 'All work and no play, et cetera. Come back in the afternoon.'

Amy left the table and returned to AEON, itching to remove Cerys and Owain from her space. She wanted to rant, throw cushions, play screamo at top volume. She wanted to open a bottle of cheap red wine and swipe the books from Jason's shelves.

But she wouldn't do those things. She would watch more CCTV footage and research North Walean gang connections, and try not to refresh the GPS tracker every five minutes to see if it had picked up a signal again.

And she would find out more about Frieda bloody Haas.

The National Crime Agency staff database was easy to infiltrate, but its employee information was sparse. Where could she find more intel on Frieda Haas? She seemed to shun social media and Amy couldn't even construct a basic family tree from the scraps found through Google. The woman was a ghost.

Amy went back through Jason's phone data, looking for significant interactions around the time he'd first met Frieda. She got a hit off Cerys' phone, then an unknown, and then a flurry of data including Owain's number. Therefore the solitary unknown must be Frieda's phone.

The number was unlisted, unsurprisingly, and registered to the NCA. Of course, it was currently in the wilds of Mid Wales, so interrogating its data was pretty much impossible.

Amy returned to the CCTV. But after five minutes, she knew she wasn't seeing much of anything, the museum's visitors passing in a blur before her tired eyes. She was getting too old for all-nighters, twenty-five years weighing heavy on her bones. She brought up the calendar – twenty-five years, eleven months and twenty-two days. Would Jason be back for her birthday?

She wanted to curl up on the sofa and take Jason on a guided tour of early noughties alt music, or watch him watching a *Die Hard* movie or some other mind-numbing action flick.

But Jason wasn't here. And there was a murder to solve.

She checked her search, the trawling of dark corners for something about gangs and the art trade. Nothing yet, but she now had another reason to delve into the deep web to find their hiding places. She ghosted into a few IRC channels, hoping to get lucky, but nothing beyond the usual trade in drugs and women caught her eye. She sent out a few more feelers into the darkness, hoping for a vibration down the line to lead her in the right direction.

'We're going to catch a late film,' Cerys said, Owain following like a lapdog.

'See you tomorrow,' Amy said, averting her eyes from their joined hands and the smudge of pale pink lip gloss at the corner of Owain's mouth.

When she was alone, the need to work fuelled her on. The need to think about anything apart from Jason and that woman. Owain and Cerys. Other people's happiness.

She made coffee and tackled another day of footage. She'd hit the last twenty-four hours now, and found nineteen suspicious people who warranted further investigation.

The girl was back, she noted, the checker of frames and statue bases. She was wearing a school uniform this time and Amy tried to make out the logo on her jumper. What was a secondary school student doing mixed up in an art heist?

Amy followed her to the exit, trying to get a good angle on the jumper, when a man stepped in front of her. Amy vaguely recognised him, froze the footage, and flicked through her gallery of suspects. He was one of the sitters in front of 'The Blue Lady'.

Amy watched their interaction. The girl was grinning, practically dancing from foot to foot, as the man looked increasingly irate. He reached for her arm, then withdrew, looking about him anxiously. *A barely controlled temper and a guilty conscience.*

The girl used the opportunity to give him the slip, and he fumed impotently in the centre of the hall. Then he went back upstairs to the gallery and made for the bench in front of 'The Blue Lady'. Except someone was already sitting there, the middle-aged woman from before.

However, instead of replacing her, he sat down beside her and studied 'The Blue Lady' as before. They did not acknowledge each other until she accidently swung her handbag into his leg, and he said something sharp to her. She ignored him and walked away.

Amy watched their exchange again, but she couldn't see any notes or code pass between them. They were successfully ignoring each other, as strangers in public places were wont to do, until he'd snapped at her.

Nothing about this canvassing operation made sense. A teenage girl in the crew, operatives openly confronting each other, lingering on the changeover without any exchange of information yet drawing attention to themselves.

How did such bungled surveillance lead to such a successful heist?

Chapter 13

River deep, mountain high

The bike was like a temperamental stallion – barely tamed, constantly trying to kick out and wanting to show off exactly how fast he could run.

Jason felt Frieda laughing against him as he understeered again and clipped an overgrown hedgerow. They were in the middle of Snowdonia National Park, now less than an hour from Bangor, and the exhilaration of the journey was morphing into the nerves of reaching their destination. One hotel room or two? One bed or two? And how exactly did he feel about those options?

And what the hell was he thinking? He'd agreed to accompany a woman he barely knew on a trip across the country to investigate a crime by … what? Asking questions? Surveillance? Breaking heads? He'd had a lot of time to think on this journey, and he was no closer to figuring out what he was doing here.

As they neared Mount Snowdon – not that he could tell much of anything in the dark – Jason was forced to slow down. The midnight air was cold and thick with a descending mist, the bike's driving lights only illuminating a few short yards ahead. Jason crawled through the fog, the bike barely topping thirty miles an hour in the dense clouds that were forming around them.

He had the sense of being watched, as if the towering yet unseen mountains were looking down and judging him. He shivered from the chill, or maybe just the creeping feeling over his spine, like someone was walking over his grave. The silent forests and majestic lakes rang with the magic of King Arthur's court, age-old monuments to a former glorious time when knights fought dragons and women rose from the frigid waters to present the one true king with his almighty sword.

The stone edifices absorbed all sound, so that all he could hear was Frieda's breathing and his, out of step and harsh in the night air. If he could see more than a few feet in front of him, he was sure the view would be breathtaking. As it was, he was confined to predicting the curves of the road ahead and not falling through the flimsy-looking barriers preventing them from a drop into God knows what.

A sudden chill swept over him, a strong breeze blowing from the right. Jason glanced over, but he could see nothing but inky blackness shrouded in swirls of mist. He fought to keep the bike's line, cornering into the wind. Frieda's hands shifted on his waist, and he felt her fingers flex through the leather as she leaned with him.

The lorry came out of nowhere.

The horn blast warned him a few seconds before impact. Jason swerved the bike to the left and braked hard, but the bike fishtailed and he felt the rear wheel lift as if a weight had been thrown off. *Frieda.*

The bike toppled, skidding across the lorry's path and taking him with it. The asphalt tore up his leathers, the agony in his trapped leg fighting to be heard over the death knell in his head.

Inches from the front wheels of the lorry, Jason closed his eyes.

And jerked them open, as the heavy lorry whistled past his head and the bike slammed against solid rock.

Jason flew through the air, an ungainly ostrich in flight, and plunged into the lake.

Amy couldn't sleep.

The coffee had done nothing for her, and the red wine chaser made her heart beat unpleasantly fast, her face flushed and too hot. Where was Jason? Bangor had plenty of mobile phone signal but his GPS locators all remained off-grid. Her mind supplied the 1001 ways that he could die in the Middle of Nowhere, Wales, but she tried to fight away those thoughts.

He was fine. He had to be fine.

Unable to monitor Jason's wellbeing, she sought out a distraction. When flash games and Sporcle quizzes failed to hold her attention, she indulged in her favourite loathed pastime – checking in with her parents.

The bank account opened up for her easily enough. It was her father's third new account in six months, which deepened her suspicion that he was involved in something unsavoury. Tax avoidance or money laundering for the obscenely wealthy. Something else she could hate him for, while he remained blissfully unaware.

From their recent transactions, they were in Monaco. Expensive restaurants and wine by the case and private casinos. Amy wondered if Lizzie was going to join them, play happy families without her. She had forgiven her sister for reaching out to their parents, but something about the image still stung.

Lizzie remembered living with their parents better than Amy did. Lizzie had lived with them in their beautiful Whitchurch house, while Amy clung to her grandmother's skirts and stayed in the little Cardiff terrace, away from the light and the outside. Of course, when they'd abandoned their children to see the world, Lizzie had been forced to share Amy's attic and the burden of Gran's fading mind.

It was the theft that set them free. Amy had watched their travels for months, yearning for some connection to them when the postcards and calls dried up. Taking the next step had been difficult only because it crossed a moral line – the child who stole from her parents.

Her phone buzzed. She pounced on it but was disappointed to see Owain's name staring back at her. He'd added a few more names to their rogues' gallery. Amy matched a couple to faces she'd flagged, and added the others to her list.

She glanced up at the clock. 02:13. Yet another sleepless soul in the city of Cardiff tonight. But Cerys would be lying in their bed, waiting for him when he decided to rest his eyes or wake her for an embrace that would make him forget sleep, forget the nightmares.

Amy had her cold, lonely apartment. No assistant sleeping downstairs or making her hot chocolate in their kitchen.

No one to wake when her darkness was too deep and she just needed someone to hold close.

Jason touched her shoulder, her arm, and sometimes he hugged her – when she was teetering on the edge of panic or despair. The times he knew about. But he was a friend, nothing more. He would always retreat, to his family, to his women.

Amy shut down her banking program and watched the gallery footage again. Anything to distract from the chill in her that was nothing to do with loss of heat, the emptiness of the silent rooms, the lack of *him*.

Chapter 14

Lost property

The shock of the water robbed him of his breath and Jason fought not to gasp and drown himself in his panic.

But he hit the bottom immediately, free to kick up to the surface if he could ignore the raw agony. Adrenaline won over pain and he broke the surface into the mist on the water, no way of telling where he was in the bloody lake.

His helmet was a goldfish bowl and he wrenched it off his head, letting it sink. He heard the shouts from somewhere behind him and he tried to turn, his sodden leathers weighing him down.

A powerful flashlight swept across the water from the bank and Jason raised an arm to wave, sending a surge of frigid water over his nose and mouth. He spluttered but kept waving, until he heard an answering shout.

'I see him!'

Jason wasn't going to wait around to be rescued, the cold already sinking deep into his bones and no Amy to send the emergency services to his exact location within moments. He started swimming towards the light, surprised when his legs hit the bottom within seconds. He got the gently sloping bank under his feet and staggered the last few feet to the safety of the shore.

'Fuck, you all right, mate?'

The man's voice was trembling as he seized Jason's hand, helping him stumble out of the water pooling around his ankles. Jason couldn't see anything of him behind the strong light, but he was grateful for the strong arm steadying him.

'Bit c-cold,' he stuttered, his body starting to shiver in the night air.

From behind the man, he heard someone or something come down from the road.

'Where the fuck is my bike?' Frieda grabbed his jacket and shook him. 'What have you done with my bike?'

Jason was startled into silence, unable to resist her angry hands on his jacket. But his flashlight-wielding saviour got between them.

'Leave off, love. He just came out of the water. Your bike's probably smashed against the wall up there.'

'You bastard!' she screamed, and any illusions he'd been harbouring about Frieda vanished in the face of her naked fury. 'I never should've brought you here!'

'Love, he could've died in that water. Or under my wheels. You need to calm down.'

Belatedly, Jason realised that the man must be the driver of the lorry. The memory of his up-close encounter with the vehicle's wheels threatened to buckle his knees, but Frieda still had a tight grip on his leathers.

She let go of him, shoving Jason onto his arse before rounding on the lorry driver.

'Who are you? You were all over the road!'

'It's been a long night,' the man said evasively.

'Asleep at the wheel? This is a police investigation now. Hand over your licence and registration.'

The man bolted, scrambling for the barrier and dropping his torch. The light threatened to roll into the water, but Jason flapped at it with his arm, dragging it towards him. He pointed it at the barrier, to see Frieda pinning the man to the ground and handcuffing him.

'I am arresting you for dangerous driving...'

Jason missed the rest of the spiel, though he knew it off by heart by now. He reached inside his leathers and pulled out his phone. It was dead, dripping filthy water. Amy was gonna kill him.

'Get off your arse and help me!'

Frieda's words finally penetrated and Jason prised himself off the grass, the torchlight guiding him to where she had her handcuffed prisoner sitting beside a scraggly bush.

'I don't know—'

'I don't care. Watch him while I call it in.' She wrenched the torch from his hand and shone it at her face, as if she were telling ghost stories around the campfire. 'If he escapes, I'm arresting you for aiding and abetting.'

She marched off, taking the light with her, and Jason felt his way to their captive in the dark. He had no idea what to say – the man had saved his life, but he had tried to run, so was definitely guilty of something.

'Sorry about this, mate,' he said, which was ridiculous.

'Don't worry. Bitch cop caught me out, didn't she?'

They sat together in the dark, Jason massaging water out of his leathers as he tried to keep moving, stop himself stiffening up. He couldn't hear Frieda's voice, so she must've wandered farther down the road. Didn't want to be overheard – or couldn't get signal. They could be here a while.

'Would you mind reaching for my fags? Inside left pocket. And help yourself – you look fit to drop.'

'Could still get the drop on you,' Jason said lightly, feeling his way to the cigarettes and lighter inside the man's jacket. 'My neck's on the line too.'

He placed an unlit cigarette in the man's mouth by the flame of the lighter, before lighting him up and helping himself to the offered cigarette. He might have quit, but if this wasn't a time for vice indulgence, he didn't know what was.

He replaced the lighter and fags, before taking back the man's cigarette – he probably shouldn't let the prisoner choke on his own fag.

'What you done then?' Jason asked, in the conversational tone of the prison yard.

'You police?'

'Nah. Work for a PI, but nothing official.' He suddenly seized on an idea. 'You've come from the port, right? Holyhead?'

The man leaned forward and Jason let him take another drag, his grimace lit only by the crumbling glow of the ash.

'What's it to you?'

'We need to know a thing or two about what's going on up there. And you'd be in the perfect position to tell us. Can't speak for Her Ladyship, but that might be worth something. See what I'm saying?'

His companion was silent for a long time. Jason brought the cigarette back to his lips, but he shook his head. Jason stubbed it out against his boot and smoked his own to the stub. He'd quit again when he felt less like Frosty the Snowman.

'I may know something about what's coming in and out of the docks. And … who you might talk to, to make it run smooth, like.'

Jason grinned in the dark. He'd show Frieda exactly why she'd brought him along.

At six o'clock on Sunday morning, Bryn was tucking into a bacon butty at his desk when the phone trilled.

The sound echoed in the deserted office and Bryn picked it up curiously. 'Hesketh.'

'Bryn, it's me. Jason.'

Bryn glanced at the clock to double-check the time, and glanced out the windows for good measure. Still dark, and definitely not a decent hour for a Sunday.

'You're up early,' he said, before a stab of fear hit his heart. 'Is it Amy?'

'No, she's fine. I think. Listen – I'm in Bangor with Frieda.'

Bryn gawped. A blob of ketchup dripped off his butty and onto the keyboard.

'Well, that's … something.'

'I got a bit … I can't get through to Amy, let her know I'm all right. And you know what she's like.'

Bryn knew enough about his pet hacker to figure she was pretty pissed off that her assistant had buggered off to North Wales with some pretty girl from London. But on that point he kept quiet. 'What should I tell her?'

'I'll try her again when I get settled in a hotel. And not to worry. Cheers, Bryn.' Jason sneezed loud enough to wake the dead. 'Shit, I'm coming down with something. Fucking water.'

All Bryn's detective instincts kicked in. 'What happened to you, exactly?'

Jason paused. 'Promise you won't tell Amy?'

'Second thoughts, best you don't tell me.' Bryn didn't want to get between those two, curiosity be damned.

'I'll keep you updated.'

'And how will Agent Haas like that?'

'She'll learn to live with it, won't she?'

The edge in his voice told Bryn that at least some of the shine had come off. He'd seen the way Jason had looked at Frieda in the detectives' office. He'd obviously fancied her enough to tag along to Bangor, but he'd hopefully got the measure of her now.

Bryn had seen enough London coppers to know they were hewn differently to Welsh police, and the National Crime Agency knew how to find a humourless hard-arse. The local divisions were a different story, but Bryn's mind skirted away from those thoughts. The Welsh Division of Organised Crime Command was lying dormant and no one had any desire to resurrect it.

'Bryn? You still there?'

'Yeah, I'm here. Just keep an eye out, will you? NCA may be leading on this but I … well…'

'I'll keep you in the loop,' Jason said, and it was as good as a promise. If there was one thing Jason wore well, it was loyalty.

'Stay in touch.'

Bryn hung up the phone and absently picked up his cold sandwich. Why was Frieda Haas in Bangor? And why hadn't she mentioned she was leaving the capital? She had commandeered his investigation and then left him to it, no word of what she was doing or when she'd be back.

While the cat's away… It seemed the investigation was back in his hands and he intended to make full use of that time – and his secret weapon.

It was time to bring his hacker back into the fold.

Chapter 15

Show me yours

Frieda was giving him the silent treatment.

Her beloved bike was under a tarp in the Bangor Police Station car park until she'd had a chance to look it over and decide on scrap or salvage. The way she was glaring at Jason, however, made him feel like she'd rather be making that decision about him.

Jason had turned down a trip to the local hospital, assuring their police escort that he was just a little scraped up and soggy, but he was grateful for access to the locker rooms and some dry clothes. He also raided their first aid box for bandages to cover the road rash on his leg, and the contents of his wallet were drying out on the radiator in their tiny kitchen.

He'd told Frieda that their new lorry-driving friend was willing to make a deal, but she'd ignored him until they got to the station, when she presented the idea as her own. Jason was beginning to realise how much of a cow she really was and regretted ever swinging a leg over her bike.

Wearing a mixture of odd gym clothes, Jason made his way to the briefing room, where Frieda was filling in the local officers on the purpose of their visit and the accident. She was still wearing her leathers, her cold eyes barely registering his entrance as she continued to hold court.

'It seems our driver was in a hurry, but we have no idea why. The back of the lorry was entirely empty except for some pallets, a couple of crisp packets and a full bottle of what looks like apple juice.'

'He was on his way back from Dublin,' Jason chipped in. 'Made his drop-off yesterday evening and caught the last ferry back.'

The lead uniformed officer turned to him. 'And who might you be, son?'

'He's with me,' Frieda said, with obvious distaste. 'He's …
a consultant for the South Wales Police, and the driver made
some comments to him while we were waiting for backup.'

The officer looked at him appraisingly. 'Nye Thomas, Duty
Sergeant. You think you can get him to talk some more?'

Jason shrugged one shoulder. 'That was for free, but I reckon
he'll be after something in exchange for more. You've got nothing on him otherwise.'

'Nothing? He destroyed my bike!'

'Treacherous bit of road,' Nye said. 'And not a drop of alcohol in his veins. I don't think we can hold him accountable for
your bike, Miss Haas.'

Frieda looked between Nye and Jason as if she wasn't sure
who she wanted to eviscerate first. 'I'll talk to London.'

While the Icewoman made her phone call, Jason bummed a
cigarette off one of the constables and went outside for a quick
fag with him. Nothing like a dash of cold water and a near-
death experience to send him running back to nicotine. The
morning sun had burned off most of the mist and Jason was
grateful for the warmth settling into his skin.

'You're up from Cardiff then?' the PC asked, probably a year
or two younger than Jason and still keen.

'Checking out some leads,' Jason said, like he knew what he
was talking about and hadn't just followed Frieda up here to
get away from his boss.

'It's to do with that museum theft, isn't it?'

'Could be.'

'We've been keeping an eye out, but truth is that our boys
aren't up to much about here. Snatching purses and growing
weed, that's about it. I don't think any of them have got the
brains to traffic a painting.'

'We think it's an international operation. Any strangers in
town?'

The PC considered. 'Usual tourists, but most of them have
gone home now. If you wanted to sneak about, you wouldn't
come through Bangor, or stop off anywhere. People are right
suspicious round here, unless you're local. If you were smart,

you'd drive up the A470 or take the A55 along the top of the country. Never see another soul.'

Jason nodded – that made a lot of sense. One painting would be easy enough to hide in a bag, and it wasn't like North Wales was swarming with border control. You could stroll onto any ferry coming in or out and no one would be any the wiser.

He returned to the office, where Frieda was writing in a little black notebook, a firm do-not-cross perimeter in a five-foot circle around her. Jason had never been one for heeding warnings, though, and he stopped beside the desk she was leaning on.

'What did they say?'

She didn't look up. 'I can question the suspect. If he gives me enough specifics, he can have immunity from prosecution. If not…'

Her tone was neutral, her cold mask firmly back in place. Jason thought he might prefer it that way. At least she was tolerating him and not calling for his head.

'Can I watch?'

'I thought you might be a voyeur.'

Her flirtation was careful, cool, and Jason wasn't in the mood to play games.

'I'll be behind the screen then,' he said, and made to walk away.

Frieda caught his arm, a firm warm grip on his bare skin. 'Jason … I'm sorry. About before. Are you sure you're all right? You should get the police medic to take a look at you.'

Her eyes were earnest, her voice pitched low so they weren't overheard. Was this another game, or did she genuinely care about what happened to him?

'I'm fine,' he said, practising his own distance, the aloof voice he'd perfected during his time inside. 'Let's get on with it, yeah?'

She nodded, released his arm, and led the way out of the room as if nothing had passed between them. Nye joined them outside the interview room, gesturing at the ajar door of the observation room.

Jason had been in an interview room more times than he cared to remember, but never on the outside looking in. The one-way glass tinted the harshly lit room with a shadow, the miserable lorry driver leaning against the table edge.

Frieda and Nye entered the room together, Nye sitting opposite the driver but Frieda choosing to remain standing.

Nye set the old-fashioned tape recorder and laid out the preliminaries. Jason watched the man's face carefully for a reaction, but he was a study in misery, downcast and defeated.

The lorry driver gave his name as Benjamin Stock, living in Canton, Cardiff – a couple of streets over from Dylan's garage.

'What were you transporting, Mr Stock?' Frieda was straight to the point.

'I thought … I thought this was about my driving.'

'I think it's about a lot more than that, isn't it? Forensics are crawling all over your lorry and they're making some very interesting discoveries.'

Jason had seen the lorry when he went for his smoke – it was cordoned off in the corner of the car park, right next to Frieda's battered bike, with not a soul in sight. She was playing him.

'Please – that bloke before, the one who went in the lake. He said you were after information. I can give you that.'

'I think you'd better.'

But then Benjamin seemed to regain a semblance of control. 'What's … what's in it for me, like? I mean, I'm happy to help you but if I … there are nasty people involved, see. I got a girl-friend, a kid.'

'Tell us what we need to know, and we will take care of everything. You want witness protection? I can give you that – if you tell me everything. If not…' She paused, leaving his imagination to fill in all the potential consequences.

Benjamin winced at the thought. 'I'll tell you what I know, but they don't let on to all of us. I can take you to the spots, get you some other fellas who are involved.'

'Let's start at the beginning. To ensure we can rely on your information. What was your latest shipment?'

Benjamin swiped at his forehead, sweat erupting from every pore. 'I picked … the shipment up in Port Talbot yesterday morning, drove up to Holyhead and went over just after lunch. Dropped … it off outside Dublin, then came back with an empty. I was heading back to Cardiff when I, uh, ran into you.'

'I didn't ask you for the route. What was in the shipment?'

Benjamin mumbled something that Jason didn't pick up.

Frieda slammed her hand down on the table, startling him up and away from the surface. 'For the microphone, Mr Stock. Do not waste my time.'

Benjamin hugged himself. 'I don't look at them. Someone else loads them up and I just drive.'

'Loads up what?'

He closed his eyes, as if he didn't want to see, to remember. 'Girls. Working girls.'

Jason had never disdained a prostitute, had been in awe of the right hook of quite a few when he was running around Butetown. But herding girls up from their homes, promising them a new life and giving them only ugly, sordid work in back alleys … He thought of Cerys in that position, a more vulnerable Cerys from only a year or two ago, and he wanted to smack Benjamin and all the other bastards until they bled.

'Trafficking,' Frieda said, and Benjamin flinched. 'Call it what it is, Mr Stock. Ignorance is not a defence.'

'When I first took it up, I thought it was dodgy tellies. Not girls. I didn't agree to that. But once you're in…' He gave half a shrug, like a man afraid to move more than an inch in case the monsters in the dark should see him, catch him.

'I am offering you a way out.' Frieda's voice was softer, kinder, as she slid into the seat opposite him. A friend in the night. She was playing both good and bad cop.

Benjamin nodded quickly, as if he was acting before he could take it back. Nye narrated it for the tape, the first words he'd spoken since the date and time of the interview. He was letting the master do her work.

'Do your lorries carry anything else, besides girls?'

'I told you – I don't look. But I've seen boxes a couple of times. The others … they're local to Neath and to here. They do smaller jobs as well, white van stuff. I don't know what they're moving.'

Jason's ears pricked up. A valuable painting wouldn't be stuffed on the back of a lorry full of women, but it might be part of a smaller haul. Jason itched to know the details of those local drop-offs, but Frieda had to weave her spell in her own sweet time.

She might be an ice-cold bitch, but Jason liked the way she worked. And he wanted to see a lot more of her in action.

Chapter 16

Hide and seek

Teenagers were a hacking goldmine.

They were power users of social media, always connected and sharing everything about their lives 24/7. A young person couldn't eat a meal without taking a picture on Instagram, couldn't stop at a shop without checking in on Foursquare. They exchanged cats on Tumblr and collected clothes on Pinterest, all while browsing Twitter for the latest unfiltered news.

Which made investigating a teenager something like child's play to Amy Lane.

The first step was identifying the school uniform. After trying and failing to focus in on the badge, she turned instead to the colour scheme. She found the culprit – a Welsh-speaking secondary school in Cardiff.

Schools rarely networked their pupils' information in a readily accessible way, but the pupils themselves were expert in shouting that from the rooftops. She found several Facebook users who had added their school, as well as some groups and events connected to it. But Facebook was fading in popularity with teens. If she didn't find what she needed there, she had several other social media avenues to explore. Teens were all too eager to vomit out information, to be known, a habit rarely broken in their twenties and thirties.

She estimated the girl's age as somewhere between thirteen to sixteen to narrow her search. As Amy got older, it was getting harder and harder to distinguish ages. No wonder aged shop assistants were IDing up to twenty-five. Not that Amy had ever been ID'd, but she'd heard Lizzie and Jason whine about it enough to know the score.

Scanning the pictures, she narrowed down a type – white, shoulder-length dark hair, no glasses, around five foot. But she didn't recognise their suspect, and AEON couldn't muster up more than a fifty per cent match on facial recognition. Perhaps teenagers involved in high-risk art heists managed their privacy a little better than the average social media user.

Amy slipped down into the next layer, the bowels of Facebook's machinations, but even the locked-down accounts didn't yield a positive match. Next she turned to Instagram, hoping that the glut of photographs would widen her window into life at the school – and let her find her mark.

Of course, the uniform could be a ruse, getting in under the radar by appearing as an innocent schoolgirl. However, given the general suspicion around teenagers in society, the girl was more likely to be watched in that uniform than if she'd dressed older, more like a college or university student.

Instead of searching by school identifiers, Amy looked at the upload location for the photos, narrowing it down to the area immediately around the school. Even if the pupils weren't allowed mobile phones in class, the teachers could never keep them locked down during break and lunch.

The pictures were mostly of food – what else? – and selfies, groups of friends, laughing and chatting. Some pupils were more artistic, playing with composition and filters, but replicating supposedly 'unique' experiments that Amy had seen repeated a hundred, a thousand times.

She found her by accident. Skimming through one user's detailed account of the first day of term, Amy caught sight of a face in the background and stopped. She was out of focus, but she fitted the type exactly. Amy browsed photographs around that time and caught her turning towards the camera, a frown at the antics of the girls taking selfies, as if she was above all that.

The girl had her phone clamped to her ear. Amy itched to trace the outgoing call activity for the timestamp, but the school would be a hive of connectivity – the likelihood of locating that specific signal was miniscule. She tried to narrow down the make or model, but it was a rectangular smartphone in black, surrounded by hundreds like it.

Amy browsed the likes and shares for the photo series, making a note of the usernames that cropped up frequently. She checked out those accounts, but they seemed like hangers-on for this particular Instagram fanatic rather than huge content producers.

Rubbing her forehead, Amy blinked away the blurring of her vision and reached for the red wine bottle. Unfortunately, only the dregs remained, standing next to its empty twin. Perhaps it was time to return to the coffee.

She stumbled to the kitchen, legs made of jelly and the floor constantly moving away from her. She made a strong cup of filter coffee, digging out some chocolate digestives to accompany it. She needed fuel if she was to find this girl, and keep out the thoughts about what could've happened to her assistant.

The doorbell buzzed. Amy frowned, milk slopping from the carton in her hand onto the countertop as she instinctively turned to look towards the door. Who the hell would ring her doorbell in the middle of the night?

Amy looked at the clock on the microwave: 09:07. The night had sped by, but it was still bloody early for a Sunday. She set down the milk and crossed to AEON, flicking up the external camera feed. It was Bryn, reaching up to buzz again. Amy opened the door and waited for him to come up in the lift, her mind racing through a hundred possibilities of why he was there, every one of them terrible.

She called up the GPS locator – nothing. Where was Jason? She had a police officer at her door and her assistant was missing. She tried to breathe.

The lift doors opened and Amy leapt towards the corridor, but Bryn had already held up his hand. 'He's fine. He called to tell me because he couldn't get through to you.'

Amy had disconnected the landline, to ensure Lizzie didn't disrupt her work. She'd forgotten her mobile was still busted open on the coffee table.

'He said he would call you when he was in a hotel.'

With that woman. Amy scowled and went back to the kitchen to fetch her coffee. Bryn followed her, helping himself to a mug.

'Anyway, I thought I'd better check in on you.' He looked at her with his sharp detective's eyes. 'You haven't gone to bed, have you?'

Amy retreated back to the living room, her sanctuary under AEON's protective shadow. 'I am not a child. I don't need a nursemaid.'

'You do have an assistant, though. Who isn't here.'

'Jason doesn't own me. I go to bed when I please, I work when I please. You don't ask questions when I deliver results.'

Bryn held up his hands in surrender. 'I'm not nagging. I came to bring you some more titbits.'

'Since last night?'

'Last night?' Bryn looked at her blankly.

'Owain was here. Before he left with Cerys.'

Bryn's confusion faded. 'Oh, right. This is privileged stuff, you understand? Need-to-know.'

Amy wasn't surprised that the right hand had no idea what the left was doing. But Bryn and Owain were close – it must be awkward not telling his team what was going on behind the scenes. Like Jason deciding to go to Bangor with a total stranger without discussing it with Amy first.

'I'm listening.' She pushed Jason away from her head and hoped the coffee would sober her brain enough to listen to Bryn. She was out of practice with red wine, and her body left her control easily, even if her mind stayed sharp enough to dig up evidence.

'Before she left town, Frieda was convinced that this couldn't be an inside job, but I'm not so sure. They seem the folks most likely to have means and opportunity.'

'Why steal the swipe card if you already had access?'

'What better way to deflect suspicion? In fact, start with her. Talia whatsit. Nothing says professional like breaking into your own car.'

Amy gestured at her computer. 'I have my own angle here.'

Bryn crossed to take a closer look at the monitor. 'Schoolgirls?'

Amy pointed to her suspect. 'She was hanging around the museum, checking the frames and statues. Had a confrontation with an older man in the hall.'

'Amy, this is a professional operation. They're not hiring kids for this.'

She folded her arms. 'Owain believes me.'

Bryn sighed. 'Can we concentrate on the museum employees for now and look at this kid later?'

'What if Frieda's right?' Amy said obstinately. 'What if you're wrong about this?'

Bryn's mouth settled into a hard line. 'Maybe I am. But I need you to look down those alleys for me. Frieda's got a hundred NCA bods working for her back in London. I've got you.'

'And what are you going to be doing?'

'I'll interview the museum staff, cross-reference my answers with what you find, press their weaknesses.'

'Make sure you ask about secret passageways and hidden doors.'

Bryn looked at her incredulously. 'Seriously?'

'We have no evidence the painting left the museum. None. Either it's still in there somewhere or there's a secret door we don't know about.'

'Secret door or not, someone must've seen something unusual, at least.'

'None so blind as those who will not see.'

'What do you mean by that?'

Amy looked at him pityingly. 'If one of your colleagues was doing bad things under your nose, would you want to know? Or would you look away?'

Bryn's jaw tightened. 'You know the answer to that.'

Amy hesitated, before her months-old grievances came to the fore. The police force was rebuilding after a spectacular collapse, where officers had lost their jobs and others their lives. She knew Bryn was doing the best he could, but sometimes it didn't seem like enough.

'Will you help me?' he asked, a note of pleading in his voice.

'Only if you trust my instincts. I'm going to keep hunting down that schoolgirl.'

Bryn grinned. 'I expected nothing less.'

Chapter 17

Post hoc ergo propter hoc

The next two hours were tedious for Jason. Dates and times of past shipments, the ships they came in on at Neath, descriptions of people Benjamin saw at either end of his journey, any piece of information they might have let slip, officials who were in on it, any hints of corruption within law enforcement in Wales or in Ireland.

By the end, Benjamin, Nye and Jason were exhausted, but Frieda was a machine, powering through her questions and demanding exacting answers in return.

'I need the names of any other truckers involved in this. And I need the name of one white van man operating locally.'

Jason roused himself from his slouched position and forced himself to pay attention again. Benjamin gave the names of four truckers like him who operated around Port Talbot, Holyhead or Dublin, but not necessarily between them.

'And the only man I know what does small work up here goes by Jonah Fish.'

'Jonah Fish?' Frieda repeated incredulously. 'Is that supposed to be a joke?'

Benjamin scrubbed a hand across his face. 'It's not his real name, like. He's a Fish but his mates named him Jonah when he was little, after he almost drowned in Colwyn Bay. His brother pushed him off their dinghy.'

'Charming family. Where can I find him?'

'I only met him once. We were stopped with some other truckers in a pub by Menai Bridge – just having a steak, we were. And he came in, sat down with us, because he knew one of the boys from doing jobs. Let a few things slip when he had a few in him, but that's all I know.'

Frieda nodded and sat back in her chair. 'That will be all for today.'

Benjamin looked up, hope in his eyes. 'Is it enough? Will I … am I all right?'

'I'll hear from London shortly. You'll remain here until then.'

He nodded, defeated, as Nye signed off the interview and Jason went to meet Frieda at the door.

'Nice work in there,' he said, admiring despite himself.

'You would know,' she said. 'Faced many opponents like me?'

'None like you.'

She smirked and walked away, as Jason cursed his traitorous tongue. He still fancied her, and that was a huge problem. Not least because she could turn on a hairpin – one moment mysterious ice queen, and the next raving harpy. That combination did not make him want to try his luck.

Yet he followed like a faithful lapdog as she stood with Nye in front of the incident board, brandishing a marker pen and noting the most relevant details for the two cases.

'London will dispatch an agent from Organised Crime Command to deal with the trafficking issue. Jason and I will continue to pursue the painting angle.'

'The white van men,' Jason chipped in, eager as a schoolboy to please Miss.

Frieda wrote *WHITE VAN?* in a box on the board. 'We need to find Jonah Fish.'

Nye laughed, startling them both. 'Oh, that's not hard. We know Jonah of old. Thieving, mostly, and drunk 'n' disorderly. We can lean on him easy enough.'

'We need to do it discreetly,' Frieda said.

'If the higher-ups get wind he's been rumbled, they'll scarper,' Jason agreed.

'Though a hold on their operation could work in our favour, we have no way of knowing what they'd do next.'

'That pub by Menai Bridge? It does a good carvery of a Sunday. That's where he'll be,' Nye said.

'Lunch, boys?' Frieda said with a smile. 'My shout.'

Bryn was surprised when the curator confirmed that most of the fine art and pottery experts were in the museum on a Sunday.

'They're running a children's workshop on conservation,' Lucila explained. 'It's the end of our summer programme.'

While the gallery remained sealed off, the museum couldn't afford to close for another weekend day. Entry might be free, but the gift shop more than made up for it. As Bryn passed the packed shop, he noticed the sticky notes stating that all post-cards of *La Parisienne* had run out. People were grabbing their mementos in case they never saw her again, like mourners at a funeral.

In one gallery two experts on archaeological conservation were explaining their processes to a few bored children and keen college-age students. Bryn interviewed them in turn, but they knew very little about the comings and goings of the fine art department. They might share a lab space but they inhabited different worlds.

Slipping behind the scenes, Bryn made his way to the security office, where the guards had nothing new for him. Paul was a nice guy, but they didn't really know him. He loved his work, loved the paintings. He would be heartbroken at the disappearance of 'The Blue Lady'.

Finally, Bryn popped his head round the door of the conservation lab, not really expecting to find anyone. Instead, he was greeted with three overalled conservators, two women and one man, surrounding a familiar empty frame.

'You're letting in a draft,' one complained.

Bryn dutifully shut the door and approached cautiously, peering over the shoulder of the nearest person to get a closer look. They were dabbing at the ragged edges of the painting with cotton buds, painstakingly removing every drop of blood.

The nearest woman turned to him and Bryn recognised Talia Yeltsova from her photograph. 'Yes?'

'Detective Inspector Bryn Hesketh,' he said, holding up his warrant card. 'I have a few more questions.'

Talia sighed impatiently. 'We are grateful to have our lady back, Detective – what's left of her, anyway.' The man flinched and looked at her as if she'd murdered his mother. 'But every moment we leave this … stain on the oil, the more risk to the work beneath.'

'I won't keep each of you long.' Bryn tried to placate her. 'But we need to find the rest of her urgently.'

Talia turned back to her work, gesturing at the man. 'Noah, go first. Don't be long.'

Noah carefully backed away from the frame, disposed of his cotton bud in a bin liner stuffed full of them, and allowed Bryn to lead him to the other side of the workshop.

'What are you using on it?' Bryn asked, curiously.

'Natural enzymes,' Noah said solemnly, before laughing nervously, more hiccup than giggle. 'Also known as saliva.'

Bryn was stunned into momentary silence. 'You're cleaning a priceless painting with a bit of spit and polish?'

Noah fidgeted awkwardly. 'Not exactly priceless now.'

Bryn took pity on the boy – who was probably in his early thirties, at least – and returned to his notebook. 'Did you notice anyone hanging around the museum before the break-in?'

'The other detective – Jenkins, I think – already went through this.'

'I'm just being thorough,' Bryn said, pleasantly. Unlike the boy revealing the conservators' darkest secrets, Bryn intended to keep his methods to himself.

Noah scratched the scraggly beard on his chin. 'We don't really see anyone. We come in at opening time and leave after closing. You want security for that.'

'Anyone ask any strange questions at the talks? Bit too interested in the paintings?'

'Oh no, that's not me. I'm just a technician. Lia deals with all the classes. Her brain's amazing – she remembers every little thing about every picture.'

The star-struck wonder in the boy's voice made Bryn suspect he appreciated more than just Talia's artistic knowledge.

'Talia did have an appointment though,' Noah said suddenly. 'The day the painting was stolen. You'd have to ask her about that, though.'

'Did you see her visitor?' Bryn asked casually. The details were always useful for double-checking between witnesses – or on camera.

Noah nodded. 'Tall, blonde woman, dressed really well. She had an accent of some kind – maybe a bit German? Does that help?'

For the second time in as many minutes, Bryn was floored. He'd need to double-check the identification, but the boy's description perfectly matched their NCA agent.

'And you're sure that was the day you saw her?'

'Yeah, definitely. I remember because she came back the next morning, but obviously the police weren't letting anybody in. I saw her in the car park – and then the next minute she was gone.'

Bryn shut his notebook. 'Thank you. You've been very helpful.'

As Noah trotted back to his painting, Bryn struggled to process this new lead. Frieda Haas had lied about being assigned this case – she had already been in Cardiff, at the scene of the crime before it had even been committed.

What else was the NCA agent hiding?

Chapter 18

Gangster diplomacy

Awake for twenty-eight hours and counting, Jason was instantly revived by the smell of roasting meat and real Welsh ale.

The waitress recognised Nye and gave them a nice table by the fire. The lunch trade was just starting up, locals passing the table and nodding to Nye as they took their regular Sunday tables. Jason salivated at the rich scents wafting from the carvery table, shredding his paper napkin as he waited impatiently for the waitress to take their drinks order.

'Arrested him for smacking his missus last weekend,' Nye said, as another man nodded to him. 'Poor girl dropped the charges, though, said she'd made a mistake.'

Frieda ordered a pint of lager, Nye a small orange juice, and Jason asked for water. He fancied a pint or three, but at his current level of exhaustion and with a roaring fire at his back, he was likely to pass out in his Yorkshire pudding.

Finally, he could scurry up to the feast and only when he had cleared half the plate did he feel more human. Nye kept up a constant commentary of regular arrestees, the petty criminals and hidden abusers, all coming together for Sunday lunch like one happy Bangor family.

Jason watched Frieda eat out of the corner of his eye. She ate mechanically – if the food were cardboard or caviar, she wouldn't care. It felt more like a refuelling. She reminded him of Amy wolfing down pasta or toast, desperate to return to AEON and whatever offender or gamer's reward she was currently chasing.

The resemblance ended there. Where Frieda was tall, blonde and strong, Amy was slight, mousy and shrunken. Frieda sported designer suits and an air of cool confidence, whereas

Amy wore faded, nerdy T-shirts and ripped jeans with an overcoat of anxiety. Both had fascinating eyes, but Frieda's were blue and chill while Amy's were vivid, passionate green, her emotions flashing through them too fast for either of them to process.

He was also currently working for both of them, a slave of two masters, but he wasn't doing a very good job for either. He'd trashed Frieda's bike and he'd drowned his connection to Amy. And despite disliking her, he had a strong attraction to Frieda which distracted him from thinking clearly around her. As for Amy...

Amy was his friend. And when she was consumed with the glow of a case, she was radiant, all her fears and worries washed away by the love of the mystery. A love he had grown to share, which powered him from one case to the next.

But she was also his dependent, using him as a crutch to get from day to day. She seemed broken, taped together and worn thin in places, threadbare. She had given him a sense of hope and optimism about his life again, but as much as he wanted to do the same for her, she was still fragile, delicate.

Jason didn't know how to fix that. Didn't know if anyone could.

'Your surveillance of the middle distance is excellent, but can we concentrate on the suspect?' Frieda's words broke his reverie, that teasing note back in her voice.

Jason ignored her, turning instead to Nye. The sergeant was looking vaguely to his right.

'Two o'clock,' he murmured.

Jason almost checked his phone before remembering that it was still drying in the police station and realising that was probably not what Nye meant. When they ran together, Jason and Lewis had briefly embraced clock position, mostly to shout 'on your six' while whacking each other's arses with planks of wood. Simpler times.

Jason looked slightly to his left. A table of young men, about his age maybe older, were laughing together over pints and cleared plates. The man facing towards their table had a stylised shark fin tattoo over one eye. If that wasn't Jonah Fish, Jason would get that job-stopper scrawled over his own face.

He was a scrawny boy, without the height and muscle of a lad like Jason. He was playing second fiddle to the other guys at the table, echoing their laughter and riffing off their jokes, but never brave enough to start something of his own. Years of being beaten down and told to shut up. Jason knew plenty of boys like him, had moulded a couple to be just that way when he and Lewis were running around Butetown like they owned it.

'How do we get to him?' he asked Nye.

He was already sizing him up. The gang law and prison survival tactics never really left you, and Jason's eyes flickered over him, assessing his weak spots, his pressure points.

'I got a couple of things to try,' Nye said, casually. 'But I reckon his mam should do it.'

'His mam?' The word came out wrong in Frieda's mouth, short and sour.

'Yeah, she won't be too pleased to hear about the girls. I think he'll do most anything to avoid her getting another phone call from me.'

Jason recalled vividly the day his mam had come to court, wearing the same suit she wore to his dad's funeral. 'Yeah, that should do it.'

It turned out that Welsh gang runners were the same all over, and Jason hardly needed a reminder of that. He wanted to say he'd been clean for months, years now, but his record said different. And he still pulled stupid shit, even if it wasn't entirely illegal.

Amy's kind of illegal suited him better. At least no one got hurt her way. It was justice, in a warped way, with both the police and the private cases. She didn't take on anything if she couldn't square it with her conscience, championing the underdog. One time she'd been approached by a man wanting to fabricate an affair between his wife and the gardener while concealing his own mistress until after the divorce went through. Amy had followed the man for a week, jumping from camera to camera, before posting the dossier of incriminating photographs to the soon-to-be ex-wife.

Jonah and his mates headed outside for a smoke, and Jason rose from the table. 'Two minutes.'

Outside, he removed his new tobacco, filters and papers, rolling up a thin one to smoke in the beer garden, now the sole province of smokers. The soft, warm rooms of the pub stood in stark contrast to its ugly exterior. The grass was damp with mist off the Menai Strait, soggy umbrellas striped with mould over rotting picnic tables.

As he lit up, the lads were making plans for a curry and a drinking session Monday night. Jason caught Jonah straining to be included, invited, looking forlornly between each of them. Eventually, one guy cracked.

'You coming, Jonah?'

Immediately, his demeanour changed, with an attempt to look bored, disinterested. 'Nah, mate. I'm going down Cardiff tonight. Won't be back in time.'

'Another one of your specials, is it?' a young lad asked, obviously impressed – and a little envious.

Jonah just tapped the side of his nose, as if he were actually secret keeper for nuclear launch codes. The others, despite themselves, appeared a little in awe of Jonah's work on the side, even if none of them would want to take on the risks.

'You'll soon be treating us to nights out, cash you've got coming in,' the lad continued.

'Hazard pay.' Jonah was revelling in the attention, preening like a peacock at his elite job status. 'There's two of us, just in case.'

Two of us… Jason didn't react, took another drag of his cigarette, and thought fast. The crowd were returning indoors and little Jonah, a medium fish in a small pond, brought up the rear.

Jason stuck his foot out.

Jonah went flying, face crashing into the cracked tiles at his feet as he tried to save his pint over his nose. His mates watched and laughed, as Jonah turned over and stared accusingly at Jason.

An expert in broken noses, Jason figured it would take another few hours before he had two beautiful black eyes, too swollen to see much of anything – and definitely not fit for a drive to Cardiff.

Jason reached a hand down to him. 'Sorry, mate – feet like a clown's, me.'

Jonah warily took his hand and let Jason pull him to his feet, saying nothing. He wasn't brave enough to start a fight with a bruiser like Jason, and his mates figured it wasn't their problem.

'Let me buy you a pint, yeah?'

Jonah's supposed friends abandoned him to his fate, as the two of them drank their pints in a secluded corner of the pub. Frieda and Nye hadn't moved, and he didn't look at them again. He was flying solo.

'Guess you'll have to give Cardiff a miss,' Jason said casually.

Jonah lowered his pint, knuckles white on the glass. 'Don't know what—'

'Come on now.' Jason smirked at him, a technique of inter-rogation perfected on snot-nosed kids with too much lunch money. 'You wouldn't lie to a man while drinking his beer, would you?'

'What do you want?' Jonah said, finally understanding the game being played.

'The man I work for has an interest in the man you work for. He's sent me to find out what's going on.'

'I'm no grass,' Jonah said quickly, as if afraid he'd chicken out if he held it in any longer.

'Of course not. Which is why I'm going to Cardiff in your place.'

Jonah gaped like his marine namesake. 'You can't do that.'

'Why not? You're unfortunately injured. You've got a mate who can help out this one time. I do the job, tidy like, and everyone's happy.'

'If my boss finds out—'

'If you don't help me,' Jason said, casual, as if Jonah hadn't spoken, 'your mam finds out you've been dealing in whores. What do you think she'll say to that?'

Jonah blanched, a spot of blood welling on his lip where he'd bitten it. 'You can't. It'd kill her.'

'Which is why you're gonna be a good boy and play the game.'

Jason drank his pint in silence for a minute or two, just watching Jonah and working out if he'd pressed the right buttons. Blackmail, extortion – old tricks he'd grown out of, but Jonah was a little shit and Jason couldn't quite feel guilty about it.

'I can … introduce you. It's up to Kyle whether he takes you or not.'

Still got it. 'Where's the meeting point?'

'I'll pick you up here, half-eleven or just before. Kyle hates it when we're late.'

Jonah chugged the rest of his pint and bolted, almost knocking Frieda over in his haste to be out of that pub, away from Jason and his charged words.

Jason calmly finished his pint as Frieda sat opposite him.

'Well?' she asked.

Jason grinned. 'I've got a date.'

Chapter 19

Loose ends

Amy woke to AEON's alarm, her face smushed against the keyboard, and three pages of *V*s in the middle of her notes.

The coffee hadn't helped, her mouth parched, and a distinctive red wine headache at her temples. She dragged her dry carcass to the kitchen for water, paracetamol and a couple of diazepam. She needed to keep the edge at bay, just a little longer. Hangovers always brought the tremors back, the uncontrollable fear of life outside her front door.

She struggled now to remember her last trip outside. It would've been with Jason, a short drive to somewhere within the city, but the details escaped her, the date, the feeling. How had she ever had the confidence to step outside the door, voluntarily, with only her assistant at her side? How had she not collapsed in panic, stared at by everyone in the street, knowing her flaws so entirely?

Because Jason was her equilibrium. And she was feeling off-kilter because he was miles away and out of contact. The promised phone call had yet to materialise, adding to the churning in her gut. But she couldn't wait for certainty, not with a murderer and thief on the loose.

Shoving down her anxiety, Amy shuffled back to AEON and checked out the source of the alarm. She found two new alerts – the museum staff's basic profiles completed, and the school's Instagram photos scanned for her elusive suspect.

She looked at the photos first – two matches only, both within the last week. Another blurry background shot, adding no new detail, and the other...

It was a perfect portrait. The girl sat cross-legged on the grass, her phone cradled in her hand. But she had looked up for one moment, some blur in the air catching her eye, and she had smiled. The picture was simply captioned '*prydferth*,' which a quick Google search revealed to be *beautiful* in Welsh.

The photographer was anonymous, no distinguishing aspects to the profile. The other pictures were artistic but had no human subjects. He had a few followers, but none who went to the school, and Amy knew a loner when she saw one, recognised a kindred spirit. But obviously he knew the girl – and liked her. He would be able to identify her, or so Amy hoped.

But how to reach out to him? Amy connected his email address to several other social media accounts, including a dormant ask.fm account which only held a couple of questions about photography techniques.

She composed the message carefully, debating the use of Welsh – but online translators were dire and she didn't have time to wait for the human touch. In the end, she kept it simple:

I saw the picture you took on instagram. I really liked it. Let's meet after school tomorrow – prydferth.

While waiting for an answer, Amy looked over the museum profiles. A few speeding tickets, one outstanding parking fine and a couple of minor shoplifting offences. One count of domestic violence, but the archaeologist in question was on secondment to Rome.

Then Amy saw it, and a grin spread her lips, the dry skin at the corners cracking with the movement. Talia Yeltsova's work visa had expired three years ago, and her last employer was registered as Oxford University in 1999. Putting her in the perfect place for the millennium heist.

Amy focussed her efforts on Talia, digging out her social and professional networks and setting AEON on a path to dig dirt. She needed much more than a coincidence for Bryn to work his magic, though the expired visa was leverage in itself. Without an assistant on the ground, however, Amy was reliant on the police to do her legwork.

Owain and Cerys had not returned, which she tried not to dwell on. Clearly, they had better things to do, even when a murder was involved, and she tried to rein in her anger, her envy. Her emotions were rumbling too close to the surface, though the pleasant buzz of the diazepam soothed her slighted feelings as well as her anxiety.

AEON beeped. It was too soon for Talia's search, so Amy checked the ask.fm reply.

C u there x

Bryn's attempt to find information on Frieda Haas was tedious and fruitless.

Talia had slipped out while he was talking to Noah, denying him the chance to interrogate her. The NCA would only confirm Frieda's status as an agent, and he had no colleagues within their ranks to push for information. The rest of her career history was unknown to him and he had no way of checking it out on a Sunday afternoon.

Well, that wasn't entirely true, was it? He had Amy, but he was strangely reluctant to share this new lead. How could he tell Amy that his latest suspect was running around with her assistant, while she had no way to reach him? The panic alone might kill her.

No, he'd have to do this the old-fashioned way. Frieda must be ex-police or ex-military for a job like this. Those organisations kept lists, detailed records of their employees. And there, at least, he had contacts in personnel, the kind who would answer his calls on the weekend and not ask too many questions.

Unfortunately, the Met and British armed forces both drew a blank. Checking out individual police forces would take time, and he didn't have friends nationwide. Of course, if her service had been in Germany, his connections didn't stretch that far.

He was about to admit defeat and call Amy when his phone rang. 'Yeah?'

'Bryn, I've got a Matthew Boateng down here for you. Says he's NCA.'

'Send him up.'

Bryn replaced the handset and tried to puzzle this one out. Why was the NCA sending in another agent? Had they discovered something awry with the first one?

One of the uniformed constables escorted the NCA agent into the detectives' office, making a beeline for Bryn. The slim black man in his perfectly tailored suit, probably around Owain's age, made a sharp contrast to the ageing tubby Welshman greeting him, mustard-stained jacket gaping open to reveal yesterday's shirt.

'Matthew Boateng, NCA – but please call me Matt.'

'Bryn Hesketh. Just Bryn. We weren't expecting you today.' *We weren't expecting you at all.*

'The NCA prides itself on a fast response in these situations,' Matthew said, all politic and polite. 'What's your progress?'

Bryn decided to test the water. 'Frieda Haas not given you an update?'

Matt hesitated only a moment. 'The last report I had was that she was interrogating a possible accomplice in North Wales. I'll be handling things from here.'

Something about his response made Bryn uneasy, but he couldn't put his finger on it. He showed Matt to the murder board, such as it was, only the barest details outlined so far. That was mostly thanks to Indira, who had camped out in the lab all weekend and bullied the technicians into prioritising her samples. She was taking her role as senior pathologist very seriously, determined not to mess up, to find the truth at the heart of things. It was the same passion that drove Bryn, and he admired her for it.

When it ignited in Amy, it could power her for days, but he'd heard nothing from his hacker since he'd visited her that morning. He worried about Amy without her assistant to hold her up, but he couldn't head this investigation and check on her every two minutes. Maybe he could enlist Owain and Cerys? Though he had no idea where they were either. It might be the detective sergeant's day off, but it was usually all hands on deck during a murder investigation. And while Cerys technically wasn't his to command, she had never managed to keep her nose out before. Too much like her brother, that one.

Matt made notes on his tablet as he silently reviewed the board, while Bryn checked his phone. Nothing from Jason. He was surprised he hadn't heard from him and that he had to hear about a possible accomplice from the NCA man. Maybe Frieda was proving a bigger distraction than Bryn had first anticipated.

'Are your cyber crime unit on this?'

Bryn managed not to laugh. 'We don't have one. Only an … outside consultant.'

Matt looked at him strangely. 'Who's not involved here, right?'

'That was the NCA directive,' Bryn said carefully.

'Good. Don't want to complicate things.' Matt tapped one particular report. 'What caused the security alarms to fail at the museum?'

'They didn't fail. The motion sensors and automatic police callout were turned off from the security office.'

Matt looked bemused. 'By the killer?'

Bryn consulted his notebook, clutching it like a talisman to ward off harm from criminals and national agencies alike. 'From what we gather, Paul regularly went up into the galleries at night – to get up close and personal with the art. He was a big fan.'

'A routine? So our killer knew that he would be up in the galleries that night?'

'Doesn't narrow it down much. According to the other staff, pretty much everyone knew he was nuts for those pictures. They say he belonged to some online art societies, and I doubt he kept his special access privileges quiet.'

'Do you think he was approached through one of those sites? Bribed?'

'If he was bribed, why is he dead? Makes no sense to pay a man and then kill him.'

'Change of heart?' Matt waved his hand, theorising. 'Couldn't stand the damage to his beloved painting, interfered when he shouldn't have?'

'It didn't look that way from the CCTV. He was surprised, shocked. If you knew someone was planning a break-in, wouldn't you stay in the security office and turn a blind eye?'

'Plausible deniability means he had to be elsewhere,' Matt reasoned. 'Maybe Paul Roberts was in on it all along, and then he was disposed of. What do we know about him?'

'Nothing much,' Bryn said, flicking back through the notebook. 'Thirty-eight, white, Welsh. Lived alone, no significant relationships. Parents both deceased. Worked security at the museum for seven years, mostly night shifts.'

'Searched his apartment?'

'We didn't prioritise it,' Bryn said defensively.

Matt sighed. 'Hopefully, we haven't lost any evidence by dawdling. Let's take a SOCO over and secure the scene.'

'What's there to secure?'

'We need the deceased's laptop, books, personal artwork. What was he into, what were his connections? I'll ship the evidence up to London by courier and we should have something concrete by tomorrow evening. If he was acting as the mole, we'll soon know about it.'

'Frieda seemed pretty convinced this wasn't an inside job,' Bryn said. The NCA agents didn't seem to even be on the same page.

'Frieda was the first agent on the scene, but art theft isn't her speciality. I'm leading this investigation now.' The polite tone had been replaced with a no-nonsense dismissal.

'I'll find that SOCO,' Bryn said neutrally, giving nothing away.

Frieda wasn't just the first agent on the scene – she had been hanging around before the crime, but for what? And if art wasn't her specialty, why had she been at the museum talking to an expert in oil painting conservation? Nothing these NCA officers did was making any sense.

But Bryn would just have to play along. If they thought him a biddable pet, all the better – when their guard was down, he would find out the truth of this game.

Chapter 20

What lies lurk

'How could you be so stupid?'

Jason sat on the edge of the bed, his head in his hands, waiting out the latest phase of Frieda's rant. She had been harping on about his stupidity, carelessness, irresponsibility, recklessness and idiocy ever since he'd revealed his scheme to her in the pub. Nye had dropped them off at their hotel and made a quick exit, leaving Jason alone to face this harangue. The ice could melt pretty damn fast when she was pissed off, turning the chill fortress into an avalanche.

'What gives you the right to decide how we pursue a suspect? What are you going to do in the middle of Wales with no backup?'

'If you're that concerned, you can follow me.' With Amy, he'd learned to wait out the rants but it seemed Frieda actually wanted answers to her questions.

'My bike is wrecked, remember? And how would I track you in the dark?'

'GPS?' Jason offered.

'Oh, I left my mobile GPS tracker in my other pocket,' Frieda said sarcastically.

'Amy can do it,' Jason offered.

He really should call her before she started phoning Bangor's cops every two minutes or commandeering the city's CCTV cameras to hunt him down.

Frieda's anger died away suddenly. 'Your boss Amy? She tracks you?'

'Constantly.'

Though his phone was still at the station and whatever bugs she'd planted on him might be water-damaged. By tacit agreement, they didn't talk about her surveillance of him – she did what she liked and he pretended it wasn't happening. It was oddly comforting to know that she could rescue him at any time.

'I'll need to be in constant communication with her.'

'Amy doesn't play well with others.'

And if she discovered he'd given out her personal contact details, it would be over between them. Amy could forgive him many things but she took her privacy and security very seriously. Jason had seen the consequences when that line had been violated, and he had no desire to see a repeat.

'What good does that do me then?' Frieda's rage returned, her cheeks flushed and her blonde hair in disarray.

She looked like a woman who'd run a marathon or just woken up from a long night of … Jason pushed those thoughts away. This was business, not his personal fantasy.

'Amy will let you know if there's a problem.'

Jason knew there was no chance she would do anything of the sort, but she'd tell Bryn and the local cops at whatever location he happened to be in.

'How am I meant to protect you?'

Suddenly, Frieda was on her knees in front of him, kneeling up so her face was only a few inches from his. He wanted to get up, move away, but the tiredness and the beer kept him immobile. And maybe something else too.

'I'm a big boy,' he said, finally. 'I can take care of myself.'

Her hand came up to his cheek and Jason tensed like he'd been struck. It was an unpleasant tension, sitting uneasy in his stomach. But why? Wasn't this exactly what he had wanted?

'If anything happened to you, how would I live with myself?'

She leaned in and kissed him, an insistent press of lips before her tongue sought to dance with his, her hand on his thigh.

For a moment, he kissed back – and then he pushed her away.

His eyes opened – when had they closed? – and he realised that those cool blue eyes were not what he wanted to see.

'Why did you stop?' she asked, a girlish begging that didn't suit her.

'Because we're working here,' he said, too quickly, a half-truth at best.

'We haven't stopped in hours. And after this, when will we see each other? I want you.'

She made to kiss him again, but he stood up this time, her hands falling away from him.

'I don't want you. Not like that.'

Frieda stood, indignant. 'Why did you follow me here then?'

'For the investigation,' he said, though that was also a lie.

The ice mask was back now, as she stood, shouldering an air of dignity that seemed to say that she would kneel for no man.

'You'd better sleep before you take on this fool's errand. After tonight, you're on your own.'

She slammed the door behind her, leaving him alone in the hotel room. One bed, just as he'd suspected. She had asked him here because she wanted to know if he was all talk, if the tiger bit in the dark. She'd thought he fancied her, wanted her, enough to follow her across the country.

And she was right. He had taken up her offer because she fascinated him, but he felt nothing for her. She was ice and fire, but nothing in between. How could he know a woman who flitted between masks like shrugging on a coat?

And that mattered to him now. He wanted it to mean something, and he wanted to look into eyes that cared for him, that knew him. He had worked out now what bothered him about seeing Frieda's eyes after that kiss, and it wasn't their unknowable blue depths.

It was because he'd wanted to see green.

Amy had nothing to do. The CCTV was catalogued, the schoolgirl was baited, AEON was scavenging information about Talia, and she was left alone with Minecraft.

But she couldn't settle to building or browsing webcomics, her usual internet haunts a dull parade playing the same faux hysteria and tired jokes over and over. She wanted distraction, diversion, but her brain just consumed this internet junk food, articles and quizzes and fun remixes.

She was tired. She was lonely.

Amy had been used to being alone, perfectly content with her own company. But since Jason entered her life, she'd grown dependent on even the sparse smatterings of conversation throughout the day and the succession of tea mugs and biscuits that appeared silently at her elbow.

More than that, she missed his opinions, his questions. Explaining herself and her leaps of faith, of technology, and devouring the carefully observed breadcrumbs he collected for her. Without him, her world shrank back to a dull apartment with an internet connection. She felt strangely limited.

She absently flicked through the case files again, hoping her mind would seize on something and stop examining her inner struggles. But there was nothing to catch her attention – except the beautiful painting she'd saved absently during her search – the woman with the flame-red hair, Rossetti's beautiful vision in colour.

With nothing else to do, she delved further. The Pre-Raphaelite Brotherhood, though possessing a pretentious name perfectly suited to well-educated artistic radicals, were masters of colour. Everything was vivid, untamed – where the Impressionists sought to capture in haste, the Brotherhood created studies in classical tragedy, decadence. Rossetti, brother to Christina, had dabbled in both painting and poetry – before dying in drugged misery.

Her ringing phone startled her from her contemplation and she answered without thinking. 'You took your time.'

'I had to follow a lead. I'm coming back to Cardiff tonight.'

Amy couldn't help the joy that leapt into her chest, the thought of her world returned to order. 'When?'

'I'm leaving at midnight, or thereabouts. But I need you to follow me on the GPS.'

Amy brought up the tracker and checked the status of her bugs. The trackers in the Micra and the jacket had been left behind in Cardiff, the motorcycle helmet was out of range, and the phone was sitting in Bangor Police Station.

'Are you with the police?' she asked, cautiously.

She tried not to let on the extent of her hacking prowess in front of law enforcement unless she trusted them absolutely.

116

'No, I'm at the hotel. My phone's down there, drying out, but at least it's not totally busted.'

'Drying out?'

The alarm in her voice must've carried, because Jason answered immediately.

'Accident with a puddle,' he lied, the casual tone giving him away. She would get it out of him when he returned home, but the loss of his motorcycle helmet was telling.

'Where is Frieda's bike?'

'Police station. Listen, the police caught up with these two blokes involved with trafficking up here – girls and other shit – and I thought you could, y'know, look into them.'

Amy called up her notes. 'Names?'

'Benjamin Stock, a lorry driver from Canton. And Jonah Fish – first bit's a nickname, but doubt that will stop you.'

She could hear his smile, and she felt her face stretch unconsciously. Smiling for him.

'Got it. Anything else?'

'Not right now. I've got to get ready for this thing. See you tomorrow.'

'Wait, what are you doing?'

But he was already gone, leaving Amy silently fuming at the end of the phone. He told her to follow him, which meant it was dangerous, but didn't give her any information about the nature of what he was doing. She hadn't been able to warn him about the lack of signal, the unreliability of her tracking through a mountain range and an area mostly populated with sheep. When the ovine population needed mobile phone masts, the apocalypse would truly be upon them.

She checked on AEON's search, but Talia used social media in Russian and it would take time to translate, assimilate. She should get some sleep before her midnight vigil for Jason, but she was listless, too tired to sleep and too worn out to concentrate.

She turned instead to her new names, fresh meat, starting the long journey to knowing someone through what they chose to leave on the internet. And all the secrets they wouldn't share.

If Jason used social media like a normal twenty-something, maybe she would know him better. Or maybe she just wasn't used to a relationship that existed outside bits and pixels. But, for now, she was left with the mystery – and if there was one thing she loved, it was a mystery that needed solving.

Chapter 21

Hidden depths

It was the waiting that killed her.

As the clock ticked down towards midnight, Truth had to prepare. Unlike that night in the gallery, she felt nervous. She had never been in danger then, not from the security guard and not from the police. But tonight, she was entering a different world – and the potential consequences could destroy her, one way or another.

Moving the large canvas without scrutiny would be difficult, but she had it all planned. The delivery men would pose as official couriers to avoid arousing suspicion and they would remove *La Parisienne* in an unassuming long box. No one would suspect it contained a priceless Impressionist painting.

But first Truth needed to know they had kept their end of the deal. She wouldn't throw away her only bargaining chip until she was certain. Truth knew the kind of men she was dealing with and they would not hesitate a moment before breaking their agreement – and clearing up the evidence.

Truth had therefore insisted on certain securities. And as they were profiting absurdly from this deal, they had agreed. When she'd first approached them through her contact, she had been the supplicant, cowering and weak. But now she was strong, holding something of great value to tempt them.

Truth couldn't wait to give up that insipid bitch to those hard men. She wanted to be free of the lady's damning eyes, her demands. Eyes that reminded her of the woman who had held her hostage all her life, eyes that shamed her for never being as good as her older sisters, her brother.

But where were they now? Living lives of value, leaving Truth to bear this burden. She alone could save the one they called mother. And, perhaps, finally, she would be recognised as having value of her own, and not as a mere shadow, a failure.

What if they don't come? The fear continued to gnaw at her. What could she do to protect herself, protect her interests? What other means did she have at her disposal? But she wasn't a little girl now. She was a killer. Perhaps they should be afraid.

She was no closer to learning if the hounds were closing in. The museum was open again, except for the galleries, and the police were sniffing around in all the wrong places. But that private investigator, the one called Amy Lane, was also keeping an eye on them. What did she know? What could be hidden from her?

Should Truth strike first before she was known?

After tonight. She could not risk losing her fragile alliance with the men of the dark. First, she had to wait. Sitting in the cold, hard plastic chair, she stared down the pale green walls, that uniform colour that decorated every cold institution across the world, and she waited. She would wait all night, if that was what it took – it was a small price to pay, in the end.

For what greater prize than truth and, finally, her mother's respect.

The pair of SOCOs were unimpressed about being dragged out on a Sunday to inspect an apartment that probably wasn't even a crime scene.

But Matt was apparently oblivious to their discontent, ordering any and all technology bagged and a thorough search of the premises conducted. Bryn was grateful for the two uniforms beside him, who at least knew how to conduct a thorough search and not disturb potential evidence.

The flat was barely more than a studio, a small kitchen-diner-lounge with a pokey bedroom and a shower room. It had been recently decorated, the cream paint barely marked, and a series of prints from the National Museum's collection hung on the walls. Including the missing *La Parisienne*.

'Photographs of all this,' Matt said to no one in particular and disappeared into the bedroom.

A chorus of mimed affront was turned on Bryn, which he silently pacified with open palms. At least the place was small, and one SOCO took the bathroom while the other scooped up the laptop on one side of the dining table.

A small rucksack was hanging off the back of a chair, which Bryn opened up. He found a notebook, a set of Tupperware boxes and a series of gadgets that baffled him. He called over the nearest SOCO and together they bagged the collection, which also included some old 35mm film canisters, a compass and a couple of magnetic cylinders smaller than his little finger. What the hell was Paul Roberts into?

Bryn opened up the notebook. A set of dates, locations and reference numbers, many in Cardiff but others much farther afield. Was he a train spotter? Bird watcher? But then where were his binoculars – and his camera?

'Look out for a camera,' Bryn called out to the room.

If he'd taken pictures of something incriminating, he could've ended up in the grip of the gangs, forced into helping them and then dying for knowing too much.

Matt returned from the bedroom and cast a glance over the items. 'Perhaps these—,' he tapped the bags of canisters and plastic boxes, '—were for making drops. Weatherproof, waterproof, unobtrusive. Maybe that's how he communicated with his contact.'

Despite Matt's matter-of-fact tone, Bryn was worried they'd fallen down a rabbit hole. They had nothing to suggest that Paul Roberts was the linchpin in some grand conspiracy. And did this flat look like the haunt of a spy? The cupboards were stacked with instant noodles and soups, the fridge and freezer full of ready meals for one. The wardrobe was full of sensible jumpers and well-worn shoes.

But perhaps affable bachelors made for the best agents precisely because they appeared too boring to attract comment or attention. They knew next to nothing about Paul and searching his apartment had only brought more questions, none with ready answers.

Though who would have those answers, now that he was dead? Who really knew him? Hunting down those online art societies would be a good first step, but Bryn only knew one way to do that and Matt had expressly asked him to keep Amy out of this.

Yet Bryn hadn't informed Amy she was off the case. He hadn't contacted her at all. She was probably still working on the leads he'd given her, while Jason was away playing his part in North Wales. If Amy wasn't involved, Jason wasn't either, except they were both in the thick of it.

'I think we're done here,' Matt said, and Bryn made his decision.

While they were collecting the evidence bags, making one final sweep, Bryn tapped out a quick text and hit Send before he could regret it.

Look at guard again.

Chapter 22

The secret life of vans

Frieda returned at eleven, all business, her cool manner chilled to Arctic frost.

She had a list of questions to which she wanted answers from his trip – route, cargo, rendezvous point, outgoing transport, names. Having watched her interrogation of Benjamin, Jason had a pretty good idea already, but he patiently listened to her instructions.

'What's your cover story?' she asked.

'The one I gave Jonah or the one for the guy?'

'Both.'

'I'm working for a rival gang, finding intel for my boss. As for the other, I'll work it out with Jonah on the way over.'

'Too many potential holes for your arse to fall into.' Frieda's face was impassive, her tone disapproving. 'You need something clear. You're the one calling the shots, not Jonah. Don't give him an inch.'

'If I say I'm his cousin—'

'You're his cousin. I don't care if his parents were both only children and everyone in town knows it. Keep it simple. Why are you going to Cardiff?'

'I live there. My car broke down. I need a lift home.'

'Where should he drop you off?'

'I don't want to put him out—'

'No. Be firm.' Frieda looked like she wanted to slap some sense into him. 'Pick somewhere close to the centre, nondescript.'

'Canton. I'm meeting some mates for breakfast.'

Frieda paused, the barest movement of her lips visible as she considered. 'It will do. Don't make small talk, don't give too much of yourself away. If you have to speak, answer as your best friend. His likes are now your likes. His family is your family. Clear?'

Jason thought over his best friends. Lewis was banged up in Cardiff Prison, his baby brother dead and his mum a wreck of her former self. And Amy was an elite hacker with a sister in Australia and parents she'd stolen millions from. He settled on Dylan as his model, a nice, dependable bloke with simple tastes in cars and beer.

Jason checked his backpack, now retrieved from the saddlebags on Frieda's bike. He removed all of Amy's business cards from his wallet, and slipped his returned phone into his pocket. He left his bike leathers folded on the chair – they didn't fit with the cover story, and were stained with crusted sediment from the lake.

'I expect a call as soon as you part ways,' Frieda instructed.

Jason had given her Cerys' number in place of Amy's, but he hoped she wouldn't have cause to use it. Even allowing for frequent stops and a wild detour, he should be in Cardiff before dawn.

He opened the hotel room door and turned to say goodbye. Frieda was at his side and, for a moment, he thought she might kiss him again.

But she merely patted his arm and offered a small smile. 'Good luck.'

Jason trudged out of the hotel and walked the twenty minutes back to the pub by Menai Bridge. Despite being in the shadow of the city, the road was surrounded by green fields and only disturbed by the odd house.

Walking in the near-total darkness, Jason felt the full weight of what he was about to do. He would be alone in the night with a stranger, a man who worked for a dangerous criminal and could choose to turn on him at any moment. It was at times like these that Jason longed for his old knife, or his father's long-lost gun. But he had only his fists and his wits tonight.

He arrived at the pub just before the meeting time, the building dark and closed up, with one solitary van in the car park. The lights flashed once as he approached and Jason crossed to the passenger door, hoping he was heading for Jonah Fish and not some dogging enthusiast.

Jonah was in the middle seat, his eyes purple and swollen as predicted, and an unshaven middle-aged man was driving. He drove off before Jason could say anything, but he thought he detected a family resemblance. Drunk uncle perhaps?

They immediately crossed the narrow Menai Bridge to Anglesey, the arches barely large enough for their van, the dark water flowing beneath them. They skirted past Llanfair PG, the town with the longest name, a challenge kids in Wales had long been trying to wrap their tongues around, and down another road surrounded by fields.

Jonah said nothing and Jason didn't start anything. The driver whistled tunelessly as the hedgerows, trees and clumps of houses flew by, occasionally broken up by what passed for a small village round here. After about half an hour of fields, they skirted a town that proclaimed itself Newborough and slipped into the embrace of a forest.

The road was little more than a single-lane track, branching and curling through the trees seemingly at random. Jason quickly lost count of the turns, and he realised that if they were to throw him out of the car, he might not be found for days, weeks. He doubted Amy had a fix on him out here and Frieda only knew he was on Anglesey. By the time they found his body, the crows would've ruined any chance of his mam's recognition.

Eventually, the trees parted to reveal a clear open space with only the stars to light it. The moon was wreathed in clouds, a couple of days off full, staring down at them like a giant unblinking eye. The driver stopped the car and killed the engine.

'We're meeting on the island,' Jonah said.

It was the first time he'd spoken since their departure. He sounded like he had a particularly bad cold from the swelling in his nose, and it was clear why he hadn't piped up before.

Jason got out without saying a word, Jonah following him. They walked down towards the beach together, the night silent save for the occasional bird and the susurrus of waves on the shore. The long thin island jutted out from the beach, joined to the shore of Anglesey by a narrow trail of rocks that would fall victim to high tide, a squat white lighthouse marking out the end some seven hundred yards out.

Jonah led him down the beach towards the tide mark. The sharp taste of salt in the air reminded him of weekends spent at Barry Island, stealing Cerys' ice cream before their dad chased him down the beach. That was a long time ago and memories of his father didn't belong in a place like this, on a night of dark deeds.

Jason knelt down on the shore, pretending to tighten his shoelaces while surreptitiously filling a small specimen pot with sand and slipping it into his pocket. Frieda had been clear that they needed a comparison sample to prove the route.

'He'll believe me,' Jonah said suddenly. 'He trusts me. I don't want this to get back to me, okay? So if I help you, I need some insurance.'

'If you help me, you might live to see Christmas,' Jason said casually, as if he was talking about the weather. Threats were the currency of the street, on the inside. He could threaten as easy as breathing.

Jonah said nothing, but Jason read the tension in his shoulders, the hesitancy in his step. If he wasn't believed, for whatever reason, he would have two problems to deal with. Jason hoped the men they were meeting weren't carrying. He was already at a disadvantage, away from his home turf and his electronic minder, and he didn't want to run into the trees away from an unhinged shooter. He'd had enough of that for one lifetime.

The rocks were slippery and Jason's socks were soaked in seconds, the unpleasant briny water oozing into his shoes from the shallows. Jonah navigated them like a pro, before giving Jason a hand up onto the island proper. In the distance, Jason could see a lone figure holding a powerful torch, flicking it on and off in some coded message.

'Boat's on its way in,' Jonah translated.

They crossed the rough ground by the light of the moon alone, the orb overpowered by the flashlight as they neared the man Jason assumed to be Kyle.

He turned as they approached, similar height and build to Jason with his face in shadow. He stared at Jonah, silently demanding an explanation.

Jonah gestured towards his face and the torch was flashed into his eyes.

Kyle returned the torch to play across the sea, beginning his flashing rhythm again. 'Name?'

Kyle didn't even look at him, his face impassive in profile as the moonlight played across it. He was in his forties, his cheeks weather-beaten, and scowl lines ingrained into the flesh.

'Dylan.'

'You police?' Straight to the point.

'No.' Jason spat on the ground.

'Don't like cops?'

'Did time inside.'

'For what?'

'Thieving a car.'

'Why you helping this scum?'

'He's family. And I need a ride.'

He realised too late that he hadn't cleared the official story with Jonah, checked what he'd told his mystery contact, made sure they were on the same page.

'You packing?'

'Can't,' Jason said, with a hint of bitterness that wasn't entirely feigned. 'Cops know my face.'

'Good. I need you to look scary and say nothing. We get the package to Bridgend in the next five hours or we don't like what happens. You slow me down, I ditch you. Are we clear?'

'Clear.'

Kyle was English, Jason realised, heralding from somewhere in the Midlands, maybe Manchester. Jason had never been much for accent geography beyond Wales, save for Scousers and posh BBC.

Jason also hadn't realised they were headed for Bridgend. Owain – and now, technically, Cerys – lived in Bridgend, which was only forty-five minutes from Cardiff. Not too far from backup, but far enough for the worst to happen while his cavalry were still getting their boots on.

After a moment or two, Jason caught his first glimpse of the boat. It was a fisherman's trawler, much abused by the sea, and a small light was flashing the same sequence as the torch on shore.

It took another few minutes for the boat to close in, before a little dinghy dropped from the side and a solitary figure rowed to the shore. Kyle walked down to him, as he beached the little boat. The rower handed out what looked like a large plastic beer cooler and Kyle passed him a thick envelope from beneath his coat, before shining the light for him to count. It was practised, routine, and Jason wondered how many times these two men had enacted this scene on the beach.

The count complete, Kyle pushed the dinghy back out and the rower returned to the fishing boat. Wordlessly, Kyle returned to Jason and Jonah before walking past them with the expectation of being followed. The pair fell in silently behind him, as Jason tried to suss out the mystery box. However, the light was too poor to tell more than it looked like a plastic picnic hamper, with no distinguishing markings and a combination lock on the lid. Why would a picnic hamper need a lock?

Of course, Kyle probably wasn't carrying sandwiches and cake. Drugs, maybe? But why hadn't the man checked the goods before accepting them? Seemed like a big risk to take, unless the power he was leveraging was so great no one dared cross him. Yet the guy in the dinghy counted the money. It didn't make sense.

When they were off the island, Jason and Jonah parted ways. Jonah stepped forward and hugged him, which Jason tried to accept without flinching.

'Kyle don't talk much. Safe trip.'

Jason pulled away first, before following Kyle towards his car, which was parked by the other stretch of beach. It was a Land Rover, two or three years old and kept tidy. Kyle placed the cooler in the boot, surrounded by a nest of blankets and covered by an old tarp. Whatever was in the cooler, it was fragile.

Could it be an antique? One of those Chinese vases or a delicate statue? Was that why he didn't look at it, in case the salt air got inside and ruined it? Jason's mind ran wild with the possibilities, as he waited for Kyle to let him into the passenger seat.

Once inside, he sat still and quiet as Kyle started the engine and Bruce Springsteen filled the cab. 'You don't like The Boss, you get out now.'

'No arguments from me.'

If it had guitar, Jason was all over it – from Queen to Bon Jovi, his father's favourites. He'd got in trouble with Amy for his passwords reflecting his taste in music, and she had started a rotating system for him that changed every month. He still locked himself out of his accounts at least once a week.

Kyle took a different route back through the forest, which Jason only realised after they emerged on the other side of Newborough. They followed another lane, this one even narrower than the last, before emerging onto the A55. The vast road carried them quickly out of Anglesey across the large Britannia Bridge, and away into the wilds of North Wales.

Jason was truly on his own now.

Chapter 23

A needle in a needlestack

Jason's GPS signal skirted the edges of Bangor and then vanished once more.

Amy scowled at the map, as if she could will the two-dimensional landscape to give up her assistant with the force of her ire, before returning to her perusal of spy-grade satellite tracking systems. The market leaders were a little out of her price range, but she could possibly MacGyver a more reliable device out of a satnav's innards.

Her electronics knowledge was self-taught, like most of her education, but it shouldn't be too difficult if she refreshed her knowledge via her favourite greyhat forums. Her lieutenants were always happy to gather knowledge for her in exchange for the odd code review or workaround for their pet projects.

However, her mind slid away from this new area of interest, her concentration barely lasting five minutes, even on the most fascinating of subjects. Her limbs were lead, the old aches stealing across her joints from too long at her desk, and even coffee failed to hold back the fatigue.

But she couldn't sleep now – she had to watch out for Jason. He was relying on her, and she couldn't let him down. She needed to keep working, keep pushing at this case. She might only be one or two puzzle pieces away from a breakthrough.

She had tried to address Bryn's cryptic text about Paul Roberts, but what was there to investigate? The man was an internet ghost. Without access to his tech, she had little to no chance of finding out more about him. If Bryn had listened to her in the first place, his laptop would be secure in her custody and not being held hostage by the NCA.

She checked the results on the North Wales names – Benjamin Stock seemed to share Jason's aversion to social media, with only the barest Facebook account on display, but she learned he lived with his girlfriend and daughter. He also worked for a reputable haulage company in the main, with his dodgier trips only a side project.

The advantage of happening upon a casual social media user was that they usually weren't very security conscious. Within minutes, she had Benjamin's date of birth from his profile and his address from his frequent location data. That was more than enough to look for a bank account via a simple credit rating search.

He only had the one bank account, with an attached credit card and a second card that he used exclusively for online porn shopping. Perhaps he had some clue about privacy precautions after all. The account received his regular company pay cheques every month and then more irregular payments, but for double the amount. These were attached to a vague company moniker – LogiPair – and Amy immediately switched her focus.

LogiPair had a bright corporate website, which used phrases like 'logistics solutions' and 'close links with key stakeholders'. Their motto was 'change in exchange', which made little sense to her. It had the air of a hastily constructed front, a page merely to satisfy the casual Google searcher but not actually for the business. Amy suspected that the men behind LogiPair did most of their business transactions on the streets and on the deep web.

LogiPair's bank transfers came through as a supposedly secure international account, which meant it took about ten minutes longer to break in than usual. The transfers were mostly to the same few names, which led her to Jonah Fish's real first name – Kevin. She noted it for later, along with the other recurrent names on the list, before she stopped short.

The account also made regular payments to a hospital.

A little Googling revealed a private hospital in the South Wales Valleys, catering for anything from private GP services to major operations, including a cancer investigation and treatment wing. Was one of the gang members receiving treatment there? Or did some of their trafficked girls go there at the insistence of their masters, to rid them of the unintended consequences of the work?

Medical records were difficult to hack into and harder still in the middle of the night. The best hacks exploited the weakest link in the chain – i.e. the human-computer interface. She only needed one surgeon with a weak password and she would be in.

But for now she only had the transaction data. She looked at the recurrent names on the list – with money deposited directly into their accounts, finding out their personal details was child's play. Opening a bank account under a false name was difficult even for an experienced forger, and Amy's heart had been in her mouth when she'd opened her first. Of course, once you have one bank account, the rest follow easily enough. Banks don't like to think their fellows can be duped.

She mapped out the home addresses of the main payees from LogiPair. They were concentrated in small patches around port towns in Wales and Ireland – Cardiff, Swansea, Port Talbot, Holyhead, Dublin, Cork, Rosslare. A quick cross-reference to the database of the Driver and Vehicle Licensing Agency revealed which of the men had HGV licences, lorry drivers capable of large hauls. The rest were more likely to be small van couriers – the kind who might stash a painting on board.

All three accounts resident in Cardiff were HGV drivers. Amy accessed their phone numbers from their bank accounts – Benjamin Stock was in Bangor, of course; another was in Germany and the third was crossing the Dutch-Belgian border.

If the painting was being moved by LogiPair, it was probably being collected by one of the other vans. Amy checked the non-HGV drivers' accounts for recent payments. A pair of accounts from Swansea had been paid on Thursday, but checking up on their mobile signals had them placed in France. The only other pair to be paid recently were Kevin Fish and Kyle Atherton, both living near the North Wales coast. The money had been deposited on Friday, exactly double what the Swansea boys had been paid.

Was the work considered twice as dangerous? Or were they being paid for two journeys, both with precious cargo on board? Amy checked the mobile signals for the two phones – Kevin Fish was snug in his bed in Bangor, but Kyle Atherton's signal was nowhere to be found. With a sinking feeling, Amy looked up the recent location data. Kyle had left Bangor at exactly the same time as Jason.

Her assistant was accompanying a gang shipment across the middle of Wales. With a man who had got into this business God knows how. This was exactly the kind of shit that she needed to be kept apprised of.

If shipment one was being delivered tonight, did that mean that the second leg of the journey would start tomorrow? Was the painting on the move?

It was a lot of guesswork, which she hated. She had data but she didn't have answers. LogiPair might have nothing to do with the painting at all – only rumours linked the art heist to North Wales in the first place.

She had to concentrate on the immediate threat. She debated calling Bryn but didn't have anything concrete for him yet. She had to rely on Frieda to keep the police updated as to her plans. Her only course of action was to find out as much about Kyle Atherton as she could.

If Jason was in danger, she needed to know exactly how much. And when that niggling anxiety in her chest should turn into full 999 panic.

The chronological recital of Bruce Springsteen's greatest hits was almost enough to reassure him. Yet Jason had better instincts than that, honed by years of rounding a corner and reading a street's atmosphere like it was written in flashing neon signs.

The silence was telling. Kyle said nothing, but he glanced over at Jason every so often, studying him. Working out his story. Judging it against the sparse information he knew.

Maybe Jonah Fish had no family. Nye said he had a mother, but what did that prove? Maybe Kyle was Jonah's best friend, or his real-life cousin. Maybe he'd seen straight through that bullshit.

Or perhaps Jason was working himself up for no good reason and Kyle could smell the fear, the anxiety oozing out of his pores. Jason concentrated on the music, the rhythms, keeping an eye out for place names he knew and wishing his Welsh geography was up to scratch.

Kyle drove like a man possessed, in keeping with his strict deadline and the vast emptiness of the roads. Unlike Frieda's bike, however, the Land Rover was more than a match for any vehicle that came along – except, perhaps, an HGV. Jason had the feeling that Kyle would let nothing stop him delivering this package. Not even Jason.

Now he was along for the ride, Jason needed to figure out a plan. If the changeover happened the same way in Bridgend, he would never get to see what was in the hamper. How would he find out? Could he sneak a look if Kyle stopped for a piss? Unlikely.

And what guarantees were there that these men were also moving art? Admittedly, Wales wasn't exactly a hotbed of organised crime but half a dozen gangs could have a hand in transit across the desolate middle of the country.

As the miles slipped by, the darkness pressing in on him from all sides, Jason realised why Frieda had been so pissed off at him. He was taking a huge risk on what might be nothing at all. They could be shipping rare caviar in that hamper for all he knew. Maybe one of the bosses had a taste for it, got his boys to transport it by special delivery.

Jason didn't want to die for caviar.

After about two hours, the unforgiving mountain roads started to level out, the terrain smoother beneath the wheels of the 4x4 as they left Snowdonia National Park behind.

'We'll stop in Aber,' Kyle said, breaking the silence like a sledgehammer shatters a frozen lake.

Jason guessed he meant Aberystwyth, an isolated town in the middle of the west coast. As a city boy, he was naturally suspicious of any place that was most accessible by boat. In its heyday, it had been a profitable tourist trap, but its past glory had faded. It boasted a university miles from anything except Aberystwyth, where English students came to be stranded and learn something about the pregnancy bump of the UK.

The pit stop would probably mean a quick toilet trip and maybe a snack at a petrol station or twenty-four-hour supermarket. The back roads of Wales weren't renowned for their service stations or wayside taverns. Could he use the stop to his advantage? Would they bond over soggy sandwiches? He doubted it.

Would Kyle leave the hamper unattended long enough for Jason to discover its secrets? He didn't know the code and maybe Kyle didn't either. He didn't need to open it, after all. In fact, maybe Kyle didn't even know what was inside – or had decided he didn't want to know. Like Benjamin and the girls in the back of his lorry.

The cell structure would suit the men at the top, no one below them knowing anyone else's business. Just do your job, keep your head down, and if you get busted by a cop, you don't know nothing important. Which would work particularly well if you were smuggling antiques that were worth more than these men would see in their lifetimes.

Though what would you do with a Ming vase in your living room? It wasn't as if the local pawnbroker would give you a fair price for it. A local gang boy might as well use it to house his mam's flowers for all the money it would bring him.

Aberystwyth loomed out of the night before Jason had really decided what to do. The opening harmonica chords of 'The Promised Land' filtered out of the speakers as they crossed into a town that typified the sort of dead-end place that Springsteen had in mind. The back alleys of Cardiff weren't exactly a fertile breeding ground for success stories but they had more going for them than poor, tired Aberystwyth.

The petrol station was bright, radiant, where the surrounding houses were grey – but it was also closed. Kyle turned in anyway, parking up away from the pumps and the deserted shop.

'I'm gonna take a leak.'

As Kyle went round the back of the garage for some privacy, Jason had five seconds to make a decision. He reached over for the boot release and rounded the 4x4 in a minute, lifting the boot and looking inside. The cooler stared back at him.

Glancing up to check Kyle hadn't returned, Jason reached for the cooler with a tremor in his fingers. It was cold to the touch, cooler than the blankets cushioning it. Had it been filled with ice? *If it's fucking caviar…*

Jason's fingers brushed something stuck to the side, and he shifted a folded jumper to see it better. It was a faded sticker, half peeled away, but Jason couldn't make it out in the light. He took his phone out of his pocket to shine a light on it – a wing, and the head of a snake.

What did it mean? Recognition tugged at the corner of Jason's mind. He had seen that symbol before, part of a larger whole, but where? Was it Masonic? Or was it the coat of arms of some arts institute? For all he knew, it could be the symbol of a well-known butcher or something he'd seen down the supermarket.

'You can't get in.'

Jason froze.

Kyle grinned back at him, a flick knife held in his hand with the air of a man who had used it many times.

'And you won't be needing that ride.'

Chapter 24

Remote control

The GPS came online in Aberystwyth.

The beeping startled her from the Wikipedia hole she'd fallen into, starting with 'proctologist' and ending somewhere in early twentieth-century literature. Amy stared at the blinking dot on the screen as it skirted the edges of the town, AEON automatically zooming and re-centring the map as she watched.

The dot stopped. Amy waited for it to move again, but it remained static for five long minutes.

And then it vanished.

A box flashed up on the screen: SIGNAL LOST – RECONNECT?

Amy slammed down the enter key, sitting forward in her chair. She felt uneasy, anxiety seeping into her mind as she fought to stop her body from panicking.

Another message: CONNECTION ERROR.

Jason's phone was offline. Amy tried to reason with herself – the battery was dead, the phone was faulty, he had walked into a lead-lined hole in the ground. But Jason was a trouble magnet and, despite her nervous nature, Amy had a finely tuned sense of when he was in deep shit.

She scanned the last known location – a petrol station attached to a supermarket, both closed hours earlier. Aberystwyth was not a late-night party town, especially not on a September Sunday. Why had they stopped there?

It was in the middle of a retail park, which wasn't prime CCTV territory. However, she found a cluster of local traffic cameras close by. Taking a few minutes to exploit a weakness in Aberystwyth Council's firewall, she tapped into the live feed and tilted the angle of the camera on the adjacent roundabout.

Just in time to see a dark Land Rover emerge from the road leading to the supermarket. She tried to catch the number plate, jumping to a second camera for a better angle. She couldn't see through the windscreen, no way to tell who was driving or the status of any passenger.

The vehicle was moving fast and Amy was on foreign soil, the camera locations unfamiliar and scattered. She managed to find the next camera just as the 4x4 disappeared out of shot and by the time she found the next, he had sped away into the night.

Amy hurriedly changed the location of her online phone router to Aberystwyth and called 999.

'999 – what's your emergency?'

'I saw…' Amy trailed off. How could she get their attention? What would bring the police running?

'Hello? Miss, can you hear me?'

'I heard a fight at the petrol station, in the retail park. Lots of shouting. And this 4x4 drove off really fast. I think someone might be hurt.'

'Where are you, Miss? Are you safe?'

'I was driving past,' Amy said. 'I'm not there now.'

'Can you tell me anything else?'

'It was a dark colour. With BG at the front. Heading out of town.'

'That's good. Can I take your name?'

Amy hung up and resumed her search for cameras leading out of town, while setting AEON to connect to the local branch of the digital police radio system. She didn't have a Bryn or Owain on the ground to give her personal updates, so an improvised police scanner would have to do.

A clear female voice came to life. '—station ETA five minutes. Can you respond to escape vehicle, Lampeter? Over.'

'This is Lampeter. We can have a bike out in twenty minutes. Reg, over?'

'ANPR data coming through now.'

Twenty minutes was a long time. The 4x4 could be long gone by then, if the automated number plate recognition had even picked it up. However, the petrol forecourt would soon be checked, inspected. For blood and bullets.

'Aber Town to dispatch. State 6.'

'Reading you, Aber Town.'

'I've got a clean knife and a smashed phone here. Knife's illegal. No blood. Over.'

The lack of blood was a good sign but she knew Jason didn't carry a knife anymore. So his mystery companion must've brought the weapon to the party. And the destruction of the phone explained her lost GPS signal.

'Check immediate location and secure for forensics, over.'

Amy waited, the silent radio and empty map taunting her.

When he couldn't sleep, Bryn liked the solitude of the detectives' office at night. Except tonight he wasn't alone.

Owain was sitting at his desk, a closed laptop beside him in a clear evidence bag. A series of cables connected the device to a computer on Owain's desk, a brand new PC that Bryn swore hadn't been there when he'd last visited the office.

At his approach, Owain started, almost flying out of his seat like a boy caught with his hand in the biscuit tin. 'Bryn.'

'Late night for you?' He wanted the boy to be at his ease before he started asking him what the hell was going on, but Owain knew all his tricks.

'NCA wanted me to start work on Paul's computer straightaway.'

Bryn frowned. 'I didn't know you could do that.'

'I've always had an interest. And not all that much to do for the past few months.' He gestured at the new computer with a faint smile. 'It does most of the job by itself, to be honest.'

'Found anything?'

Owain nodded. 'Lots of art, of course, and his own photographs from all around Wales. Though they're not of anything in particular – a random bench or an empty bird's nest. Nothing to write home about.'

'What else?'

'This is really interesting. When the computer was last booted, the password was entered incorrectly three times. And then the lid was shut without turning it off, sending it into hibernation.'

Bryn nodded like he understood why that was significant, waiting for Owain to put him out of his misery.

'The boot log says it started up Saturday lunchtime.'

'After Paul had been dead for two days?' Bryn felt an odd shiver, as if the man's ghost was looking over his shoulder.

'Yeah. SOCOs dusted for prints but they're smudges on smudges. Not even a workable partial.'

'Who would be after Paul Roberts' computer?'

Suddenly, Matt's theory that Paul was the inside man didn't seem so ridiculous.

'They didn't get in, so we don't know what they were after. But there's nothing here that's incriminating.'

'That we can see. Can you take this to Amy tomorrow?'

Owain hesitated. 'I thought Matt said—'

'Owain, I don't doubt you have some idea what you're doing, but Amy is the expert.'

'Her evidence is also inadmissible in court.'

Bryn gritted his teeth. 'Do you work for me or not?'

'I work for the department,' Owain said, squaring his shoulders. 'And I can do this! You have to believe in me!'

Bryn reached for Owain's shoulder but he shifted it away. Bryn withdrew his hand and Owain went back to typing, steadfastly ignoring him.

'I do believe in you,' Bryn said. 'But Amy—'

'Amy isn't police, Bryn,' Owain said bluntly. 'Do you want more sky falling on our heads?'

The phone screeched to life, causing them both to jump. Who the hell was calling at gone three in the morning?

'Hello?' Bryn said.

There was a burst of static, a terrible line. '—you hear—?'

'Who is this?'

The line went dead, the connection lost.

Bryn rang through to the switchboard. 'Who did you put through?'

'Said it was urgent, sir. J-something. Didn't hear the rest. Bloody awful line.'

What the hell had happened to Jason now?

Chapter 25

Evening, officer

The blues and twos surged over the crest of the hill, the police motorcycle drawing alongside the dark 4x4 and flagging it down.

Winding down the window, Jason gave the officer his best smile. 'I'm sure I was under sixty.'

'Licence and registration please.'

Jason pulled his driving licence out of his wallet and handed it over. 'It's my mate's. He asked me to drive after he had a skinful.'

Jason jerked his thumb towards the back seat, where Kyle was snoring with a rough blanket hauled over him. Concealing the trickle of blood down the side of his head and the jump leads tying his hands. The vodka miniature Jason had found in Kyle's coat pocket added that smell of authenticity.

The cop wrinkled his nose. 'Where are you headed?'

'Carmarthen,' Jason said, sure that was vaguely in the right direction. 'It was our mate's stag do – bit of a late one up in Aber.'

'You're not from around here,' the officer said, handing back the licence.

'Cardiff.' No point in hiding it when the man had seen the address on his licence and could hear his native accent. 'Staying the night round Kyle's before heading home.'

'And you weren't drinking?'

'I had a pint with my lunch,' Jason remembered. He didn't want the inevitable breathalyser to make him a liar. 'But I knew I had to do the driving. Kyle always likes one too many.'

'I'm sure you won't mind a breathalyser.'

Jason stepped out of the car and blew into the little device. A big fat zero – it had been over twelve hours ago, after all.

'Did you stop at a garage a few hours ago?' The police officer's voice was light, but Jason realised that was the crux of the matter. They had been seen.

'Kyle needed to take a piss,' Jason blurted, as if he were confessing under duress. 'He wouldn't get back in the car, so I had to … sort of lift him in. Lost my phone in the dark.'

'Lose anything else?'

Shit, the knife.

'Don't think so.' Jason played innocent. 'There was a fair bit of rubbish about, though. That's why I couldn't find my phone – didn't want to rummage through that lot.'

Kyle moaned, shifting in his sleep. Jason prayed to whatever gods might watch over ex-cons and hackers' assistants that he stayed asleep long enough for the cop to let them go.

'His missus is gonna go spare,' Jason said ruefully.

That seemed to decide it for the cop, who let him go with a friendly warning to drive safe and bring his full licence to his nearest police station within seven days. Jason fully intended to do just that, hoping he could get through to Bryn when he next found a phone. The payphone in Aberaeron had several loose wires sprouting from it and he'd been cut off as soon as he reached Bryn.

Of course, he could've come clean to the cop on the bike, but he didn't think he would look as kindly on Jason knocking out a guy to steal his car and his treasures. Not that he was any damn closer to finding out what was in the box.

When Kyle had come at him with the knife, Jason had moved before his brain had time to catch up. Swinging the picnic cooler, he'd connected the heavy box with the side of Kyle's head. The big man had gone down like a sack of potatoes and Jason had hurriedly loaded him into the back seat. A few miles down the road, he'd stopped to truss him up, cover him with the blanket and splash the vodka around. Kyle had woken up a few times, cursed Jason for a bastard, and then fallen asleep again. Hopefully, there wasn't more damage beneath the surface but Jason would get him to a hospital just as soon as he made the drop in Bridgend.

Or before, if he could just get hold of his backup in Cardiff. But there was nothing about but fields and quaint villages, no twenty-four hour petrol stations in these parts, and their proud red phone boxes had likely been vandalised and scrawled with 'CALL ME 4 GR8 SEX' graffiti.

It was coming up to four in the morning, the night still clinging stubbornly to its hold over the gently sloping landscape, as Jason looked keenly for any flash of red that might indicate a phone box. A bruise was developing on his right arm from bashing it into the door every time he turned the wheel – he'd thought his Micra was a cramped drive, but this thing was a nightmare to even keep on the road. He was sure it was great over fields but it was an unwieldy juggernaut on the roads. Dylan would laugh his arse off if he saw him now.

'You cock-sucking wanker!'

At least Kyle's headache must be improving.

'That's quite a talent,' Jason said mildly. 'Could earn me some admirers with that one.'

'How the fuck do you think you're gonna pull this off?'

'Guess we're not talking about the wanking.' Jason had hoped for another hour or two of silence, but his luck had never been that good.

'The bosses will carve you up and chuck you in the harbour.'

'"Sleeping with the fishes"? You can do better than that, Kyle.'

'You arrogant little sod!'

In the rear-view mirror Jason caught sight of Kyle struggling to sit up and realised he was in a precarious position. A man didn't need full use of his hands to take a swing.

He pulled into the nearest lay-by, fetched the wheel wrench from the boot and opened the passenger door nearest Kyle's head.

'Get out or I hit you again.'

Kyle looked up, past Jason's head and out into the surrounding darkness. 'You can't leave me out here.'

'Maybe I will, maybe I won't. Out.'

Kyle slowly swung his legs round, sizing Jason up as he slowly got out of the car. He teetered, falling against the side of the Land Rover. Jason made no move to help him – he wouldn't have his mercy turned against him in the Middle of Nowhere, Wales.

Jason shut the door and nudged Kyle in the back with the wrench. 'Move.'

He opened up the boot, removed their precious cargo and gestured with the wrench.

Kyle shook his head. 'Fuck no.'

'Get in or get this.' Jason raised the wrench, wanting to make himself absolutely plain. He wasn't going to tolerate any messing around.

Kyle tried to run.

Which was an error because he had a recent head injury and Jason had a heavy metal rod in his hand. Thwacking Kyle across the shoulder, Jason grabbed his arm and swung him into the boot. Kyle yowled as he fell into the nest of blankets and Jason shut the boot. The grill across the back – usually for keeping dogs in line – should keep him out of harm's way for now, but it would be harder once it started getting light.

A disturbing thought stole through his mind – had there been any women in the back there, a special delivery for someone who just couldn't wait? It made him feel sick, a feeling that reminded him he'd had nothing to eat since lunch.

Strapping the cooler into the passenger seat, Jason took the driver's seat once more. Kyle started shouting about his rights and his boss, so Jason turned the CD player up to full volume, drowning out his prisoner's protests. *Prisoner* was a strong word – did this count as a citizen's arrest? Jason hoped Bryn could spin it that way.

Finally, a phone box loomed out of the night and Jason nipped out to make the call, sure to take the keys with him.

He was put through to Bryn immediately. 'Jason? Where are you?'

'Somewhere after Carmarthen. I'm heading to Bridgend to drop off a mystery package, but the driver and I had a bit of a disagreement.'

'How much time do you have?'

Jason didn't wear a watch and his phone was smashed. 'Hang on.'

He set down the receiver and peered through the car window at the satnav, before returning. 'Just under an hour to go and I reckon they're expecting me about then.'

'What's the meeting point?'

'Satnav location is for the Bridgend industrial estate just off the motorway, behind the hospital.'

'Come off a junction early and we'll meet you there.'

The pips started in his ear. 'Bryn, I've gotta go.'

'Drive safe now. Don't get pulled over – again.'

Jason laughed and hung up.

Chapter 26

Too many cooks

Bryn didn't want to wake Matt Boateng, but there'd be hell to pay tomorrow if he neglected to keep the NCA agent up to speed.

Bryn wasn't a glory hog, desperate for the spotlight like some eager officers – even Owain could be a bit of a fisherman for career-making cases. However, he wanted to keep his hand on the tiller where Jason was concerned. If Matt had taken against Amy, what would he reckon to her assistant being right at the centre of this operation?

Though he only had his colleague to blame for that. It was Frieda Haas who had led their boy a merry dance across the country, only to leave him on his own with a gang runner in the middle of the countryside.

But Jason could hold his own, as long as they could back him up. And that was what Bryn intended to do, whether Matt liked it or not.

'Boateng.'

Matt had barely a trace of sleep in his voice. Bryn envied his youth.

'It's Bryn here. We've got a situation that I thought you should know about.'

'Yes?'

'Your agent up north – Frieda Haas – has sent one of our boys down here with a gang runner on a delivery. But it seems the runner got wise to it and Jason had to—'

'Jason Carr? Amy Lane's assistant?'

Bryn paused. It was odd information to have on the tip of his tongue. How did he know about Jason?

'That's the one.'

'Go on,' Matt said, his voice giving nothing away.

'Well, the drop is in Bridgend. I reckon the reason he's on this run is that they might try to give him something to take back.'

'The painting. ETA?'

Bryn glanced at the wall clock. 'We've got fifty minutes to get out to Bridgend.'

'I'm at the Hilton. Two minutes.'

The bloody Hilton – of course he was. No expense spared for Bryn to have yet another boss to answer to.

Bryn hung up and grabbed his coat. 'Owain, we're going to Bridgend.'

The boy hesitated, his cheeks pale and his grip on his pen tight enough to warp the plastic. 'I…'

'You'll be all right,' Bryn said gently, seeing the echoes of fire in his partner's eyes. 'We'll be in the car the entire time.'

Owain nodded, a rough jerk of his head, and Bryn shepherded him to his car at a brisk trot. If they made Jason late for this drop-off, the consequences did not bear thinking about.

Amy paced like a caged tiger, her muscles trembling with every frantic step. The familiar surge of panic was rising in her, clawing at her throat and causing her heart to flutter like a trapped sparrow in her chest.

The radio burst into life.

'Dispatch, this is Lampeter, over.'

'Go ahead, Lampeter.'

'Our bike found your 4x4. Said it was a squabble at the garage. False alarm. Over.'

Amy wanted to scream at the monitor, rail against the idiotic West Walean police officers who couldn't see through a simple lie. Of course he would say that. Of course he would deceive them!

'You have a name for the book?'

'Jason Carr – that's Charlie, Alpha, Romeo, Romeo.'

Amy collapsed onto the sofa and closed her eyes. *Thank fuck.*

'Any record?'

'He's that boy what was on the news early in the year. If we'd known at the time, we might've brought him in, but the boys in Cardiff aren't fussed. Over.'

'Ta for that, Lampeter. Over and out.'

The boys in Cardiff. Which meant that someone at Cardiff Police Station knew and hadn't called her. And who would've been confident enough to dismiss Jason as harmless? Amy could name those people on one hand – and Bryn and Owain were top of the list.

If they knew Jason was safe, why hadn't they rung? They didn't know she was looking for him, but Bryn had kept her up to speed before. Had Bryn spoken to Jason? Had Jason asked for her not to be in the loop?

Amy returned to AEON and called up her GPS tracker again, inputting both Bryn and Owain's phone locations. Maybe they were both safely in their beds and someone like Catriona Aitken had taken the call. Jason might not get on well with the detective sergeant, but she now knew he was one of the good guys.

The GPS beeped. The two signals were side by side on the edge of Park Place – Central Police Station.

Amy reached for her phone, typing a sarcastic text – before stopping. Was it deliberate? Did they not want to worry her? Or did they think she couldn't handle it? Jason had gone off with Frieda with barely a word – maybe they thought he didn't report in to her anymore. Did they know something she didn't?

Suddenly, the GPS signals were on the move, little flashing dots speeding out of Park Place. Was Jason in danger?

Amy tuned the police radio back to Cardiff, activating her CCTV camera network to track the car. Bryn's number plate was now logged on her automatic recognition software, so she followed them easily – across the main road to the Hilton entrance.

She changed the camera angle, an unfamiliar man getting into the front of Bryn's car, before they were off again. Heading out of town, she reckoned, and onto the motorway. Towards Jason?

Amy was determined they would not keep her out. If Jason was in trouble, she would follow him, find some way to be part of this. She wasn't some child to be coddled while the big boys played cops.

Forcing her body under control, Amy sat stock-still in her chair, following the little dots and the cameras as they sped away into the night.

Chapter 27

Somewhere only we know

Ten minutes before the exchange was due to go down, Jason took the slip road off the M4 down to a quiet roundabout. The satnav squawked at him to get back on track, Kyle warning him that the blokes didn't like to be kept waiting, that they would hunt him down and dismember him.

Jason saw a pair of static headlights just beyond the first exit of the roundabout and he pulled up on the opposite verge. Bryn and a man he didn't recognise got out of the car and crossed over to him.

'Nice Land Rover,' Bryn said, then caught sight of Kyle's scowling face. 'I like your little cage back there.'

'My boss is going to fuck you all up,' Kyle seethed.

'Not unless he wants to be known as a cop killer,' the new man said coolly, and Kyle subsided into shocked silence.

'This is Matt Boateng, NCA,' Bryn said, as Jason got out of the car. 'He read through Frieda's report on the way over.'

'There's very little evidence, isn't there?' Matt said shrewdly.

'Close to none,' Jason admitted.

'Well, at least we can break this chain. What you carrying?'

Jason winced. 'I don't know.'

He pulled the picnic cooler out of the passenger seat and handed it to Matt, who gave a low whistle.

'You know what this is?' Bryn asked.

'Yes, I do.' Matt turned to Kyle. 'Code?'

'Don't open it!' Kyle said, a panicked note in his voice. 'You'll ruin it.'

'No one's getting what's inside now,' Matt said. 'Code?'

'8008.'

'What are you, five?' Bryn said.

'Not my idea,' Kyle shot back.

Matt entered the code and removed the lock, before opening up the box.

Chipped ice filled the cooler to the brim. Matt used his gloved hand to gently separate the top layers. Beneath, under several layers of plastic bag, was a bright blue curved bowl containing a chilled human kidney.

Jason gawped at it. 'That's ... shit.'

'Human organ trade. Never used to touch us much here, but the waiting lists are getting longer.' Matt shook his head. 'I'll call it in, make sure we're not treading on any toes.'

Matt repacked the kidney and replaced the lid of the cooler, before passing it back to Jason. He held it awkwardly, like a squalling baby unceremoniously dumped in his arms.

'What ... what happens to it now?' Jason asked Bryn.

'Nothing. It goes into evidence.'

'So, some poor sod's lost a kidney for nothing?'

'I expect he was paid for it. He ... or she.' Bryn squinted at the closed box, as if he could somehow divine the gender of the donor by his stare.

'And what about the person on the other end?'

'They wait their turn.'

Jason cradled the box in his arms, suddenly reluctant to let go. 'Can't we just ... let this one go?'

'That's an illegal kidney. Who knows where it came from? Maybe some junkie, or a man offed in Ireland for his organs. We're doing everyone a favour by taking it into custody.'

Jason's fingers brushed the sticker on the side again, the snake and wings aligning in his head to form a symbol of medicine, a long staff with two snakes and wings at the top. *First, do no harm...*

'How desperate do you have to be to take an organ off the black market?'

'Jason, this isn't a discussion,' Bryn said sharply. 'You're gonna deliver that organ to the gangs to complete the chain, and then we're gonna arrest the lot of them. Backup's already on its way.'

'What about the doctor? And the patient?'

'We'll have to deal with them too, in time. Since when did you care so much about the consequences?'

Jason knew the answer to that, knew that it was Damage Jones' blank staring eyes that had altered him, changed him. The boy who had died merely to frame Jason for murder.

Drugs and women and now organs – nothing gang life touched came away untainted. Needing a kidney had led to someone seeking the only solution they could think of, and look where it had landed them. No kidney, maybe doing prison time on dialysis, before dying behind bars. What was the penalty for handling stolen goods, if those goods were sewn inside you? What about all the others in receipt of those organs – what price would they pay?

Jason thrust the cooler into Bryn's arms. 'I can't do it.'

'You can and you will. There is no one else.'

'I can't condemn them all like this.'

'You want to work for the police, you play by our rules. You don't play and you're out, you and Amy.'

Jason baulked at Amy's name. He could decide for himself how much he was prepared to sacrifice, but he couldn't decide for Amy. Except he could – losing her police work would cripple her, and he could never be the cause of that pain. Not even for his own guilty conscience.

'Fine,' Jason said. 'But I don't like it.'

'I'm not taking a vote.' Bryn pushed the cooler back towards him, as Matt came over.

'Problem?' Matt asked.

'What's happening?' Jason deflected, not looking at Bryn.

'We've got the go-ahead from HQ. Make the drop as planned and, as soon as you've got the money, I'll come in with the uniforms to make the arrests. I've formally noted you as an undercover, so there's no issue of prosecution. We ready?'

Jason nodded his reluctant agreement, feeling inexplicably dirty. He also didn't let on to Matt that there was no plan for the drop – Kyle had that knowledge and he was unlikely to share. Matt and Bryn hauled Kyle out of the car and into the back of theirs, while Jason replaced the cooler in its nest of blankets in the boot.

'They always work in pairs,' he called back to Matt.

The NCA agent returned to his side and beckoned someone out of the back of the car – Owain. 'I think a black face will draw too much suspicion around here,' he said.

Jason privately agreed, but he saw the way Owain's hands trembled, shoulders hunched over as he approached.

'You all right with this?' Jason asked.

'We've got three minutes to rendezvous.' Matt was already moving back towards his car, leaving the two of them alone.

Owain said nothing, just slid into the passenger seat and did up his seatbelt, like a robot running on autopilot.

'Let's hope I don't cop a speeding ticket,' Jason quipped, trying to garner a response. Nothing.

Jason sped off towards the meet, his heart throbbing painfully in his chest. He was signing someone's death warrant tonight and he felt the Reaper looking on, judging him and his. He didn't feel like chancing his karma tonight, but surely Owain had earned a reprieve from yet more trouble?

The dots departed the motorway just after Bridgend and stopped. She didn't have a camera on that spot, so Amy had to content herself with manually refreshing the GPS every thirty seconds.

Suddenly, one dot moved away from the rest. Amy double-checked the ID – Owain. After a minute, Bryn's dot followed, heading towards Cardiff. But instead of continuing down the motorway, they took the Bridgend turnoff, making their way past the shopping centre and into the industrial estate beyond.

Her fingers itched to call Owain, demand if he was with Jason. It was entirely possible – enough time had elapsed since the altercation in Aberystwyth to allow him to reach Bridgend, especially with his somewhat reckless driving style. But why wasn't he coming home? Was he persisting in whatever ridiculous mission Frieda had sent him on?

She didn't have enough data. How was she supposed to work this out, calculate the risks, if she didn't have data? Why were they keeping her in the dark?

Owain's dot stopped at the edge of the industrial estate. Amy hunted desperately for cameras, but only caught one at the end of the road. She turned it as far as it would go, just able to make out the shape of a tall car – a 4x4? – parked up in the middle of the street.

No one moved. Amy checked several times to make sure the image hadn't frozen, but the time code continued to rise, much slower than her frantic heartbeat.

Then a second car arrived, parking up on the opposite side of the street. After a moment, the doors opened together, like it had been perfectly choreographed. Two figures met in the middle of the road – while Amy couldn't see faces at this distance, the man was too tall for Owain and Amy had watched Jason on too many cameras to mistake him.

The man seemed to be arguing with Jason, before another couple of men emerged to flank him. Three against one – with Owain in the car. Why wasn't Owain moving to help him? Where was the backup?

But whatever Jason said reassured them, as the newcomers backed off a step. Jason handed over a large box and took something in return. A small powerful light source blinked on, whiting out the low threshold of the camera. Amy desperately tried to see around the edges of the light, but it obscured everyone in the road. Anything could be happening and she wouldn't know. She wouldn't know until it was too late.

The light died, and the camera readjusted along with Amy's eyes. Jason turned and got back in the car. Suddenly, the road was filled with flashing lights, cars blocking both ends of the road. The cavalry had arrived.

But the gang boys weren't going down without a fight. Little bursts of light surrounded their car – and Amy belatedly realised they were muzzle flashes. They were shooting at Jason.

The 4x4 was stuck between the barricading police cars, unable to escape. Amy's heart was in her mouth. Would she watch him die here, helplessly separated?

But Jason wasn't easily beaten. The 4x4 heaved up onto the pavement, reversing away from the shooters and scraping past the police car nearest her camera. The flashes from the surrounded car stopped. Had they run out of ammunition? Or had they realised, as Amy had, that the police weren't shooting back? That the cars carried no SWAT team, no guns at all.

All they had to do was leave their car and execute the police officers one by one. And there was nothing that could be done to stop them.

Chapter 28

Fighting fire with fire

The first spray of bullets took out the driver's side windows and rained down glass. Jason cursed and ducked, yanking Owain down behind the dubious cover of the dashboard. When the fuck had everyone started carrying guns?

The suspicious hard men had only just bought his story about Kyle being taken ill and only reluctantly parted with their cash when Jason had threatened to take the kidney away. He had seen the weapons distorting the lines of the coats and wanted to get the hell out of there as soon as possible.

The thick smell of diesel filled his nostrils. The tank had clearly taken a hit, haemorrhaging the last of its fuel, much depleted after his night's journey. But Jason wasn't planning on this car becoming his coffin, or one large roasting tin when a stray spark set the whole lot on fire.

He turned the key and the engine miraculously turned over, enough fuel in the lines to give them a little time. Jason slammed the Land Rover into reverse and, still ducking his head, steered them up onto the pavement and back towards the waiting police car.

But Owain, without his restraining hand, starting yanking on the passenger door – desperate to open it, escape the thunderous sound of bullets with their names on.

'Calm the fuck down!' Jason yelled, as the door opened and scraped against the fence. 'And shut that bloody door!'

When Owain showed no sign of complying, Jason steered closer to the fence, effectively shutting the door for him and meaning that they only destroyed a wing mirror when scraping past the cop car. Except the front of the Land Rover was too broad to pass completely and Jason was wedged tight against them. No escape except through the boot, and that was denied them by the dog cage.

Then the noise stopped. The officer in the passenger seat of the police car glanced over to him, just above the line of the window, and Jason met his inquiring gaze with equal confusion. Why stop shooting now?

Owain whimpered softly beside him.

'Are you hit?' Jason asked, his voice sounding muffled to his ears.

Owain shook his head, but something wild had overtaken him, adrenaline overriding all his better sense. Jason had no idea what Owain would do next and that frightened him.

A phone was ringing. Owain pulled it out of his pocket and stared at it like it was some mysterious artefact from the planet Zog. 'It's Amy.'

Jason snatched the phone out of his hand. 'Amy, we're—'

'They have guns.' Her voice was taut, flat – she was barely holding it together. 'They can execute you. You can't fight back.'

Slowly, it dawned on Jason that he wasn't surrounded by Armed Response Vehicles, but ordinary police cars. The ARVs would be in Cardiff, maybe Swansea, but that was about half an hour's drive away. The gang boys could pick them off one by one before backup materialised.

'You got a plan?' he asked, hopefully.

'Stop them getting out of the car.'

Easier said than done. They had no covering fire, no projectiles. It was Jason who couldn't get out, not them, so unless he managed to wedge them between the wall and a police car, that wasn't the best plan.

He peered through the windscreen to examine the road for potential obstacles. But the lighting was poor here – he could barely make out the slick of diesel he'd left behind during his frantic reversing, and that was all...

That was all he needed.

Jason killed the engine and snatched a crumpled packet of fags and a cheap lighter out of his jacket pocket. He could light the oil nearest them easily, but then they would go up in seconds, taking the cop car with them.

He motioned for the police officer to roll down his window. 'On my signal,' he told him, 'you have to make a run for it.'

The cop saw the lighter in his hand and blanched but only nodded.

'Owain, you need to get that cage off, so we can get out.'

'I can't—'

'You fucking can.' Jason shoved him towards the back seat of the car without further ceremony.

'Jason, what's going on?'

'I need to hang up, Amy. Do you know when—'

'Ten minutes for the ARVs.'

'We'll need a fire engine.'

Amy, thankfully, didn't question him. 'Try not to die.'

'Do my best.' He threw the phone into the back, rummaging under the seat for anything to stick down the lighter switch. Electrical tape or even a pack of gum…

His fingers seized on a thick A-Z map, folded open to show the back roads of Anglesey. He hauled it out triumphantly.

'Owain, is it—'

But he didn't have time to finish, the doors of the gang's car opening and three shadowy figures emerging. Jason crouched on his seat and lit the A-Z. It smouldered, the plastic cover giving off an acrid stench, before the cheap insides caught in a burst of flame, devouring the roads of North Wales in an instant. Jason stepped on the smashed remains of his window and the cop's, enough leverage to fling the burning book towards the oil.

A shot rang out and Jason fell back into the car, just as the book landed in the middle of the road. And … nothing.

'Shit. Owain—'

A burst of flame streaked across the road, driving the men back towards their car. Jason crawled into the back of the Land Rover, to find Owain still wrestling with the screw at the top of the cage.

'Almost,' he said, but they didn't have time for 'almost'.

Jason flung his full weight at the cage and the screw snapped, bringing down the cage with Jason on top of it. The boot released from the inside and the two of them tumbled out, the police officers herding them behind Bryn's car.

Sirens filled the air once more, as Bryn and Matt joined their huddle, fleeing like a large multi-limbed monster away from the fire and letting the huge red engine see to the mess they'd made.

'You're bleeding,' Owain said suddenly.

Only then did Jason feel the searing mark across his temple, blood coursing over his cheek and down his neck.

'Jason, you've been shot.'

Amy hated this part more than any other – waiting for Jason to come home.

In the heat of the moment – literal heat, in this case – her anxiety still ruled her but she had purpose, direction. She could call for reinforcements, she could provide intelligence to the field. But in the aftermath, when the fire was out and the bad guys were carted off to the cells, she only had inertia.

She could not run to him, wait by his A&E gurney and press his hand like Cerys. She couldn't awkwardly pat his shoulder and offer him a lift home like Bryn. No, she could only wait for him to return, make a cup of tea and try not to fuss like her anxiety demanded of her.

It was most important that he didn't think he had to worry about her, not tonight. So she removed the empty wine bottle, dumped the multiple coffee cups in the sink, and pulled on a clean T-shirt. She could keep it all together just a little longer.

The lift ejected him as the midday sun was streaming through the gaps in the curtains. She surveyed him critically, taking in the white patch of gauze taped to his head and the way he walked unaided to the sofa, despite Cerys hovering at his elbow.

'It only took off a few layers of skin,' he said immediately, without preamble. 'It's gonna scar but it's not gonna stop me doing anything. I feel fine.'

'There's blood on your shirt.'

162

The dark cloth was saturated with it, his right shoulder to his elbow starting to shed rust-coloured flakes.

Jason glanced at it and scowled. 'Aw, shit.'

'Head wounds bleed a lot,' Cerys chimed in.

Cerys' comment irked her. Amy had watched enough medical dramas to know that. She didn't need Cerys coddling her as well as Jason.

'Where's Owain?' she asked, a little pettily, just to see Cerys flush.

'At home,' Cerys said, brusquely. 'He doesn't like hospitals.'

'You should get back to him,' Jason said.

His voice was neutral, but Amy knew he was trying to get rid of his sister. As much as she hoped it was so they could spend some time together, she knew it was more likely he simply wanted to avoid an argument between her and Cerys.

'Is he…?' Cerys trailed off, glancing at Amy. Whatever she wanted to ask, she obviously thought Amy was too fragile to hear it.

'A bit shaken up,' Jason said.

Cerys left without another word, as if she'd heard more in his words than had been plainly said.

The kettle finished boiling, the button having been pressed as soon as Amy saw Bryn's car pull up. She didn't know why he hadn't come up, merely waiting for Cerys' return so he could deliver her to Owain. Maybe he suspected Amy would ream him out for his involvement in Jason's nocturnal activities, and he would be right.

She made the tea and delivered a mug to Jason, her hands steady as a rock. She was in control. He would never know. 'Do you have a headache?'

'I told you, I'm fine.'

'*Fine* is a broad spectrum.'

'Like when you use it?'

It wasn't quite teasing, the way he said it, and Amy's smile was shadowed in return. They both knew that *fine* was relative for her, and that she had never yet said otherwise anyway. It could be more accurately called a polite fiction, a very British way of dodging that awful question 'How are you?'

'Where is Frieda?'

She hadn't meant the question to be so abrupt, but when she'd thought it, she had to know immediately. But the real question lurked beneath the surface of her words. *Why wasn't she with you?*

'Still in North Wales, I guess. Matt's going to fill her in.'

'Who's Matt?'

Amy guessed he was the man Bryn and Owain had picked up at the Hilton, but even she needed more than a first name and a blurry CCTV image to identify a person.

'NCA agent. He turned up to run things down here while Frieda was up north.'

'So that was his operation, last night?' Amy had found a new target for her anger.

'I guess so. I think it was a bloody mess by the end.'

Amy chewed on her tongue, suppressing the urge to rant about how he'd been shot in the head – as if he didn't know. 'It was clever, what you did with the fire. What did you throw?'

'A-Z.' Jason wore a self-satisfied smirk.

At least it had gone better than his last piece of arson, but Amy kept that thought to herself. He didn't need reminding of the fire that had almost cost Amy and Owain their lives, flames that still haunted them now.

'You need to rest,' she declared. 'And then you can debrief.'

'I do need a shower,' he said.

It took her a moment to make the connection, before her cheeks flamed scarlet. 'About your trip!'

Jason grinned, the long tail of tape beside his right eye crinkling at the motion. 'I know what you meant,' he admitted. 'Just like to see you blush.'

'No one likes that,' she muttered darkly, sure her face had come over all splodgy and pink, like a blancmange.

'It's pretty on you,' he said, before heaving himself off the sofa and heading for the bathroom. 'I'm gonna nick your shower cap.'

Amy watched him go with a slack jaw. *Pretty?* No one had ever called her pretty, not when there was Lizzie beside her, with her blonde curls and perfect smile.

If Jason thought her pretty, did that mean…?

She pushed the thought aside and returned to AEON. He had been hit by a bullet, she reminded herself. He wasn't in his right mind.

But a feeling of warmth curled in her belly, delighted beyond words. With a new-found enthusiasm, she returned to her case files, collating all the evidence from last night and adding it to the records.

Now Jason was beside her again, they would be able to make sense of this. She had a feeling it was all coming together for them. Any minute now, Bryn would ring with the news that the painting had been found and they were only one step away from the killer.

Chapter 29

Secret admirer

'They know nothing about the painting.'

Bryn snorted. 'Of course they'd say that.'

'Except they've happily confessed to human trafficking, drug smuggling and the organ trade.' Matt counted the list off on his fingers. 'Why cover up the theft of one painting?'

'The price tag?' Bryn hazarded, but it sounded thin even to his ears.

At least the press officer had something positive to spin on a dreary Monday morning, even if they were no closer to finding the damn painting or their killer.

'Where are we on Paul's possessions?'

'Lab's still processing,' Owain said.

Bryn spared a glance at his detective sergeant. He'd tried to keep him at home, get him to take the day off, but Owain insisted on returning. Even after a shower and fresh clothes, the smell of burning diesel hung around him. Too close.

Matt sighed, as if he had momentarily forgotten he was working with Cardiff's finest and not some fancy twenty-four-hour London lab. 'Then what do we have?'

Bryn's sleep-deprived brain informed him that Amy had never replied to his text last night, but then she had spent most of that evening fretting over her assistant. Maybe he should give her another nudge.

'Bryn?'

He snapped back to the room, as the chief constable lurked in the doorway.

'A word?'

Bugger, he couldn't avoid him any longer. Bryn followed, meek as a lamb, his brain struggling to think of excuses why he couldn't accept a promotion. But the fog in his brain proved to him exactly why he should take the job – he was getting too old to go haring about in the predawn hours before working a full shift of a Monday. And his daughters would sleep easier at night knowing Daddy was home and only going to a desk in the morning.

'Bryn,' the chief said, pressing a plastic cup of machine-made tea into his hands, 'I think you're the man for chief super.'

No beating around the bush here. Bryn decided to be equally candid. 'I'm not sure I am, sir.'

The chief tsked softly. 'Don't play coy now. The budget's protected for another year, after the special measures, and you can pick whoever you like for the four new detectives.'

Bryn was surprised at the numbers. 'Four?'

'Well, naturally we'll cover Jenkins and Aitken after they move over to Cyber Crime. On top of the two vacancies, that makes four.'

Bryn froze. *Cyber Crime.* That was why Owain had been so keen to hang about with Amy, had spent all those hours with the new equipment. Why he'd been ordering Catriona about as if he were her boss. Why he'd protested so strongly against Amy's further involvement in the case.

'Everything all right, Bryn?'

'Yes, sir. Fine. I'll think about it.'

But his mind was elsewhere, reeling at the betrayal. Owain had never said a word to him. And Bryn knew exactly why.

The chief's smile was tight, superficial. 'Think fast. I have fellows from all over asking after the job, DCIs of five years or more. I won't be able to hold them off forever.'

'Thank you, sir.' Bryn made his exit, his tea slopping over the edge of the plastic cup in his haste to get away.

But he couldn't go back to the office, couldn't look Owain in the eye when he felt so wounded. He resolved instead to go to the museum, walk the galleries, speak to the experts again. Catch Talia and ask her about Frieda Haas.

He dumped the cup into the nearest bin, still full, and walked out into the rain without his coat. He was soaked through by the time he made it to the museum – only to find it locked up. A small sign declared they were closed on a Monday.

He went round to the side door, but security declared no one was at home and wouldn't even open the door. Instead, he walked into Cathays, towards a collection of mostly deserted cafés and pubs holding their breath in anticipation of the students' return.

Bryn drank his tea slowly, ignoring the buzzing of his phone, sure he would see Owain's name on the screen and not wanting to deal with that. What could he say to him? The immediate feelings of anger had died away to be replaced by confusion, guilt. Had Owain been trying to tell him something and he hadn't paid attention? Had his injuries affected him so badly that he now no longer wanted to be part of the street work?

Owain had always liked the scientific side of evidence, particularly computer forensics, and he was rapt with attention for Amy when she explained how she had dubiously obtained this titbit or that. But to spearhead a new investigation division, without saying a word?

Bryn knew it wasn't personal, not to him. Owain hadn't said anything because of Amy. Because an official police Cyber Crime Unit would end their work with her and leave her bereft. He remembered how passionately Jason had argued for her inclusion on this case. What would this do to her?

It might also explain Owain's coolness towards Cerys, this sudden desire to avoid her, fob her off with work excuses. It would be hard to explain to his girlfriend how he'd put her brother out of a job.

Jason would go spare. Bryn started planning how he might break the news, and then stopped. This was Owain's mess – let him deal with it. Their partnership was on the way out and Bryn would no longer be his direct superior officer, no longer responsible for him except as a friend.

If a friendship could survive a betrayal like this.

Jason woke in the middle of the afternoon, tangled in the blankets of Amy's bed.

He lurched upright, completely disorientated. How had he ended up here? Had Amy invited him? Had they…?

But the memories trickled back in around the pounding in his head. After his shower, he'd been asleep on his feet. Amy had helped him from the sofa to her room, not wanting him down in the basement where it was harder to keep an eye on him. He'd put up a token protest before letting her tuck him in and falling straight to sleep.

He had a couple of missed calls – one from Dylan and one from Bryn. The bike could wait, as he was in no fit state to ride it and he'd need to buy a new helmet to replace the one at the bottom of a mountain lake. And he hoped Bryn had reached Amy without his intervention, though they both often failed to get through to her.

Blanket over his shoulders like an old woman, he shuffled into the living room, glad for once of the muted light filtering through the closed curtains. Amy twisted in her chair and smiled at him, video playing on her third monitor as she worked with pictures and a spreadsheet on the other two.

'You've only been down for a few hours,' she said, checking her clunky wristwatch. 'I've got this.'

Jason ignored the hint to go back to bed and shuffled closer to the monitor. What he'd originally thought was CCTV was actually a full-colour live broadcast from Amy's badge-sized camera. After he'd lost the last one, she'd made its successor out of a gaudy plastic daffodil, which he hated wearing in public.

But who the hell was wearing it now?

'Just heard the bell. Hopefully out in five.'

Cerys' voice rang out from AEON's speakers and Amy turned back to the monitor.

'What's she doing?' Jason asked, caught between curiosity and irritation. It had only taken two days of absence for Amy to replace him in the field.

'Checking out a lead at a school.'

'You could've woken me,' he protested. He was home now and Cerys had probably missed some lectures to run around for Amy.

'You're too old to be at school.' Tact was not Amy's strong point. 'And you have a massive bandage on your head. I only need her to confirm a meet-up and then I can work remotely.'

'Why are you even looking at a school?' He'd missed a lot in forty-eight hours, it seemed.

'One of the girls was acting suspiciously at the museum. I found a boy who took a picture of her and sent him a message from her to meet after school.'

'You impersonated a teenage girl to the boy who fancies her?'

'Yes.' Amy looked up at him. 'Problem?'

'You don't think this might … have some consequences?'

Amy existed in a world of data and investigations. Sometimes, she seemed to have no concept that her techniques might have an impact on the people involved in her machinations.

'They might hook up. That would be nice. Unless she does turn out to be a criminal mastermind. Then not so much.'

'Amy Lane, matchmaker,' he teased.

'Hooking up gang spies and introverts since 2014.'

Pupils were pouring out of the school now, and Amy fiddled with something on Cerys' microphone feed to filter out the background noise.

'I've made the suspect. Eleven o'clock.'

'She's as bad as you,' Jason muttered, as Amy tagged that region of the video feed.

'There she is,' she said, after a moment, pointing out the girl with her mouse. 'On her own, as I suspected.'

Cerys slowly turned, as the girl came closer, watching her approach the main gate.

'This should be it,' Amy said, a white-knuckle grip on her mouse.

Suddenly, a girl bumped into Amy's suspect, grinning awkwardly and holding up her phone.

'Damn! Get out of the way!' Amy yelled at the screen.

But the girl didn't move, trying to engage their suspect in conversation, though the target regarded her suspiciously.

'Cerys, get closer,' Amy said, suddenly, even though she had no way to hear her. She typed on her screen, sending a text, and heard Cerys' phone buzz through the speakers.

'Right you are,' Cerys mumbled, and moved in.

Not that her proximity helped any, because they were both speaking in Welsh and Cerys' command of the language was as bad as Jason's. However, the word 'Instagram' featured heavily.

'Gotcha,' Amy said, opening up another window. 'Now let's grab our suspect's number.'

'How can you do that just by looking at her?' Jason asked, incredulous.

'Because I have the phone number of that girl talking so earnestly to her. Our little Instagram fanatic. Phones make a connection when they come into close contact and so … ha!'

She copied and pasted the new number into her text app and typed a message. Jason leaned over to read:

she likes you. be kind. @

Their suspect withdrew her phone from her pocket and stared at it. Then looked about her as if searching, as her admirer struggled to hold her attention. And looked right at the camera.

'Think I'm made,' Cerys said and started to move.

'Hold position,' Amy said, then texted the command to Cerys. She was too used to the headset communication, Jason realised. How they worked together. This was an improvised op from the beginning.

The suspect extricated herself from the photographer with difficulty, and marched over to Cerys, waving her phone in her face.

'Is this you?' she demanded to know, thick North Wales accent full of indignation.

'Um … I guess…' Cerys said, hesitantly.

'Are you from the geocaching forum?'

Jason stared at Amy in bemusement. 'Amy…'

'What the fuck are you doing at my school?'

Chapter 30

Rhyme and reason

After Cerys awkwardly explained that she was just a go-between, the girl insisted on speaking with Amy by phone. Cerys handed over her own mobile and the girl ducked her face away, from Cerys and the camera.

'How did you get this number?'

She was pissed off, and perhaps a little afraid. Amy didn't want to come across as a creepy stalker, but if she had to lose face to solve this murder, she was prepared to take the risk.

'I found your picture on your friend's Instagram account and asked her to meet you.'

'She's not my friend. We only met a few days ago. Why are you following me?'

Amy decided to bluff. 'Confirm your forum handle. I need to know I can trust you.'

'Corelia. Who are you? What's this all about?'

Amy had a vague idea what geocaching was – hide a thing, leave clues, someone finds it – but she needed more. She searched for local geocaching groups, finding the Cardiff Geocaching Forum and quickly searching for Corelia's posts as she kept her talking. 'What's going on at the museum?'

Corelia turned back to the camera for a moment, a smug smile spreading across her face. 'You want my help with the clue.'

The posts appeared on her screen. All Corelia's latest contributions had been centred around her frustrations with the Welsh cache in the UK Treasure Hunt.

'Yes,' Amy said, distractedly, trying to skim through the information. 'I'm … I'm Ada, and we can help each other.'

'And who are you then? Her sidekick?'

As Cerys tried to field Corelia's questions, Amy looked into the UK Treasure Hunt. It appeared to be a national competition, with fifty separate caches spread around the country. The UK Treasure Hunt required cache hunters to prove their find by inputting a ten-digit code. This might be scrawled on a piece of paper, embossed on an item, or loaded on a chip that needed scanning. The first person to find all fifty caches could claim a ridiculous prize of £100,000, with smaller prizes for the 'first finder' of each cache. If Amy wasn't sitting on a stolen fortune, she'd be tempted to try her luck.

The forum thread was nearing one hundred replies, as everyone complained it was too hard and begging a user called 'LizzieSiddal' for a clue, someone who sounded like a very experienced geocacher. Why was that name familiar?

'Oi, are you listening?'

Amy tuned back in, concentrating again on the phone conversation.

'I think we can solve it if we work together,' Amy said.

She brought up the Welsh cache's details. The starting location was definitely on the edge of Park Place and the museum the most likely building. The page counter stated it was yet to be solved, one of only two in the competition.

Amy studied the riddle with her mystery-solving eye:

Yesterday was St Valentine

Water, for anguish of the solstice: —nay

Oh! May sits crowned with hawthorn-flower

And day and night yield one delight once more?

'It doesn't make any sense,' Jason said, peering over her shoulder.

Yet something about the words nagged at the back of her brain. She had read some of them before, but where?

'Isn't that cheating?' Corelia said suspiciously.

'There are forty-nine other clues,' Amy reasoned. 'Collaborating on one won't hurt. And you can have first find.'

The coveted position and prize of 'first find' seemed to sway it for Corelia. 'All right. Though I've searched the galleries every day for the past week and found nothing. And now they're bloody well closed.'

174

'Talk me through your reasoning so far,' Amy said, hoping Corelia wouldn't catch on that this partnership was rather one-sided.

'Well.' Corelia pulled out her phone, scrolling through some notes. 'Everyone's arguing over whether the lines should be taken literal, or if they're symbolic. Or maybe there's a code in it. Me personally? I reckon it's hid by a Rossetti painting – they're his poems, after all.'

Rossetti. The artist behind the flame-haired woman. Amy pasted the lines into a plagiarism analyser she'd been tinkering with last summer, a project for an exasperated professor of theology, and let AEON cross-reference it to common sources. She identified the poems in seconds, spitting out the titles for Amy's perusal.

'The first one references her handle,' Amy said, referring to 'Valentine – For Lizzie Siddal.' 'Maybe the choice was vanity.'

'Then why not Siddal's poems? That first line is the best evidence there is for a code – the fifteenth of February, or one-five-oh-two, one-five-two, something like that. It could be a catalogue reference.'

'Why all the interest in *La Parisienne*?' Amy said.

The concentration of suspicious persons had been around that painting – now most likely to be other geocachers. Amy belatedly recalled that she was meant to be solving a murder, not a geocache. Though perhaps the two were connected?

Corelia, however, laughed at the question. 'Some idiots think that the water in line two must refer to the dress and that the last line is a coded reference to Renoir – "night yield once more," again night, re-noir. I think it's a bit of a stretch. Course, we've been assuming LizzieSiddal knows what she's doing but maybe it's just a really bad clue. And she won't answer any PMs.'

Amy pulled up LizzieSiddal's forum account. Last login was Saturday morning – a few personal messages read and the UK Treasure Hunt thread checked without commenting. The email address was standard Gmail and no other social media profiles were linked. Amy checked the IP addresses on the forum posts and ran a trace.

175

'She likes to keep us guessing,' Amy said. 'I think you're right about Rossetti, but I guess you've searched around *Fair Rosamund*?'

He only had one painting on display at the museum, the one that had so captivated Amy on her browsing. She would almost be worth a trip to the museum, to see her in the flesh.

But the thought alone set her heart racing, the thought of venturing outside covering her in a wave of sickness. She took a deep steadying breath, grounded by Jason's hand on her shoulder, and sank her anxiety deep down.

'Top to bottom. It's definitely not there – unless some bastard stole it. But why not claim you found it then? And surely LizzieSiddal would check on it?'

From a quick glance at the rules, the hider was meant to maintain the integrity of the geocache, ensure that it was still findable. Of course, geocachers also took holidays, but right after they'd planted a piece in a national contest? This seemed unlikely to Amy. These people appeared to have the same obsessional interest in their hobby as she had for hers.

'When the gallery reopens, we'll take another pass. I have a portable metal detector.' Amy lied easily, her low, disinterested voice difficult to suss out. Only Jason could catch her in deceit.

'Really? All right, Ada, I can live with that.'

The promise of a gadget had won Corelia's heart and Amy smiled at how similar they were. Though Corelia was standing in the sunshine outside her school, whereas Amy was locked down in the dark.

Amy hung up as AEON beeped the completion of LizzieSiddal's IP trace. Amy brought up the results, a neat green dot in Cardiff town centre.

Right over the National Museum of Wales.

Something had gone wrong.

Truth had waited all night – and nothing. And no courier had come to fetch the carefully packed crate in the morning, leaving her agonising over why. How had her meticulous plan fallen to pieces?

Once more, she was left with nothing but the painted harlot, the last thing she wanted, a reminder of her permanent place in the shadows. Truth's anger erupted like a volcano, the long-maintained façade splintering. She seized the bunch of flowers on the side table and yanked them from the vase, throwing the faded roses to the floor.

She wanted to scream, to rage, but the door was ajar, the bed's occupant slumbering despite the noise burbling up from the corridor beyond. Truth carefully picked up every last stem and petal, mopped up the water and neatly threw them away before anyone saw.

The mask back in place. The good daughter once more.

She retook her seat by the window, folded her hands calmly in her lap. Took a deep breath. She had to remain calm, in control. Her discipline was all she had. The only chance she had to appease the forces of life and death.

It was clear that her demands were not being taken seriously. Truth was not being taken seriously. She had thought she held all the bargaining tokens, but it turned out she held nothing at all. She needed to retake control of the game, and the first step was targeting the one who had betrayed her, forced her hand to theft and murder.

Truth was not a little girl now. She was going to prove that – to everyone who would push her down, and to the mediator who would try to trick her when she should fear her. She would return to her original plan, except she would not listen to excuses this time. She was the one in control.

She took out her tablet and opened up her email, an anonymous service that guaranteed safety to political activists and women in hiding. Nothing new – no explanation, no new promises.

The bitch would respond. She would respond or she would be shown, in front of everyone, exactly what happened to those who dared to defy Truth's wishes.

The security guard had paid the price. And so would she.

Chapter 31

Symbiosis

Amy ordered pizza, leaving AEON to puzzle out the riddle of the geocache. Tomorrow, Jason would go down to the museum and demand answers, but tonight was for what Amy called 'debriefing'. Jason steeled himself for an interrogation.

'How did you lose your helmet?'

The first question was revealing. Jason had wondered where exactly she had planted her tracking devices, and she had showed her hand there. He silently objected to being tagged like a lab rat, of course he did, but he didn't exactly live a quiet life of knitting and bridge.

'I had an accident,' he began.

Amy sat on the sofa beside him with a slice of pizza halfway to her mouth as she listened in mounting horror to his story. It was easier to confess when he was sitting in front of her, presenting evidence of his wholeness, wellbeing.

'In a lake? Where the fuck was Frieda?'

Knowing the NCA agent's lack of sympathy would earn her negative brownie points with Amy, Jason attempted to side-step the issue. 'Arresting the lorry driver. I got out by myself.'

'You could've died.' Amy replaced the pizza slice in the box, her mouth twisted unhappily.

'But I didn't.' He reached out to cover her wrist with his palm. 'Just got a bit wet.'

Amy let out a shuddering breath. 'You got to Bangor?'

'We interrogated the driver and he was involved in … moving girls, through Wales to Ireland. He told us about this smaller operation, like a courier, between north and south. We tracked one of the guys to a pub and…' Jason trailed off. Was there a good way to tell Amy he'd offered himself up like a sacrificial lamb?

'You volunteered, didn't you?' Amy asked wearily. 'Someone needed to put themselves in danger and that person had to be you.'

Jason thought that was a bit harsh, but it was essentially true. He had been sick of feeling like a lackey, an errand boy, pushed and pulled around for Amy and Frieda's personal convenience. And he was in his element with boys like Jonah Fish, knew what made them tick, how to nudge at them just right to make them squeal.

He had been the man for the job. And if there was a bit of danger involved, that was no bad thing. How did you know you were alive unless you felt something?

'I made contact,' he said, thinking of the way Jonah had crashed into the floor, rising with a bloody nose and fear in his eyes. 'Arranged to meet him in the evening, so I could do the run in his place.'

'So, you spent the afternoon making arrangements,' Amy filled in. 'You called me.'

Jason's tongue caught, unpleasant warmth creeping up his neck and onto his cheeks. He should tell Amy that Frieda had protested, told him not to go, railed against his choices. But that scene had ended with her ... He didn't want to tell Amy that.

He was aware that he hadn't moved his hand, that his palm rested over her slender wrist, as she watched him with rapt attention. No computer between them, nothing except a pizza box on the table that both of them had forgotten. He had wanted to see her, across from him, in that moment and here she was.

He closed his eyes, mounted his courage, and—

'Are you all right?'

Her concern broke the moment, her hand coming up to ghost across the bandage at his temple.

'I'm fine,' he said, voice steady but only just. 'Just tired.'

'We can finish up tomorrow.' Amy stood, gathering up the pizza box to stuff it in the fridge, her concession to domesticity.

Jason fought for control, berating himself for being so stupid. It was the exhaustion, he told himself. Amy was off-limits, his boss, and she needed a level of careful handling that he, tactless oaf that he was, couldn't aspire to. He needed to shake this crush before it ruined something precious between them.

'I'm going to bed,' he called out, slipping away before he could see her again. The air was too full of possibility, and he had to escape before his resolution failed him.

'Should I change...?'

Amy returned to an empty living room, her assistant vanishing as if he'd never been there. For a moment, panic clawed at her throat – had she imagined him? Was he lost, alone, in need of rescue?

But, no, his empty mug was still precariously balanced on the arm of the sofa, his jacket slung over the back. He had been here. Why then had he fled for the hills?

They'd only been talking about Bangor, an innocuous retelling of his adventures in the north. She had reached yesterday afternoon in the story, a lull between the major events of the tale – why should that provoke such a reaction? Unless...

Unless something had happened that afternoon. Something he wanted to keep from her. When he had been alone with Frieda in a hotel room with nothing but time, about to part, to put himself in danger and not see her again for days.

An uncomfortable suspicion lodged itself in her stomach, the pizza threatening to make an abrupt return to the light. Had Jason and Frieda had an ... encounter in North Wales, a tryst? She would be the latest in a long line of women that Jason had picked up and put down without thought, taking his pleasure and then casting them aside.

But Frieda was different, wasn't she? A professional woman, an investigator, not a random student or girl from a bar. He had followed her to North Wales on a whim, preferring her demands over Amy's. *What does she have that I don't?*

The answer was blindingly obvious, of course. Confidence, poise, urbanity, worldliness – and a brand new motorbike, even if it was now ruined beyond repair. Amy enjoyed a moment of spiteful joy at that fact, but it didn't last.

He had come home to her, but for how long? When Frieda returned to Cardiff, would he beat down her hotel room door, take her in his arms and … leave for London?

The idea was preposterous. Jason Carr was Welsh, born and bred. His family were here, his mam and his sister. His friends, on the inside and out. She couldn't imagine him in any other place or time, though his music drifted him back to the eighties, surrounded by memories of his father.

But stranger things had happened. Cerys had run with gang boys, dated notorious criminals, clawed her way through fights and set innocent property on fire for nothing but fun. And now she was training to be a police officer, dating one.

If Frieda Haas had enough power over Jason after one day to summon him to North Wales, what would she be capable of now? She would only have to click her fingers and he would come running.

What was that phrase? 'If you love him, let him go.'

She didn't know about love, had never tasted it, but the pain in her chest at the thought of losing him was a cut as devastating as if she'd been stabbed.

But she would let him go. He deserved better than her. She had nothing to give him except murder, and one of them deserved the chance to live free from horrors.

Chapter 32

Masquerade

When Jason got up the next morning, half-remembered dreams lingering on his mind, he was surprised to find Amy showered, dressed and finishing breakfast.

'Bloody hell, what happened to you?'

Amy didn't turn, her thin smile reflected in her blank monitor. 'I managed while you were away, didn't I?'

Jason conceded that she had, though the idea made him uneasy. It wasn't that he didn't want Amy to grow in her life skills, her confidence, but if she emerged as a competent butterfly, what need would she have for an assistant?

He was under no illusions about who was the brains of the outfit, or exactly how far she was willing to trust him, and his legwork became redundant if Amy could just take a bus into town and do it herself. He fancied himself useful to her – how long would her interest in him last if he was no longer useful?

'What are we doing today?' He emerged from the kitchen with fresh mugs of tea and tried to insinuate himself back into her investigation.

'I've confirmed that LizzieSiddal is inside the museum, but a generic login was used to connect to the forum.' She handed him a USB stick over her shoulder. 'Insert this into any free slot in a museum computer for two minutes. It will give me a remote connection into their system and I can monitor the network in real-time.'

Her voice had that slightly posher ring to it that she unconsciously adopted when she'd been speaking to her sister, as if she triggered remote memories of a time when Amy had spoken with a plum in her mouth. Jason's harsh Cardiff accent always thickened in response, until they drifted back to their natural tones.

'You want me to ask questions?' he asked.

'Can't hurt. Cerys is meeting you there in an hour.'

Jason's stomach twisted. Since when had Cerys become part of this operation? 'She's got police stuff,' he protested.

'Bryn said he would put in a word for her. I'd ask you to look into the possible secret entrance, but I'm still flying without data.'

Jason wanted to demand answers, to shake her until she gave them up. Why was his competence being called into question? He could just about understand Amy's logic with the school, but he was perfectly capable of investigating the museum by himself. Didn't she trust him at all now?

Or was this some bizarre punishment for running away with Frieda? She was telling him he was expendable, that she had a replacement waiting in the wings. Would his sister really do that to him?

Jason tried to shake off his absurd thoughts. Of course she wouldn't – she wanted to be a copper, a proper detective with the badge and attitude to match. She wouldn't just take his place.

But how many people would leap at the chance? Amy could put a call out for an assistant on one of her forums, and her online minions would all leap at the chance, to work with the great @d@l and her high-profile investigations.

And they would be knowledgeable, in computers and in the world outside the backstreets of Cardiff. Jason might be her first assistant, but maybe she thought it was time for an upgrade.

'The organ smuggling was on the news this morning,' Amy said. 'No mention of you.'

'Good,' Jason said, with feeling. His face had been on the news enough for one lifetime.

'Apparently it crosses at least four countries, and Interpol are very pleased. They interviewed that NCA agent.'

'Frieda's back?'

His stomach lurched. The last thing he wanted was to see the NCA agent, for a cold shoulder or another amorous mistake. He had hoped she'd stay in North Wales a little longer.

'No. The man.' Amy's voice was flat, without a trace of emotion. Too controlled.

Jason realised he'd been baited. Amy was fishing for information about Frieda and he'd made it look like he gave a damn. *Fucking manipulative women.*

'I hope she stays away,' he said, voicing his thoughts. He knew Amy wanted to hear how he felt, even if she would never ask outright. 'Cares more about her precious bike than my skin.'

Amy mumbled something under her breath that was indistinguishable over the rim of her mug, but Jason thought he heard 'run off' in there. He was going to be in the doghouse for weeks over his little trip up north, he could tell. As long as she kept him around to be mocked.

The Micra was still parked up outside Dylan's, along with his motorbike, so he walked the short distance into town. The area around Cardiff's main hospital was quiet, the majority of students not yet returned from their long summer break, but the schools all back for term time. The first leaves of autumn drifted across the pavements, damp from last night's rain. The air was close, too warm for September, as the overcast, pregnant sky threatened to birth a storm at any moment.

The smells from Whitchurch Road's many eateries proved too tempting and he picked up some Indian street food to eat on his way to meet Cerys. He wiped the last crumbs from his mouth with the back of his hand as he turned down the approach to the main university campus.

The storm broke just as he passed between the Students' Union and the university Main Building, breaking into a run as he hauled his leather jacket up over his head. Cerys was waiting at the top of the stairs in her uniform, between two pillars, in the shelter of the lintel.

'So, you're here on official business?' Jason asked.

Cerys tipped his head to examine his bandage, as if she were a nurse, not a trainee copper. 'Mm. Bryn has issues with Talia's statement but he's stuck in some meeting. When Amy called to say you were heading over here, he asked me to keep you in line.'

185

'Did he now?' So they were colluding against him. 'I can do this by myself, you know.'

'Yeah, I'm just here to give it an air of legitimacy. And so anything said can be presented as evidence.'

Jason hesitated. 'Cerys, there's something else—'

'Nope! Not listening!' She shook both hands an inch from her ears and squeezed her eyes closed. 'I don't want to know what else you're up to.'

'What happened to my partner in crime?' he teased.

'She's working the right side of the law now.'

They entered together and asked to see security first, Cerys flashing her badge and a smile to get them in without questions.

The duty guards told Cerys that their systems were all run by a private IT company, as Jason pretended to drop his phone and slipped the USB drive into the tower beneath the desk.

'Who has access to the generic login?' Jason asked.

The guards exchanged a nervous glance. 'It's for staff who don't have their own, but some of the computers … they're just left logged in.'

Cerys tried to thank them for their time, but Jason had another ninety seconds to fill.

'When are the galleries reopening?'

One guard winced. 'When they've got the blood off the floor,' she said quietly.

'They might have to replace the floor altogether,' the other added. 'Not that any of the workmen will touch it – they reckon the gallery is haunted.'

'Haunted?' Jason said, even though he could sense Cerys' eye roll.

'It's nonsense,' the female guard said impatiently, but she didn't sound quite convinced.

'The workmen have heard noises, footsteps across the gallery – but no one there,' the male guard said. 'They say…' He stopped, suddenly self-conscious of his story and how ridiculous it sounded.

'What do they say?' Jason prompted.

'They think it's *her*, "The Blue Lady",' the female guard said, exasperated. 'Or Paul. A ghost in the gallery, waiting for the bloody picture to come back. It's disrespectful is what it is.'

Cerys tried to leave again, but Jason seized on another loose end.

'Any rumours of secret passages in the museum? Tunnels or the like?'

The guards both laughed.

'It's all concrete in the basement,' the female guard said. 'And the galleries have all been renovated in the last twenty years. No way something like that could stay hid.'

'No way anyone could get in or out without passing by the CCTV cameras on the entrances?' Jason persisted.

'Not that I can see,' she said. 'Even if you avoided the cameras, the doors record when they're opened and closed.'

Jason thanked them, before bending down to adjust his shoelace and palming the small USB stick before standing.

Cerys looked at him strangely as they headed for the restoration laboratories. 'Amy sent you here to check out ghost stories and secret passageways?'

'It could be useful,' he said defensively.

Actually, he thought it was utter bollocks but he didn't want his sister to know that he had just opened a door for Amy to the museum computer network.

In the lab, Talia, Soo-jin and Noah had stopped for tea, a packet of Bourbons half-eaten between them, as their colleagues continued to work independently behind them on their myriad precious projects.

Talia scowled as she caught sight of them. 'Why do you keep bothering us here? Why aren't you out looking for our picture?'

'We have questions,' Cerys said tersely, and Jason was surprised that she had shifted to 'bad cop'.

'We have answered all your questions!' Talia threw her hands into the air dramatically. 'I am tired of questions!'

'Before the theft,' Cerys continued, ignoring the theatrics, 'did anyone visit the laboratory, asking questions about the painting?'

'As you know,' Talia said, to Jason, 'we do not allow visitors in the laboratory.'

'What about Frieda Haas?'

Jason started at the name, looking at Cerys in confusion. But Talia fell quiet, the atmosphere in the room suddenly strained.

'That is a private matter,' she said. 'It does not concern the painting.'

'What did you discuss?' Cerys pressed.

'She thought I could help her with … something else, in exchange for…' Talia looked up at Jason, then Cerys. 'Why don't you ask Frieda?'

The lab door opened, temporarily saving Talia from responding. Lucila was holding a cardboard parcel tube in her hands, waving it for the restoration experts.

'Anyone expecting a package?'

Noah crossed the room and took the tube from her. 'There's no Elizabeth Siddal here.'

'Give me that!' Talia snatched the tube out of Noah's hands.

Jason's heart leapt – had they found the mysterious LizzieSiddal?

Talia tore off the plastic end of the tube and reached inside it. A long pale strip of pastels and brilliant blue spiralled from the ends of her fingers, like a magician's silk scarf, as a low moan of grief left her lips.

'What is it?' Jason demanded. 'What's wrong?'

'He's cut her,' Talia said thickly, as the impudent black shoe of 'The Blue Lady' fell from her hands.

Chapter 33

Buried treasure

The museum's computer system opened up before her and Amy started navigating the network, siphoning off data onto her personal servers for later perusal.

She located the last computer to log in to the geocaching forum, but the network map did not include the location or assignment of the machines. Useless.

The pages browsed corresponded exactly to LizzieSiddal's forum activity. The other pages accessed were news articles about the missing painting, and Gmail. Amy lifted LizzieSiddal's password from the forum, and set up her own backdated account for Corelia's benefit. She was playing two games now.

Thankfully, LizzieSiddal wasn't exactly security conscious and the passwords matched exactly – *Lovenh8*, likely an oblique reference to the vitriolic poem 'Love and Hate' by the original Elizabeth Siddal.

She'd spent some time researching Rossetti and Siddal after the forum handle had been revealed. Siddal had been a poet, painter, and muse to more than one artist, the classic model for *Ophelia* as she lay drowning, a role that had almost killed her. And then she'd fallen for Rossetti, kept in secret from his family, until he finally made an honest woman of her. But when he turned away from her, her life grew cold, empty, and she used laudanum to dull the pain. The death of their baby was the last straw, shattering the last shadows of her world, and she drank her comfort until it carried her to the grave.

It seemed that the dramas of the art that surrounded her had followed Siddal into her home, claiming her sanity and finally her life. And what had Rossetti done to stop it? Not a goddamn thing. He had watched his lover waste away into nothing, because he preferred other women, other so-called muses. A different thrill.

Why had the geocacher chosen the handle? Amy itched to ask her. As someone who had modelled her own internet identity on the daughter of Lord Byron, mathematical prodigy and mother of the computer, Ada Lovelace, Amy could relate.

Only three emails had been read since the painting went missing, the others promotions, mailing list digests, and forum notifications. The three read messages had subject lines in all caps: *RENOIR, ANSWER TRUTH, CONSAQUENCES*.

Amy clicked on the first curiously, noting the sender was operating behind a Virtual Private Network and URL masker.

i have it. exchange can go ahead now yes?

'Blackmail,' Amy mumbled, eagerly clicking on the next email.

why wont you answer? tiem running out for her.

Her mouse pointer hovered over the final email, for once her heart beating madly with excitement rather than fear.

answer me or there will be very big consaquences. I am not a child.

Despite the careless typos, the message was clear. The blackmailer wanted something in exchange for *La Parisienne*. But what did he want? There was no ransom demand here, no conditions. And why would LizzieSiddal have a personal stake in the painting's return?

Amy's phone buzzed on the desk. A text from Jason – *Talia got painting bit in post. She's LizzieS.*

Amy grinned at the new information, belatedly thinking to check the computer's other logins for information. Talia Yeltsova's name was first on the list.

She wanted to call Jason, demand more information, but AEON beeped and the third monitor spluttered to life. Talia's face took up most of the screen, sitting in a lab somewhere, as Amy flicked on the speakers.

'Thank you, Cerys,' she mumbled. She'd forgotten she still had the daffodil camera.

'Who is Elizabeth Siddal?' Cerys asked.

Talia scowled. 'What does that matter? You must send this for analysis! The killer is a madman!'

'And we will.' Cerys' voice was steady, patient. 'First, I want to know why you opened a package addressed to another woman.'

'Lizzie Siddal has been dead for over a hundred years,' a woman butted in, from somewhere off screen. 'She's a nineteenth-century artist and poet.'

'I use the name on the internet,' Talia said, as if the woman hadn't spoken. 'Who uses their real name, hmm?'

'Do you know who sent you this piece of painting?'

'No. No idea.' Her knuckles were white on the edge of the table, her voice quavering.

'But someone who knows your internet handle and that you work at the museum.'

'Everyone knows I work here,' Talia snapped. 'That is not a secret.'

'Why address you as Elizabeth Siddal?' Cerys persisted.

'I told you – he is mad!'

Amy picked up her phone and texted Jason, her eyes never leaving the video: *ask about emails @*

'What about the note? It talks about wanting answers.'

'I don't know what th-that means.' Her voice betrayed her again, the stutter giving her away.

'What about the emails?' Jason's voice came from somewhere to Cerys' right. 'Don't know what they mean either?'

'How do you – you have been spying on me!'

'Frieda sends her regards.'

Amy stiffened. Frieda? Why was that NCA bitch taking the credit for her work? But the reaction in Talia was astonishing, her face crumpling at his words.

'I think the emails … they are about the cache.'

'You owe someone money?' Cerys said, mistaking her words.

'No, no, the geocache. It is a competition, online. That is where I use the handle LizzieSiddal. I have … hidden something and this man, he wants to find it.'

'He killed a man over a geocache?' Jason said, incredulously.

'I told you – he is mad. And now he is tearing her to shreds over it.'

191

Bryn listened to Jason and Cerys' account with astonishment. 'It's about some online game, G.I. Catching?'

'Geocaching,' Jason corrected. 'That's what Talia thinks.'

'I don't know if we can trust her.' Amy's voice rang out from Jason's phone, placed in the middle of Bryn's desk in the detectives' office. 'She lied about her visa and she's working with Frieda Haas. It could be something else.'

'I guess we can't just walk up to Frieda and ask her what it's about.'

The questioning note in Cerys' words was weak. She was a Butetown girl and knew a thing or two about asking after people's secrets. If you don't want people to pry into your own, you kept damn quiet about theirs.

'And we can't ask Talia. She thinks Frieda already told us.'

'What's going on?'

Matt walked up to the huddle and Jason's hand leapt out to kill the call to Amy.

'Talia Yeltsova is being blackmailed by the murderer,' Bryn said, bringing him up to speed. 'She has answers to some online puzzle that he wants. I was just about to brief you.'

'And why are you here?' Matt fixed Jason with a look.

'Just confirming my statement with Bryn,' Jason lied smoothly. 'I was here when Cerys arrived with the evidence.'

'Your sister,' Matt said, looking between the two of them. 'Don't they teach confidentiality anymore, Miss Carr?'

Bryn quickly interjected, before Cerys could vent her spleen. 'I asked for his opinion. Because of Amy's—'

'I'm sure the Cyber Crime Unit can handle that,' Matt said. 'We don't need external consultants for this investigation.'

Jason looked at Bryn before smiling tightly at Matt. 'Only when it's convenient for me to get my arse burned, is it?'

Before Matt could reply, Jason pocketed his phone and walked away from them.

'Talia will need a formal interview,' Matt said, turning to Cerys. 'Type up your notes, Miss Carr, so the detectives can do their work.'

Cerys sat at Owain's desk without another word, flipping open her notebook and busying herself with logging on.

However, Bryn knew she would be keeping half an ear on the conversation – to report back to Amy, Jason, Owain. Carrs might be adept at keeping secrets, but they also knew the value of them.

'I will have Head Office look into Miss Yeltsova. This can't just be about a game.'

Bryn decided to play his hand. 'I wouldn't bother if I were you. I think Frieda Haas has all the information you need.'

Matt's eyes narrowed. 'What do you mean by that?'

'Oh, didn't she tell you? She was in contact with Talia before the painting was even stolen. Now that's a funny coincidence, isn't it?'

Matt tried to cover his wince. 'I'll talk to Frieda. You take Yeltsova's formal statement and get a warrant for her computer.'

'You don't seem surprised,' Bryn said, testing the waters, looking for a reaction.

Matt leaned in, his words only for Bryn's ears. 'I don't know why she was there, but I intend to find out. In the meantime, I don't want idle gossip prejudicing this investigation.'

'And I don't want a cover-up.' Bryn was blunt, as always. 'Why was she even in Cardiff?'

'Frieda was working a separate investigation before the painting was stolen.'

'Which was…?'

'Need-to-know. I'm not clear on all the details. I'm sure her dealings with Miss Yeltsova relate to that investigation.'

'And you didn't think to mention it? How do you know the two aren't connected?'

Matt's smile was enigmatic, guarded. 'I'm pretty sure on this one. And we have bigger fish to fry. My bosses want developments.'

'Are you going to call the Foreign Minister?'

'Why would I do that?' Matt seemed genuinely puzzled.

'Because of our diplomatic relations with France?'

But even as he said it, Bryn realised something was off about it. France couldn't just demand the restoration of all Impressionist paintings. How had he been naïve enough to believe anything that came out of Frieda's mouth?

'I think the French can wait,' Matt said, his voice filled with amusement, and Bryn fought down his embarrassed flush.

Before Bryn could question him further, he had walked away, presumably to bring Owain and Catriona up to speed. Owain, who hadn't even had the decency to tell Bryn he was leaving, just scuttled off to his new office without a word.

Bryn still had one computer expert he could trust. Quietly, he copied all the investigation files in the update folder, watching as they disappeared one by one. If anyone could puzzle out the contents of Paul's apartment, Talia's secret identity and Frieda's investigation, it was Amy Lane.

Chapter 34

Held to ransom

When Jason arrived home, Amy was in a hyperactive phase, flitting around the living room like a deranged butterfly.

'Hostage negotiation!' she said, stabbing her finger into his chest.

Jason captured her wrist, to protect his body from more pokes. 'Say what now?'

'We must organise an exchange, like in the movies. The geocache clue for the painting.'

'And how do we know he will keep his end of the bargain?' Jason asked.

'We'll arrange a drop. Or … something. Bryn can work it out, or the NCA. I don't know the rules.' Amy waved her hands dismissively.

AEON pinged and Amy returned to her computer, flapping her hands as if she were trying to demonstrate the sound of one hand clapping twice over. 'New files! At least someone keeps me in the loop.'

'What's that supposed to mean?' Jason said, hotly.

Amy glanced back at him, momentarily still. 'You broke your phone, I get it. But landlines still exist. I'll even accept faxes. Communication breakdown is the end of a relationship.'

The word hung uneasily between them for a moment, before she added weakly, 'Not that we have a relationship.'

Jason felt something cold pierce him, like a portion of his blood had turned to sleet. 'No,' he said, numbly. 'Course not.'

She typed on, oblivious to the nausea crawling up Jason's throat, the feeling that the floor was shifting rapidly beneath him and he might fall at any time.

What was wrong with him? It was true. Their partnership was about business.

He liked solving murders as much as she did. Or gathering dirt on arsehole ex-partners of frightened women. Or a little intimidation of business world dinosaurs with dodgy hiring and firing practices, hanging around their offices and homes, staring at them through windows from beneath his hoodie.

He liked the work, he couldn't deny that. But he liked Amy. He liked living among her chaos, trying to make sense of it, hold it all together long enough for her to settle, to smile at a job well done.

But, beneath all that, were they friends? He had been her cleaner, and now he was her assistant. All contractual, paid for services rendered. He wasn't her carer or her relative – he was the help. With her words, Amy had made her feelings clear on the matter.

Not that we have a relationship. He had imagined an intimacy where none existed.

It was the absence of the sound that told him something was wrong, the keyboard silent, the mouse unclicked. Amy was staring at a document on the screen, totally focussed on the bullet points. But she didn't scroll down, didn't even reach for the mouse, and he realised her whole body was trembling.

'Amy? What's wrong?'

His grievances vanished in the face of her distress, as he placed his hand on her shoulder and looked at the screen. It seemed like an innocuous report on Paul Roberts' computer – something about a failed login, but nothing particularly shocking.

'Amy?' The heel of his palm pressed into the tense muscle of her shoulder, trying to rouse her from her stupor.

'Owain wrote this.' Her voice was quavering, full of unshed tears.

Jason still didn't understand. 'Owain…'

She pointed at the screen, the tip of her finger leaving a greasy smudge on the monitor as it shook with the intensity of her feeling.

He read the words but they meant nothing to him. 'Cyber Crime Unit?'

'South Wales Police Cyber Crime Unit,' she said thickly. 'A new computer forensics department, headed up by Owain and that bitch Catriona Aitken.'

Computer forensics. The implications suddenly hit him and he felt that same lurch of his whole world shifting further out of alignment. 'They're replacing us?'

'Me. They're replacing me.'

The tears came then, an outpouring of grief, and Jason swung the chair round to face him, gathering her into his arms to offer some comfort. *Those fucking bastards.* How could they do this to her? When she had calmed down, he was going to call Bryn up – no, he would go round there and…

And what? Punch a detective inspector in the face? Cause a scene down the police station? How was that going to help Amy?

At least he'd figured out why Owain had been sniffing around Amy. The weasel had been stealing her ideas, learning her tricks of the trade before setting up his own stall. Shutting her out of the police work that kept her sane. Had Cerys known about this? The idea of his sister turning traitor left a bitter taste in his mouth.

But his priority right now was the woman in his arms, her shakes and sobs subsiding to muted sniffles against his shoulder. His palm cupped the back of her head, digging his fingers into the tangles that she could never be bothered to brush out. With her pressed against him, her scent filled his nostrils, that balm of familiarity putting a lid on his anger – for now.

But when he saw Owain…

Amy leaned back and away from him, scrubbing at her eyes with her hoodie sleeve, and Jason tactfully retreated to the kitchen, making a pot of tea and digging out the posh biscuits with the extra dark chocolate.

But when he returned to the living room, Amy was back at the computer, code over all three monitors, as she typed like lightning.

'Are you—?'

'We may get the data second-hand, but I won't be shut out.'

Amy stabbed at the enter key triumphantly and the code vanished, replaced by a simple set of windows with a menacing black skull and crossbones logo.

'That doesn't look friendly,' Jason said, trying to sound neutral as he placed the biscuits beside the mouse.

'A mod of one of my Trojans – one of my minions has outstripped me in avoiding detection, but he has a flair for the dramatic.' She gestured towards the skull.

'And that Trojan is where exactly?'

'Looking for Owain's new computer, particularly focussed on the Cyber Crime evidence folders and his analysis – such as it is.' She tutted like a disappointed teacher.

'Amy, are you okay?'

She had switched from sobbing on his shoulder to acting like a detached military spy, but she did not answer his question.

'What he's failed to realise is that the intruder typed exactly the same password three times. Exactly. No variation in the numbers, capitals – nothing. So they were pretty confident in the password's accuracy, but they probably weren't the originator. Which makes sense, because Paul Roberts was already dead.'

'Hold on, you've lost me.' Jason was still reeling from Amy's emotional whiplash, but he also wasn't sure she was making sense.

'If your password is rejected, what do you do?'

Since Amy had taken an interest in his passwords and started changing them monthly, Jason commonly had this problem. 'Uh … try a different one?'

'Or?'

'Try different capitals or vary the date with the name.'

Amy's password combinations hinged on significant information already in his life – from his mam's maiden name to the year he'd passed his driving test. It was just remembering which bits went together that flummoxed him.

'Yes, exactly. You don't type the same thing over again – well, maybe once, if you think it's a typo, but three times? I think the intruder only knew one password, so they must've taken it from somewhere.'

'Did they guess it?'

'Unlikely. I don't know what it means – DGRES230560. The six digit format suggests a date, but it's not his birthday. What was special about May 1960?' Her fingers flew over the keyboard, scrolling through Wikipedia pages in quick succession. 'Unless he was interested in Nazi war criminals, tsunamis or American church mergers, it's nothing particularly famous.'

'What about art?' Jason asked. 'He had a thing about art, didn't he?'

Amy stopped typing, her fingers hovering above the keyboard. 'What if it's not 1960? What if it's 1860?'

Her fingers flew again, like sparrows darting from berry to berry, alighting only for the barest hundredth of a second before hurrying away to the next, and the next.

'No, that's too early for the Impressionists. But it's right in the middle of…' She trailed off, before turning to him with a sudden smile. 'DGR and ES!'

Jason was still lost, but Amy had clearly seen the light. She hauled up a Wikipedia page before crowing triumphantly.

'Ah-ha! Dante Gabriel Rossetti and Elizabeth Siddal were married on 23rd May 1860.'

Jason still felt several steps behind. 'But this is Paul Roberts' password. Not Talia's.'

Amy held up one hand, while she continued to type with the other, only fractionally slower than when she used both. 'I'm checking their logins at the museum now. And…'

She sat back, admiring her work. 'It is Paul Roberts' password.'

'So … did he have a thing for Talia? Playing Dante-whatever to her Lizzie?'

Amy brought up the security guard's browsing history, long lists of websites visited, logins used. 'No, his recently visited sites are art forums, NFL sites, and … geocaching.'

She clicked on a link and the Cardiff Geocaching Society site appeared.

'Look – look at the login.'

'LizzieSiddal,' Jason read.

'Talia isn't LizzieSiddal – Paul Roberts was.'

'And so the Welsh geocaching clue…'

'Died with Paul Roberts.' Amy's mouth settled in an unhappy line. 'We have nothing to give the blackmailer. And neither does Talia.'

Chapter 35

Blind date

Talia walked in to the cocktail bar, scanned the mostly empty tables, and scowled.

She stalked angrily over to the table and threw down her bag. 'I suppose you think this is funny.'

Jason held up his hands. 'I didn't think you'd come otherwise.'

Talia waved her phone towards his face. 'Impersonating an NCA agent – isn't that a crime? Won't you and your boss have more trouble?'

'We only suggested you might be meeting Frieda. We never actually used her name.'

It wasn't a plan without risk, though Talia hadn't stormed out yet. The message had been carefully composed, to tell just enough without giving them away: *The police are on to you. Meet me and I can protect you. Fat Cats @ 8pm.*

'And the rest was to lure me here? Pathetic. I will tell Frieda what you have done.' She grabbed the handles of the bag and made to leave.

Jason had only one chance to stop her. 'We know you're not LizzieSiddal.'

Talia hesitated, buying him an extra few seconds.

'Why have you stolen Paul Roberts' identity?' Jason decided to make another leap. 'And why did you break into his flat?'

Talia sat down hard. 'How do you know that?'

'It wasn't difficult,' Jason said, dodging the question and continuing his bluff. 'But I don't understand why you did it – pretended to be Paul. What did it bring you except grief?'

Talia leaned in, her face taut, her voice barely above a whisper. 'You're independent, aren't you? From the police? The thief, he said no police.'

Jason leaned in, all ears now. 'This is between us. No police.'

Amy had made it very clear they were divorcing from Cardiff's finest, which would make their next family dinner more than a little awkward.

'There was a note left on my desk, before they found Paul. I had arrived early – I thought the bus would take longer, and my car was in the garage. Because of the window. Sorry, where was I?'

'The note,' Jason prompted.

'Yes. It said something like "I have her. No cops. I will email the instructions." It was addressed to LizzieSiddal.'

'On your desk? So, the killer already thought you were Lizzie?'

Something about this story didn't add up. But before he could press further, the waiter came over for their order. Talia asked for some exotic spirit-filled cocktail, while Jason earned the man's disdain by ordering a beer. When he had finally left them, Jason opened his mouth to question further, but Talia slipped off her coat, made herself comfortable. Settling in for a long story.

'When he entered the national treasure hunt, there was some press interest. Paul was very shy and he asked to use my photograph, and I agreed. That was all.'

'You were close?'

The evidence retrieved from Paul's flat made sense now in light of his geocaching, but they hadn't found any signs of a lover.

'Friends. We were both interested in the geocaching. His enthusiasm was infectious – others in the lab also started playing the games. It became a little competition.'

Their drinks arrived and she took a large gulp of the multi-coloured liquid, ignoring the straw.

'When the emails came, I panicked. I was afraid for "The Blue Lady". So I went to his place and I tried to use his computer, but I could not get in. I thought he might have left a clue there, about the cache. Where it is.'

'You don't know?'

'He was very keen on the secrecy. Because of the contests. He didn't want to give anyone an advantage, liked to give only small hints. But with this treasure hunt, he would not give any. He was very fair.'

'Why didn't you respond to the blackmailer?'

'I wish I had.' Talia appeared agonised, genuinely distraught. 'I would do anything to protect the painting, anything. What do I care about this silly geocache now? Paul is dead and the painting ruined!'

It was hard to work through the pain in her chest, but Amy couldn't escape the feeling that if she stopped, she would never start again, like a clockwork monkey running down and slumping to a stop.

The questions of how Bryn had let this happen, why Owain had used and usurped her – that all had to wait, for a time when she could detach herself from the grief lodged in her throat, threatening to choke her.

She had to carry on. She checked the geocaching forums, out of habit as much as investigative intent, and saw five new PMs from Corelia. She scanned them all, but found nothing but nagging and impatience. She fobbed her off with another set of excuses, stalling her a little longer. She could still be useful.

They had set up the meeting with Talia to confirm what she knew, but Amy didn't expect much. If Talia had the key to the geocache, she would've handed it over readily before seeing poor Henriette Henriot lose her toes. At least they now had an explanation for Talia's suspicious behaviour.

LizzieSiddal's online life was rich and explained Paul Roberts' lack. From art forums to an online dating site dedicated to transvestism, the redheaded painted lady did get about. Amy checked the evidence log for Paul's apartment, but no women's clothing had been found. Perhaps he had a secret garage somewhere? Or maybe the Cardiff forensics team hadn't been particularly interested in his wardrobes.

She made a note, but it didn't seem relevant. It was unlikely that the killer knew Paul was LizzieSiddal – why ransom a painting when you can threaten him for the clue? And why kill him if his secret dies with him? No, the killer couldn't have known LizzieSiddal and Paul were one and the same. Any clues about Paul would only be useful in answering a very different question – where was the Welsh geocache?

Amy opened up the riddle again, but knowing the real-life identity of LizzieSiddal didn't add any meaning to the words. Why had Paul chosen those particular poems?

Maybe the answers went deeper than that. Or perhaps she was starting in the wrong place. The real enigma here was not why Paul had picked out these Rossetti poems for his clue, but why he had chosen the handle of LizzieSiddal in the first place.

If his passion was for the Impressionists, what was it about this nineteenth century Pre-Raphaelite model and artist that compelled him to become her? Looking at her own experience, Amy had chosen Ada Lovelace for her online pseudonym because she was the first computer programmer and she had done everything possible to distance herself from her father's lifestyle, shunning the reckless Lord Byron for the comfort of mathematics.

What, then, was there to Siddal that drew Paul in? From what they knew of him – which was, admittedly, very little – he had a deep passion for art, but did not paint himself. Nor had they found any works of poetry. He had not been mentored by any great artist, nor sponsored by a rich patron. He had never taken an art class, though he attended many lectures on Monet.

Was it her personal life that intrigued him? Married to Rossetti, but spurned for his many mistresses – but Paul had never been married and his few interactions on the dating site were short conversations, arrangements to meet. Amy had no evidence he had ever been in a serious relationship. And he had not given birth or lost a child, though Amy made a note to check the local registries.

Siddal was addicted to laudanum – could Paul have shared her vice? Perhaps alcohol or opiates separately, but the police search of the flat hadn't found bottles, pills or needles, and his internet ordering habits didn't reveal any pharmaceuticals.

Thinking about her medicine cabinet made her twitchy. Amy had swallowed down a couple of tablets after Jason left, but she wasn't mellow enough to resist a second calling. She drifted, zombie-like, into the kitchen, boiling the kettle while she took another one, two, three for luck. Tea would help, calm her, soothe her. Until Jason got back.

Amy returned to AEON with her tea in hand, watching the colours of Rossetti's *Beata Beatrix* blur together into a pleasant, Impressionist-like sea. She was grateful to Paul Roberts, for dying to introduce her to this beauty. It was very generous of him. But he wasn't a genius, was he? Not like Amy, who was heralded as such by her online sycophants and Jason's quiet wonder. Her parents had never recognised her talents, but then they'd never really known her at all. And she would rather keep it that way.

So, if she was a genius and Paul was not, she should be able to crack his geocache with ease. If she applied herself. And why shouldn't she? With the police throwing away her expertise, she was free to show them exactly what she was capable of, without the burden of their legal qualms.

If they would not engage with the blackmailer, then she would.

She opened LizzieSiddal's email account and brought up the latest message. Altering the metadata to suggest Talia was sending from the museum system, Amy composed a short message to the thief, a proposition:

The clue is lost. But I can solve it if you return her.

Amy triumphantly hit Send and slumped back in her chair. How could the killer resist? She opened up her remote connection to the police database, idly searching for Owain's files but unable to find a networked drive that fitted the bill. He must have a separate uplink – clever, but not enough to outsmart her. She placed a monitor on Owain's email account, sure he would access that through his privileged connection without thinking and then she would have unfiltered access.

AEON beeped, displaying a new message from the blackmailer in LizzieSiddal's account. The body was blank, the subject line reading: *WHO ARE YOU*

Amy scowled. How had she been made so easily? No matter. If she could prove her offer was genuine, the killer could bargain directly with her instead of Talia. And she could shift the power balance in this hostage negotiation. She replied:

A concerned third party. I will trade my knowledge for the painting. This is a one-time offer. If you do not agree, you will never find the cache.

Amy watched the screen intently. AEON was busy trying to follow the source of the email, but it was winding and wending through an obscure series of servers, false bounces and dead ends like a vast maze with no escape. It was a slow method of obfuscation, but Amy had to admit it was effective.

The reply pinged through within a minute.

price different now. solve all clues for me and lady is returned.

Beneath the short message, the killer had listed five places: Nottingham, Southampton, Glasgow, Belfast and Cardiff. Amy pulled up the UK Treasure Hunt website – they were all cities hiding geocaches, with Glasgow and Cardiff the only two with no solvers.

The killer wanted all the glory of victory, unable to solve the riddles but willing to murder, steal and ransom to achieve his goals. It was that hubris that would be the end of him.

Amy would play his game. But she would also hunt him down like the dog he was, inching ever closer to finding him and bringing him down.

Chapter 36

Battle lines

'You want me to go to Scotland?'

Something about Amy's demeanour, her breezy words and her unsteady gait, had Jason looking for a drained bottle of red. But in the absence of glass in the recycling or scattered about the living room, Jason had to admit that her state was nothing to do with alcohol. Which left the pills.

'Corelia thinks she can get to Belfast tomorrow, because I wrote her a note – ha! And I have Southampton and Nottingham cachers willing to trade. That leaves Scotland.'

Jason swung his rucksack off his shoulder, as Amy dropped onto the sofa, her tea sloshing over the edge of her mug onto the cushion. She was stoned. He'd left her alone for a couple of hours and she was completely off her head, making next to no sense.

'What's in Scotland?' he asked, perching beside her on the sofa.

'The unsolved cache. Only one on the list – except Cardiff, of course. That was the deal.'

Jason felt something uncomfortable lurch in his stomach. 'What deal? What have you done?'

'Deal with the thief,' Amy said, as if it were obvious. 'For "The Blue Lady". Five geocaches to release her.'

'And you just … did this? This morning, without saying anything?'

Amy grinned, a childish expression that stretched her pale cracked lips. 'I'm a genius!'

Jason was reminded yet again that this wasn't an equal partnership, that he couldn't chew her out for not consulting him, but he also figured she hadn't exactly acted out of sober judgement in this instance. And that put this whole case in jeopardy.

'Amy, what have you taken?'

She blinked at him. 'What?'

'Tablets. What did you take and how many.'

She pointed an accusing finger at him. 'You sound like my sister.'

'I sound like your friend. How many tablets?'

Amy shrugged, an exaggerated movement that cost her more tea. 'Some. I don't count. What does it matter?'

'How can you investigate if you're off your head?'

Amy stared at him. 'I'm not off my head.' She hesitated. 'Am I?'

Jason rested his hand on her arm. 'Maybe you should lie down, yeah? Until it wears off.'

Amy yanked her arm out from under his palm. 'I'm fine. You need to do what I say. I'm your boss.'

'I know you are—'

'Frieda asks you to go to North Wales and you just leave! I ask you to go to Scotland, with a plan and everything, and you tell me I'm baked.' Amy stood up, the mug tumbling to the floor and soaking the carpet in tea.

'Did I say I wouldn't go? I just don't think you should be making these decisions when you're … not at your best.'

'I'm brilliant! I'm not at my best when I'm shaking and crying and can't get out of bed. This isn't that, is it?'

'Can't you be something in between?'

But he already knew he'd lost this fight. He couldn't argue in favour of the anxiety, the panic attacks that could rob her of an entire day. He didn't know nearly enough about this illness to save her from it, didn't even know if it were possible. So he turned a blind eye to the tablets and the duvet days, and hoped it would pass over. But it hadn't, and he had to face the fact that it wouldn't. Not without help, help he wasn't qualified to give.

Amy didn't answer him, moving back to AEON with the jerky walk of a woman trying not to let on how intoxicated she was. The printer spat out a couple of sheets of paper and she nodded her head towards them.

'The starting GPS coordinates and the riddle. I can't make it out yet, but being on location should help. I've booked tickets for you on the last train.'

Jason opened his mouth to protest, to argue that there was no way in hell he was leaving her like this, when the doorbell rang. Amy flicked up the image on the monitor.

'Are you expecting your sister?'

Amy buzzed her up without waiting for an answer, but Jason had read the agitation in Cerys' body. She was here for A Talk, which was the last thing he needed today. He had almost preferred it when his little sister had been running around Cardiff seducing gang runners and snorting drugs, instead of taking on all their mam's nagging qualities and trying to intervene in his life for the better. Just because she was now an applicant for the sainthood didn't mean that he had to follow suit.

The lift spat out his sister, in her uniformed best, and Jason stood in front of Amy to face her down. She didn't need to see how the hacker was handling Owain's betrayal.

'Bad time?' Cerys asked tentatively.

'For what?' he snapped back, more hostile than he intended.

Cerys squared her shoulders and he knew then the niceties were done with. She directed her next words over his shoulder. 'You contacted the blackmailer from Talia's account.'

'The account isn't Talia's,' Jason said. 'Which you would know if you hadn't shut us out of the case.'

'No one is shutting you out,' Cerys said, but he could see she wasn't convinced by that argument herself.

'Oh yeah? So what do you call not sharing vital evidence? And setting up a Cyber Crime Unit without saying a fucking word?'

'You think he told me about this?' Cerys' words were infused with cold anger. 'I found out yesterday!'

'Yet you're not fighting him, are you? You've come round here to tell us to back off.' When her denial wasn't immediate, Jason stepped closer, his voice louder. 'Haven't you?'

'Bryn said you were prejudicing the investigation.'

'We're the only people in this investigation with some bloody clue what's going on!'

'Care to share?' Cerys asked, too casually.

'So you can run back to Owain with our leads? No, ta. If he's the police's pet hacker now, he can do it himself. Don't need us, do you?'

'I am on your side!'

'Are you? Coming over here, telling us to quit investigating? Playing errand girl to your lover in your fetish outfit.'

He had gone too far, he could tell. Cerys' cheeks were flushed, her hands clenched at her sides. She'd never looked more like him.

'You can fuck around with NCA agents and then just saunter on back to your boss but I can't have both a boyfriend and a brother? Where the fuck do you get off telling me what to do?'

'I care something about loyalty!' Jason roared, ignoring the hypocrisy staring him in the face.

Cerys laughed, a bitter, ugly sound. 'You hear that, Amy? I hope you're very happy with him.'

She turned on her heel and left. The slam of the front door echoed upstairs, and Jason watched on the monitor as she stormed off down the street.

Chapter 37

A tangled web

As she slowly returned to earth, Amy realised exactly what she had done.

She had contacted a murderer and agreed to play a game. She had tied Jason and Corelia into this dangerous play, even forging a sick note for Corelia's school. And she was sending Jason to Scotland, when she had only just got him back within her sanctuary.

She stared at the whorls of plaster on the ceiling, listening to Jason washing up in the kitchen, and struggled to remember what had been important about today. Cerys, she could recall, the shouting and the accusations. But she also recalled Jason using the word 'loyalty' and meaning her, the warmth that had filled her entire body that had nothing to do with drugs.

Jason peered over the back of the sofa, looking at her with trepidation. 'Y'alright?'

'Mm,' she said, and swung her legs down to make room for him on the sofa.

He sat beside her, pressing a cup of strong, sweet coffee into her hands. She took the first scalding sip immediately, enjoying the tingling on her tongue as the liquid seared its way down her throat.

'You want to hear what I got from Talia?'

She nodded, not trusting herself to speak, trying to give the impression she was both sensible and sober in that moment. The look Jason gave her suggested she wasn't particularly convincing.

'She said the first blackmail note wasn't sent by email or post, but left on her desk. The killer thought she was LizzieSiddal because Paul used her photo. He was shy or something. But I thought the bit about the note was interesting because you would've seen that, right? On the CCTV. So she must be lying.'

Something nagged at the back of her brain, the blurry highlight reels of hours upon hours of CCTV playing across her mind. 'There isn't a camera on the laboratory corridor. Only on the end. And … I don't remember if I checked it.'

She remembered watching the exits, but had she tracked the killer inside the museum? Fuck, she was losing it.

'Later,' Jason said. 'It might be nothing. You look tired.'

It sounded like an accusation to her ears, 'tired' meaning drained, exhausted, not coping. She couldn't afford to be 'tired' in front of him. She couldn't let on exactly how much she didn't want him to leave tonight and go to bloody Scotland.

'I'm fine,' she said, sticking with that socially acceptable lie that meant anything from breezy as a summer's day to knocking on death's door.

'Yeah, sure you are.' Jason's narrowed eyes peered into hers, as if he could see the brain whirring beneath, a little off-kilter, a few thousand molecules of serotonin out of whack.

'Have you packed for Scotland?' she asked, when what she wanted to say was: *Don't leave. I'm not fine. I need you.*

'Can we talk about what happened today?' he said.

That was the very last thing she wanted to do. But it was too much effort to escape, both hands occupied by the coffee and her thigh muscles too weak to stand alone. She needed a personal trainer. She needed a new life.

When she didn't answer him, Jason barrelled on. 'You weren't right today. It's the pills, isn't it?'

She didn't meet his eyes. 'I got a new batch,' she lied. 'They were stronger than the last lot. They took me by surprise. It won't happen again.'

'A parcel arrived?' Jason asked, suspiciously.

'Courier,' she said, trying to keep it simple. The most effective deceits were simple.

'Right,' he said, a sliver of belief creeping in around the edges of his suspicion. 'Maybe you need a better supplier.'

'I'm cutting down.' More lies. 'I should be off them by Christmas.'

212

'That would be a great present.' A warm smile eclipsed that tense, worried look he hadn't shaken for days. 'Maybe we can go round my mam's for Christmas dinner.'

Her heart lurched in her chest, but Amy smiled, remembered the part she was playing. *I'm fine.* 'You need to pack.'

Jason took hold of her wrist, swept his thumb over her pounding pulse point. 'You'd tell me? If things were getting worse?'

Amy merely smiled and slurped her coffee, burning her tongue. How could she tell him how the news about the Cyber Crime Unit had shattered all her illusions? If she had the energy to argue, she would tell him that a cup of coffee couldn't solve everything. It wouldn't find 'The Blue Lady' and it wouldn't help her feel like someone who belonged on this planet, who could know and be known by other humans.

Jason nodded, apparently satisfied, and left to pack for Scotland.

Leaving Amy sinking under the weight of her own untruths.

The game was afoot.

That was what that famous English detective said, wasn't it? 'The game is afoot.' Truth had never understood the strange phrase – how could any game be a foot? Unless it was some obscure soccer reference. She had never understood football.

This 'concerned third party' could be the answer to all her problems, something to turn her frustration into joy. Truth could taste the triumph, the way her mother would look at her, recognise her. She could still fix this, make it all right for them. Become a true daughter.

She wouldn't have to watch her mother die because Truth was too weak to fight, too weak to claim what was owed to her, and save the life of a woman who hated her – yet meant everything to her.

If it was genuine. Truth knew enough about hiding IP addresses to know that the mystery puzzle solver was concealing theirs. Why were they intervening? How had they known that she needed them?

213

So many questions. But if she could solve the last few caches, she could bring this game to an end. Remove the hold all these spectres had over her once and for all. She would have the recognition she deserved.

And if they betrayed her? She had killed once. She could do it again.

All she had to do was wait for the clues to arrive. But time was running out, another day under the weight of the lady's eyes. Truth still had her scissors close at hand, to peel away another ribbon of canvas from the whore's skirts – that would make them hurry, feel her urgency to be out from under that gaze.

Truth fancied she saw fear in the vapid girl's eyes now, knowledge that the next blow would wound more than her coy toes. The temptation to eviscerate her was strong, her blood heating at the thought, but Truth forced it down. She had more important things to consider, even if it meant sparing the tart.

Truth had to make the deadline short, because she was fast running out of time, out of hope. It would increase the chance of the girl meeting another sweep of the blade, but what did she care? They would restore her, of course, no expense spared for that obscene woman and her criminally blank eyes.

Three days, Truth would give them.

Three days until 'The Blue Lady' was torn in two.

Chapter 38

Old shoe leather

Walking back to the station, after another set of tedious interviews at the museum, Bryn was glad of the distraction of his ringing phone. He was glad he didn't recognise the number, still struggling to think of a decent excuse for his daughters about why he wasn't home for dinner. Again.

'Hesketh.'

'Detective? It's Talia Yeltsova. The blackmailer says three days only! Until he destroys our blue lady.'

A chill shivered down his spine, as if it were a real, living woman who had been threatened. 'I assure you we are doing everything we can.'

'But you must do it faster. Please. I don't trust that Jason Carr, not after what Frieda said. I want only professionals.'

Bryn gritted his teeth and resisted the urge to ask exactly what Frieda said. 'Our best professionals are on it. We won't let you down.'

He replaced the phone in his pocket, his mind struggling to catch up with what Talia had told him. He was going to get hold of Frieda Haas and find out exactly what the bitch was playing at. But first he had to deal with Owain.

They hadn't said a single word to each other since Bryn had found out about the Cyber Crime Unit, not even pleasantries exchanged over the kettle. Bryn was still seething, like a wounded tiger – an old toothless one whose claws had been filed down to stubs.

He wanted to ask why Owain had planned all this behind his back, and yet he was afraid of having his suspicions confirmed. That he had been dreading returning to work but hadn't felt able to say. That he thought Bryn would take Amy's part over his.

Bryn approached Owain's new office, the fresh plate on the door bearing the legend CYBER CRIME UNIT. He pushed open the door without knocking, but Owain was nowhere to be seen. Only Catriona was in the office, typing away on a laptop and not looking up at the intrusion.

'Where's Owain?' Bryn asked.

Catriona started, but she looked him square in the eye, without a trace of guilt. She had never been his partner, owed him nothing more than any other colleague in the department.

'Urgent personal business,' she said, which Bryn took to mean he was with Cerys.

'Talia Yeltsova reported a new blackmail message.'

'Carr's on it. We think it's in response to the Lane girl's meddling.'

It took Bryn a moment to realise that she meant Cerys, not Jason. *Because sending your girlfriend round to confront her brother's boss will always end well, Owain.*

'It would be helpful if you kept me informed.' Bryn had no idea what Catriona meant by 'meddling,' but he could guess.

'I copied you into the email to Matt.'

Bryn would have to keep a closer eye on his email if he wanted to keep up with the kids. Amy had always laid things out for him, but Owain and Catriona wanted to play with the big boys at the NCA.

'We'll need a strategy meeting to address the new threat.'

Catriona's computer emitted a dull chime. 'Matt confirms eight o'clock in the detectives' office.'

Bryn left the office without another word. He walked downstairs and into the administrative corner of the forensics laboratory, hoping that some fingerprint or bundle of fibres would crack this case, instead of a smattering of data in some email.

Indira stood at the desk, in earnest conversation with the duty tech, but looked up at Bryn's approach. 'Just checking on our samples,' she said. 'The sand analysis is back – nothing like North Wales, as it turns out. Including the sample Jason brought back for us. The experts reckon it's from some beach in Cornwall. Besides, we found it in many of our elimination samples throughout the museum – probably a random contaminant.'

Another wild goose chase, with Frieda and Jason's road trip offering nothing to their investigation – but bringing down a human trafficking and organ smuggling operation. Bryn couldn't exactly say they didn't get results.

'There is one thing.' Indira gestured towards the tech's computer. 'I'm not the first person to access these results. One request came from Owain and the other via your computer.'

No prizes for guessing the identity of that particular data thief. 'Best keep that to ourselves, eh?'

Indira waved away his concern. 'It's Owain's request that interests me. The remote connection was today, but these results had a rush put on them from on high – they were back last week, before Frieda Haas left for North Wales.'

'So you're saying Frieda knew the sand wasn't a match before she left?'

Was that what Frieda's investigation was really about? Did Talia Yeltsova know something about the girls in lorries from Eastern Europe?

'Sure looks that way,' Indira said. 'I can't imagine why Owain would've kept it from her.'

'There's a lot of secrets Owain's been keeping.'

The edge of bitterness in his voice clearly took Indira by surprise.

'How's he finding his new job?' she asked tentatively.

'You'll have to ask him.'

He left the lab, his mind churning like a vat of rancid butter. His feet carried him to the detectives' office automatically but he stopped short of the door. The closed door.

In all the years Bryn had worked in the department, he'd never known the door to be closed. It was always wedged back with a folded, yellowing piece of card that was replaced every year or so when it threatened to disintegrate.

Bryn stepped forward and tried the handle – locked. What the hell was going on?

He could hear something from behind the wood and he lifted his hand to knock smartly on the door. The sounds died away and, after a few moments, the door opened a fraction to reveal Matt Boateng and behind him a host of suited men Bryn didn't recognise.

'What's this now?'

'Change of plan,' Matt said, unruffled by Bryn's sharp tone. 'The agency wants to make sure the investigation is watertight. We'll be taking this one off your hands.'

It sounded so generous when he put it like that, as if he was doing Bryn a great favour. Bryn squared his shoulders, bracing himself for a fight.

'If there are any leaks,' he said, 'they're not coming from us.'

Matt's smile was fixed, a slight narrowing of the eyes the only sign of his anger and disdain. 'In a case of national and international interest, we are keen to avoid the appearance of impropriety. I'm sure you understand.'

Bryn understood perfectly – he and his team were under scrutiny, and the NCA had poached their case, stolen their office and identified their scapegoats should they fail to retrieve the painting.

'I'll leave you to your scheming then,' he said, the false cheer causing Matt's eyes to narrow further.

Bryn walked away, up the stairs towards the top floor, where the brass sat. If Owain was truly Matt's man now, his secrets weren't safe with his former partner. All that running to Amy, the unprecedented access he had given both her and Jason to evidence, police records and even crime scenes. All the time he'd looked the other way in exchange for a lead, using her as a confidential informant and never asking exactly how she came by her information yet knowing all the same.

It was all coming back to haunt him now, his failing grasp on twenty-first century policing, his reliance on Amy when he could've been giving Owain opportunities to shine, to develop. Paying attention to his partner's dreams instead of belittling his enthusiasm for every flashy out-of-towner who could show him newer, faster ways of working that Bryn could barely understand.

Perhaps it was time to pass on the baton. Time to accept that what Bryn knew about detective work was slowly falling into obscurity.

The light in the chief constable's office was still on and the secretary buzzed him through without questions.

'Seen the light, Bryn?' he asked.

Bryn smiled tightly, feeling every single one of his fifty-eight years.

'Where do I sign?'

Chapter 39

A game of queens

The last train for Glasgow left Cardiff Central just before five o'clock, the platforms awash with commuters who had bunked off early to enjoy some rare September sunshine.

Jason felt out of place here, among the men and women in variations of grey. His leather jacket marked him as an outsider, his worn, grease-smudged jeans revealing that he didn't earn half what they did. He carried a backpack, not a briefcase, and in the era of heightened terrorist alerts, it earned him a number of suspicious looks.

He checked his phone – another missed call from Dylan, with a voicemail to call back. Jason texted instead, asking what was up and how much he owed him for the repairs. It had been too long since they'd caught up properly, and he hated feeling like he was just using his mate to tune up the bike.

He felt bereft without his Bluetooth headset, his connection to Amy. Usually, when he was out and about, he was checking in with surveillance updates or just a bit of chat as he walked from place to place. But he'd put her to bed just before he left, to sleep off the last of her drug-induced haze.

When she'd told him about the mix-up with the tablets, he'd felt disconnected from her in a way he hadn't felt since he'd moved in. He hadn't known she was running low on tablets, ordered more, popped a couple while he was out. He usually had a handle on her health, how she was ticking over, but he seemed to have lost his grasp.

When he got back from Scotland, he'd get back on top of things. Maybe invest in a medicine cabinet or look into a doctor who did house calls. Dodgy medication off the internet was just asking for trouble, and he'd let her get away with it for far too long.

The train pulled in and he glared away everyone who tried to beat him to the doors. The train would take him as far as Crewe, and then he had to make his connection for Scotland. He'd brought his new tablet for entertainment, though he hadn't got much farther than adding a couple of games. Amy, however, had kitted it out with whatever she thought useful – including an uplink to her vast and highly illegal video library.

He plugged in his headphones as the train pulled out of the station, snatching the last vacant seat after pointedly shoving at a teen's designer shopping bags. Bruce Springsteen was the first song up, but he quickly skipped it. Too soon, the oppressive atmosphere of that old Land Rover invading his skin once more.

He looked up, away, to escape the sensations of the past – and he saw her. Her pale blonde hair obscured most of her face, but he recognised the curve of her lips, her slender fingers curled around her tablet as she worked.

Why hadn't he heard from her since Bangor? Not even a check-in to ensure he'd made it home safely, though she'd probably accessed Matt's reports. How had she gone from kissing him in that hotel room to ignoring his existence?

And then there was her connection to Talia.

He told himself that was the reason he left his seat, making his way down the carriage to speak to her. If he hadn't been staring at her, unable to tear his eyes away, he would've missed the furtive look she sent his way from between her fine locks of hair. She knew he was there and she was hiding from him.

'Hello, Frieda,' he said.

Her look of surprise was well-feigned, he had to admit, but her smile was as cool as ever. 'Jason. On another little errand?'

He didn't rise to the snub. 'Surprised to see you here. Where are you headed?'

'I'm sure you understand that I can't say,' she said, flaunting her air of mystery, but the shine had worn off for him.

'Give my best to Talia,' he said, and quickly walked away, hoping he was heading for the on-board café or at least a toilet. Trying not to move too fast. Calm and cool, like a PI's assistant should be.

Had he done the right thing? Tipping their hand could blow up in his face, but he wanted to push her buttons. See if he could get the Snow Queen to melt – and, this time, it would be to his advantage.

She caught up to him in the tea queue, the crisp scent of her perfume wafting over him. She didn't touch him to get his attention, but then she didn't have to.

'What game are you playing?' she murmured to him. To any casual observer, she wouldn't have said a thing.

'I could ask you the same.'

'Are you determined to compromise this investigation? A man is dead.'

'And you were hanging around the scene of the crime – before it took place.'

He felt a huff of air against his ear. She was laughing at him.

'You still don't get it, do you? You think you have control of this situation, but you're a child compared to me. My advice? Get out now. While you still can.'

He whirled on her, infuriated, and grabbed her arm. 'What the fuck—'

She cried out, a girlish shriek that drew all eyes in the carriage. 'Baby, no! You're hurting me!'

Jason dropped her arm as if she'd scalded him. 'You bitch.'

Her blue eyes filled with tears. 'I just don't know how to make you happy!'

The server had stepped out from behind the counter. 'Mate, you're gonna have to get off at the next stop. You all right, girl?'

Frieda sobbed into the man's arm, leaving Jason quietly seething. She was a viper in the grass and her venom had infected him.

He was escorted off the train at Newport, having not even made it out of Wales, and he was surprised when Frieda followed him off.

'He's just had a few too many,' she was explaining to the guards. 'I'll get him home. Thank you for your help.'

The train pulled away, his last chance to get to Glasgow that night, and he faced down Frieda on the platform. The platform staff stood at a distance, watching the pair warily, in case something was about to go down.

'I did that for your own good,' she said flatly. 'You need to learn the rules before you screw this up for all of us.'

'You got off the train.' His mind tried to catch up with the situation, something elusive just out of his grasp.

'Brilliant deduction, Watson.'

'You weren't going anywhere,' he said, his brain filling in the gaps as the truth of it tumbled out of his mouth. 'You were following me.'

Frieda laughed, but it was hollow, as fake and farcical as the rest of her charade. 'Your ego could fill this platform.'

His phone buzzed in his pocket and he drew it out automatically, a new message from Dylan on the screen: *Someone cut the fuel line.*

'You sabotaged my bike,' Jason said, anger mounting now. 'You wanted to meet me outside the museum – that's how you already knew who I was. And then you wanted to catch me at Dylan's, concocting that whole trip to North Wales. And that's why you were pissed off when I got close to Jonah Fish – because I would be out of your clutches.'

She didn't deny a word of it, her mouth settling in an unhappy line.

'What I don't get is why,' he said. 'What the fuck do you want with me?'

'Not quite clever enough,' she said, at last. 'I hope you work it out before I'm done, Jason. I've already warned you once – next time, you won't be so lucky.'

Chapter 40

Licence to kill

Amy struggled out of bed after a night of tossing and turning, plagued by the lurching, sick feeling of a tired brain trying to keep an exhausted body upright while running on fumes.

She wanted to call time on this investigation, hard delete and never look back. But Jason had shamed her, reminding her of everything left undone, the evidence a casualty of the war between her curiosity and her weariness.

Tea was the only thing her stomach would accept, and she sipped at it like an invalid in her dressing gown, staring at the exact centre of one blank monitor while her thoughts sloshed back and forth against the sides of her mind without purpose.

The tea warmed her from the guts out and she idly clicked through comic strips, TV spoilers and BuzzFeed articles for an hour or two until her brain was capable of more than mindless consumption.

She returned to the gap in information from the CCTV – the moments immediately after the murder and the period after nine o'clock the same morning, when the surveillance had switched to a new disc.

Amy started with the murder. After the thief killed Paul, he exited through the gallery door, crossed the room with an assured purpose and went down the stairs at the back. He opened the door to the laboratories with the swipe card and entered the back rooms of the museum. As Jason had earlier observed, that was the limit of the museum's CCTV footage. The thief then had time to plant the note on Talia's desk and … what? Make his escape through the still undiscovered route below the museum?

She loaded up the CCTV post nine o'clock while she checked her messages. None of the architectural experts had responded to her emails or voicemails. Her usual errand boy was in Scotland, which limited his usefulness. Her only other option was Cerys, and she doubted Jason's sister would want to speak to her right now, let alone help her continue with the investigation. Bryn and Owain had made their position clear, and she only had three days to solve this before 'The Blue Lady' was ruined forever. She regretted sending Jason away but she needed him and Corelia to hurry back with their clues as soon as possible.

No sooner had she thought of Corelia when the girl's uniform leapt out at her from the CCTV image frozen on the screen. Outside the main entrance, just after nine o'clock, impatiently pacing in front of the police cordon. Amy knew the Welsh geocache had obsessed her, but why was she skipping school on a Friday morning? She'd used every evening to hunt for the prize, so why had she appeared on the morning of Paul Roberts' murder?

It was too much of a coincidence to ignore. Amy had dismissed the geocaching community out of hand after she'd identified them, but the content of the blackmail revealed the killer's primary passion was geocaching, not theft and murder. Was it therefore inconceivable that the killer was a member of the Cardiff Geocaching Society?

Amy had thought Corelia was too short for their thief, but her school shoes were completely flat. With a platform heel, she could fit the profile of the thief. The killer had demanded the Belfast clue, but had Amy's gift of the forged sick note allowed that same killer to pick up the clue herself?

Could a teenage girl really be their thief and murderer?

Corelia stepped off the plane at Cardiff International Airport, slipped on her sunglasses and descended the stairs like an International Woman of Mystery.

Heddwen followed in her shadow, like her personal Jeeves or Watson or whatever, her precious camera cradled close to her chest. She'd marvelled at every inch of Belfast, photographing motes of dust in front of statues and dirty street corners.

And, when she had needed a model, Corelia had been happy to oblige.

The maintenance of her alias had been a condition of Heddwen tagging along. Of course, Ada had been very specific about the fact that Corelia couldn't travel alone and so Heddwen had been a logical choice, given her new-found status as Corelia's minion.

It was good to have an appreciative audience for her ideas and opinions, and the girl wasn't entirely useless. She'd even worked out part of the clue on the Belfast geocache, but Corelia would've figured it out given a few more minutes. Still, useful.

The kissing wasn't bad either.

The airport was near-deserted, the lull of midday, with a few businessmen drinking down their liquid lunches. When Amy had changed their flight to early morning, Corelia was hoping for an extended adventure in Northern Ireland, but her boss had been adamant she return as soon as possible. 'I might have more work for you,' she'd said, which gave Corelia a little thrill, like James Bond to Ada's M.

It had therefore been a race against time to solve the clue, only a few hours on Belfast Docks to work out the cache's location and find the code. In the film version of this adventure, only a little editing would be needed to make it a taut, fast-paced thriller, instead of two girls standing around with a tourist map, staring at their phones and willing the feeble mobile signal to cough up directions.

But solve it they had, and Corelia had smugly updated her UK Treasure Hunt profile with First Finder before sending Ada the answer. The perks of this job were endless, not least the day out of school with Heddwen because she was supposedly off sick with something like glandular fever.

Of course, her dad knew nothing about it, and her stepmother had never noticed anything about her at all. Heddwen's parents were a little more twitchy, so they thought she had stayed the night at Corelia's before going to school. Her note had given her a doctor's appointment in the morning, with the supposed doctor asking the school to respect her confidentiality in regards to her parents. Heddwen would hopefully make it back for afternoon lessons, to work on her GCSE Art project. As Corelia suspected she was the subject, she was keen to encourage this.

They caught the bus to the train station, sitting together in companionable silence, Heddwen's floaty sleeve brushing against hers. It tickled, but she didn't move away. She couldn't remember the last time she'd sat next to someone on the bus, someone who had chosen to be there.

The train was a slow, local chugger which wended its way along the south coast of Wales from Swansea to Cardiff. They sat across from each other by the window, watching the coast go by. Heddwen took a few snaps through the filthy windows, probably focussing on the grime rather than the beaches behind it. Corelia had never met someone so fascinated by dirt.

And she'd never been so fascinated by another human being. For the most part, she had grown up alone, a military brat with her older siblings having long flown the nest. Unnoticed, except for when she was in trouble – for climbing the fence at the barracks, for backchatting Dad's CO. She wanted to be noticed for different reasons, better reasons. Cracking the UK Treasure Hunt would make her father realise she was worth something, more than another female trophy to trot out for occasions. Like her stepmother.

Using Ada to achieve those aims was a dangerous game, but Corelia was not above playing dirty to win. Once she had the Welsh clue, she would be the victor. The plaudits, the recognition would all be hers.

And Heddwen's. Standing slightly behind her, with her camera.

'Do you want to be famous?' she suddenly demanded of her companion.

To her surprise, Heddwen laughed. 'I prefer being behind the camera.'

Corelia grinned. One less competitor for the limelight. And Ada didn't want the exposure, a ghost lurking in the shadows. They might be a team, but Corelia was the public face of victory.

The platform at Cardiff Central was busy, packs of men in rugby tops alongside heavy-laden university students and their clinging relatives. Corelia took Heddwen's hand – so she wouldn't lose her in the crowd, that was all. Heddwen's palm was clammy, her cheeks flushed from her knitted layers and hefting her lenses. Corelia led the way, the pathfinder through the throngs and down into the tunnel below.

Something collided with her back, the sharp edge of a bag or a swinging arm.

'Traitor.'

She wanted to confront the clumsy oaf, the owner of the hissed word, but she was frozen, dizzy. The air was suddenly thin, the tunnel too hot, and Heddwen was shouting through a thick cloud, clutching at her arms.

'Help me! Please … please…'

The ground flew up to meet her, her legs crumpling like a soggy paper doll left out in the rain. She wished Heddwen would stop crying like that, shoving at the bruise over her back. It hurt, but dull and far away, like a dream happening to someone else.

'Ein Tad yn y nefoedd…'

She'd just close her eyes. Rest them a moment.

Fame could wait.

Chapter 41

Collateral damage

Too ashamed to head back to Amy's, Jason slunk home to his mam, endured her fussing and feeding, and spent the night in his old room. He caught the first train to Glasgow, keeping his head down while furtively checking that Frieda wasn't on his trail.

He was no closer to discovering her true motives. What did an NCA agent want with him? Despite what Bryn and the rest of Cardiff thought, he didn't have gang connections anymore, no inside knowledge of crime or access to its architects. And he hadn't done anything wrong, nothing that would draw the attention of a national investigation. What the hell did she want from him?

It was only after he changed trains that he realised he hadn't heard from Amy. She usually kept closer tabs on him than this, constantly monitoring his position and demanding to know why he wasn't where he ought to be. Maybe she was more off her game than he'd first thought.

He itched to call her, to make sure she was okay, but a selfish part of him didn't want to admit that he wasn't in Scotland yet. Every delay to the investigation risked the painting, and potentially more innocent victims. If this man was willing to kill over a game, then the rules could change at any time. They could end up with more than a painting held hostage.

He finally arrived in Glasgow just after midday, his open-ended ticket giving him a little breathing room. Amy had given him starting coordinates and he used his new geocaching app to bring up the location. He opted to walk across town, wanting to see a little bit of Scotland before he was inevitably summoned back to Wales.

As he walked under the glass-walled railway bridge over Argyle Street, Jason drank in the sights and sounds of Glasgow. It looked like a chimera city, beautiful yet dangerous, cultured achievement side by side with desperate deprivation. It was a darker, wilder Cardiff, on its transformation from ashes to a phoenix, but still snarling and vicious by night. Jason was reminded of Cardiff Bay, how the bright new buildings sat cheek by jowl with shabby Splott and the remnants of the old Tiger Bay.

In Glasgow, he had the shining surface of the river on one side and a wall of office blocks on the other, eventually giving way to flats and then hotels. Amy's coordinates brought him out in front of a brilliant glass-fronted arena topped by a silver crown. It looked like a space-age hotel, backing onto a giant silver armadillo that reminded Jason of Cardiff's own Millennium Centre down the Bay.

A nearby sign told him this was the SSE Hydro and the armadillo was the Clyde Auditorium. Amy had completed some rough work on the last lines of the clue, cracking the code to reveal 'FCB58'. Jason wasn't entirely sure a meaningless string of letters and numbers counted as 'cracked', but she was adamant that was the solution.

The first part of the clue instructed him to 'seek water and then shun it'. Jason headed for the river, a few paces along the service road. The Clyde was much wider than the Taff as it ran through the city centre, a slim bridge crossing the water, roofed over with more fancy glass.

If you shunned something, you turned your back on it – so Jason leaned back against the railing, gazing back at the buildings he'd just left with a cool breeze playing over the near-bare skin of his head.

The next lines made no sense to him:

Look for the large armoured one there,

The true winner between tortoise and hare.

He removed his phone to Google the strange references only to find he'd missed a call from Cerys. He hesitated a moment before calling back. His sister was more stubborn than he was

– if she was calling him, she must have a good reason. Something bigger than their last argument.

She answered in a fluster. 'Where are you?'

'Glasgow,' he said bluntly. 'What do you want?'

'What the fuck are you doing up there?' Her voice was a hissed whisper, as if she didn't want to be overheard, and he heard a crowd die to silence behind her. 'You have to get back here.'

'What's happened?' His stomach dropped through the floor. 'Is it Amy?'

'No, she's fine – well, probably, I don't know. It's not about her.'

'Stop playing games, Cerys,' he snapped, his nerves fraught. 'What is it?'

'Corelia. The schoolgirl Amy sent me to find? She's been stabbed.'

Jason froze, his heart seized with fear for that cocky girl and her shy admirer. 'Is she…?'

'In surgery. Knife hit her lung, maybe damaged her spine. She was stabbed in a crowd at Cardiff Central – no witnesses, no nothing. But she had ticket stubs from Belfast in her pocket marked for today.'

Which tied this directly to Amy and what she'd sent her to do. The chances of this being a random stabbing were almost zilch. Knife crime in Cardiff was about fights between gangs and the rare mugging, but not stabbing a schoolgirl in the middle of a train station.

He said nothing.

Cerys' breath hitched and the strained silence spread between them, like an accusation. 'Was she … Jason, did Amy…?'

She didn't ask and he couldn't answer. If Amy was implicated in Corelia's stabbing, there would be questions. Bryn and Owain had made their positions clear – Amy would be on her own. Sure, she'd have a lawyer, but she wasn't herself right now. A stiff breeze could blow her down, mind lurching about like her body, drunk and overmedicated.

233

'Jay?'

'I need to know whose side you're on, Cerys.'

'A girl's been stabbed! How can you talk about sides?'

Jason closed his eyes, praying he was doing the right thing. 'Corelia was hunting down a cache in Belfast. That's all I know about it. I don't know why anyone would want to hurt her.'

'Does Amy?'

Jason felt his stomach clench, resisted the urge to punch the fence behind him. 'I'm not answering that,' he said, indignant.

'Then I'll ask her.'

'Cerys, no!'

He wanted to protect Amy from this, as long as possible. No one could say it was her fault, no one – except her. And he wasn't there to support her, to shore up those fragile defences when the self-doubt set in.

'Someone has to. This madman has proved he's willing to keep killing over this bloody thing, and now there's a school-girl caught up in it all. It has to end.'

'I'll tell her. I'll ask.' It was the last thing he wanted to do, but it had to be him.

'Do it fast. And then I'm going over.'

The line went dead and Jason stared at the building in front of him, not really seeing it, a sheen of water blurring the silvery image beyond recognition.

An inappropriate bubble of laughter filled his throat as, out of nowhere, he saw it. Of course. *Armadillo.*

But he had no time for games now, not with Corelia's play-time all run out.

He dialled home.

She'd set up an alert for news in Cardiff. She wouldn't be caught out again, hearing about Jason's miseries second-hand from Bryn, hours after the fact and with every major news reporter already on the scene.

So, when a volley of beeps burst from AEON's speakers, she checked her news feed first. *Schoolgirl stabbed in Cardiff Central Station. More to follow.*

When she saw it, she knew. She reached for her phone to dial Corelia's number, then stopped. The police were not her friends anymore. She couldn't take the risk.

Instead, she pulled up the GPS locator in Corelia's phone. University Hospital of Wales. *No … no…*

The darkness embraced her like a lover, smothering her, drawing all the air from her lungs and sending her heart beating out of her chest. Corelia was dead, and the killer was coming for her next…

She couldn't protect herself. The house wasn't safe. Jason wasn't here.

Corelia's dead.

She had to get out, to move. If the killer could find Corelia, he would find her.

Her throat closed, and she gasped for breath, desperate to live. But she was rooted to her chair, to AEON, her fingers clawing at the edge of the desk as she fought to regain enough composure to flee. But she was lost, spiralling down and down until everything was dancing spots across her vision, and the blackness swallowed her whole.

Corelia's dead because of me.

Her phone was ringing. It was distant, muffled, and she opened her eyes to see the organised chaos of AEON's cables under her desk. Her face was pressed against the carpet, limbs sprawled awkwardly from where she had slid off the chair, crumpled on the floor like a puppet with her strings cut.

Like Corelia.

The ringing paused for a second before it started up again, refused to let her lie, dragging her back to her life – her responsibilities. Jason.

She snatched at the phone, bringing it down to her, in the shelter of AEON's protection. She answered without saying a word.

'Amy, listen. There's something I have to tell you.' Jason sounded worried, on edge.

He knows. He knows what I've done.

'Corelia.' The word was choked, thick in her throat, suffocating her.

235

'You heard. Did Bryn—?'

'The news. Everywhere. They all know. What are we going to do?'

'I'll get the next train back. Cerys is coming over. Don't open the door to anyone else.'

'Do you have it?' Her brain was slowly coming back online, the circuits realigned to their primary mission.

'Have what? The cache? Forget the fucking thing.'

'We need leverage. To protect ourselves.'

'You want to negotiate with him? That bastard stabbed Corelia! How can we trust him not to come after us?'

'We need to prove we're still useful. I'm … I'm fine. Tell Cerys I'm fine.'

'Cerys is not up for discussion. She's staying with you until I can get home.' He paused, before muttering 'fuck' under his breath. 'I'll get the cache tonight and get straight on the train. I'll be with you by morning.'

'Morning?' The bitter taste of adrenaline coated her tongue, fear rolling in her stomach. 'Why the delay?'

'I need to wait for the concert to start. I'll explain when I come home. Just hold tight. And … find out what's happening. With Corelia.'

'I will,' she swore, to him and to herself.

She would find the killer and she would bring him down. Before someone else fell before her hubris, victim to her incompetence.

Before she had to bury Jason in the ground because she had failed.

Chapter 42

Quis custodiet ipsos custodes?

The girl was dangerous. She had to go.

As soon as Truth had seen the triumphant post on the UK Treasure Hunt site, she'd become suspicious. But when the email had come through only a few minutes later, giving away the location of that exact cache, she'd known. The girl was using Truth's trusting nature to stall her, solve the puzzle ahead of her. Deprive her of the prize money.

Tracking the child was easy. She'd posted the update from her phone, revealing her true identity and placing the unsecured GPS location in Truth's hands. The signal had disappeared for just over an hour before reappearing outside Cardiff International Airport. The movement of the signal after that was fast, too fast for a car, and Truth realised she was on a train.

The main station was crowded, choked with bodies, but the girl's voice carried clearly, arrogance dripping from every word spoken. Truth had recognised her lying face instantly, slipped behind her and drove her knife into the girl's spine.

She would die. Die like a traitor deserved.

The second time was easier, killing someone. She had known what it would feel like, the cold rush of adrenaline and the bitter aftertaste in her mouth. Painful, but necessary. Another secret for her to carry, another necessary evil.

Not only had she erased her only competition, she had secured her identity. The child had seen the face of Truth and she could not allow that. If she'd known the girl's plans, she would've moved on her before she'd stolen her Belfast crown.

The time for games was over. She couldn't afford to let anyone take away her victory, let the prize slip through her fingers. She had too much at stake for that, too much judgement set to fall on her head. She had killed a man, stabbed a girl, and for what? Nothing. She had to win this or she would lose everything.

Truth was running out of options. She must either sell the painting or win the geocaching competition. But she still had yet to hear why the painting transaction had failed and she was losing her grip on the geocaches. How was she to buy her mother's health?

Stabbing the girl had been rash. She'd now lost her accomplice in hunting down the caches, lost her advantage. Risked leaving evidence that might implicate her in the crime. Her usual calm and control was slipping. She had to make it right.

Truth called up her email – and was surprised to see a new message, sent only a few minutes earlier from an address she did not know. She opened it, her heart high in her throat.

I helped you because I wanted to see The Blue Lady returned. You stabbed my friend. If she dies, you die.

Truth choked. The girl wasn't the one behind this – she was working for someone else. A power she could not reach, one who was now after Truth's blood. What had she done? She had opened herself up to ruin and she had nothing to show for it, nothing left to give. Nothing to ensure her mother lived, finally proving she was a worthy daughter.

But she could not show herself vulnerable, not to this unseen power nor to the vultures circling. She held all the cards – if she could only be patient. She, who had killed twice, had the power now. Not this unseen taunter.

She had to prove to everyone that she was strong, untouchable.

help me and no one else will hurt.

The email flashed up on her screen and Amy hesitated before opening it.

The price for no more bloodshed was her continued cooperation. But why then had Corelia been targeted?

Amy sat back in her chair and steepled her fingers like a supervillain. Perhaps they had made an error in assuming the killer's thoughts made sense, that he was entirely sane. But then he was able to plan an art heist, solve complex geocache clues and track down Corelia. Amy had been in enough psychiatric hospital waiting rooms to know that when a person's logic fell apart, most of their function went along with it.

She was sure there was a method in the madness, but she couldn't quite see it. What was driving this desperate hunt for the geocache? Why steal the painting at all? And why hunt down Corelia?

At least Corelia wasn't dead – yet. Amy had found her father's name from her phone registration details and, from there, uncovered her operative's legal name: Leah Martinez. She pretended to be a distraught aunt to get information – not a difficult role to play with her head spinning like a top – and learned that Corelia was in surgery, still breathing.

She had to be smart about this. She needed to solve the final cache, to give the impression of helping the killer, but she also needed to learn about him. As he hunted for the answers to the puzzles, so she would hunt him, more aggressively and savagely than before.

The doorbell buzzed. She flicked up the monitor, expecting to see Cerys' tufts of blonde through the camera. Instead, she saw something that made her heart stop.

Frieda Haas was standing on her doorstep.

Amy froze. Who had given her away? Had Bryn sold her out to save himself? Or did he really think her a criminal now? Did he blame her for Corelia's wound?

Or maybe Frieda was looking for Jason. She had discovered this was where Jason lived and was seeking him out. Amy wasn't sure which scenario she liked least.

'Open up, Miss Lane.' Frieda looked directly at the camera. 'You know who I am.'

Amy's mouth went dry. No, she was definitely looking for her. What did the National Crime Agency want with her?

She scrutinised the image on the screen. Frieda wasn't carrying anything except her handbag – did that mean she didn't have a warrant and was merely trying her luck? If Amy ignored her, would she just go away?

'I'm waiting, Miss Lane. Or I'll huff and I'll puff and I'll blow this house down. That's what you think of me, isn't it? The Big Bad Wolf.'

Frieda wasn't going anywhere and Amy had no one to call on for help – what could Jason, Cerys or Bryn do anyway? And she couldn't call Owain, could never call on him again.

Instead, she called up the old typing interface, something she had barely used since Jason became her assistant. She typed the letters that would appear on the simple digital display by the door, the only way she was willing to communicate with this unknown threat on her doorstep: *WARRANT?*

The beep carried back through the camera's speakers and Amy watched Frieda peer at the screen, shading it from the sun's glare.

Frieda looked back at the camera. 'Let's talk like civilised people. Not resort to threats and intimidation, hmm?'

Amy smiled. Frieda didn't have a warrant. Which meant she had nothing with which to procure one. This was a fishing expedition. She decided to wait Frieda out. Hopefully, she would just go away and leave her to get on with her work in peace.

'Your parents send their regards.'

And the world fell apart.

Amy stared at Frieda's smirking face, the agent flushed with the knowledge of total victory. If Frieda was here because of Amy's parents, then this was nothing to do with the geocaching, Corelia, or the minor transgressions she regularly committed when aiding the police.

She was here about the money.

Amy had been naïve to think she'd get away with stealing five million pounds. But it had been over ten years ago and she'd thought they were in the clear. Except that Lizzie had made contact with their parents – was it that which started the cogs turning in their father's mind, made him consider that his broken little girl could be a master thief?

She knew there was no limit on time to prosecute such a theft, and for the millions she had stolen, she would face the stiffest sentence. All her current wealth stemmed from the proceeds of a crime, invested well – her profits from that day had bought this house, paid Jason's salary…

Jason.

Oh God, she would have to confess to Jason.

She needed a lawyer. She needed Joseph Treves to get over here and tell her what she could do, if there was anything that could save her. A police investigation, a trial, prison.

She realised too late that her breathing was too fast, her face heated, her heart beating out of her chest. And Frieda was still on her doorstep.

'You're a smart girl. You understand now what it is that I know. Let me in and we can talk. Perhaps make a deal. Jason doesn't have to suffer for your crimes.'

Amy clutched at her T-shirt, clawing it away from her skin as she tried to breathe. Frieda hadn't been following Jason because she liked him – she had used him to get to Amy. And now he was going to pay for her crimes, because he'd spent her stolen money on tea and biscuits.

'Maybe you'd get away with a suspended sentence, but Jason? How many times has he been arrested now? Aiding and abetting a thief, a cyber criminal of your calibre – oh, I expect he and his friend Lewis might get out about the same time, if Jason's lucky.'

Lewis – what the hell did Lewis have to do with any of this? The non sequitur threw her enough for Amy to take a breath, and then another. She had to regain some control.

'Yes, I know all about Lewis. I imagine his transfer to Cardiff Prison will be unexpectedly delayed, probably indefinitely. After all, he's been providing information to a known criminal, hasn't he?'

Consequences. Frieda was laying out all the consequences of Amy's impending incarceration. Amy forced herself to breathe through the weight crushing her lungs.

'And Cerys Carr … well, that's one promising police career over before it's begun. Her brother's indiscretions were forgiven, but now she's tied to you? Good luck weathering that storm. As for Owain and Bryn, they might keep their jobs, but I don't think they'll let Owain keep Cyber Crime, do you?'

A small, bitter part of her felt it served Owain right for betraying her, but Cerys? Bryn? He had been nothing but kind to her, held her up when she was drowning and given her a purpose in life, shown her there was more than merely existing from day to day. He had given her these investigations and now he was going to pay with his job.

'Do you understand now, Miss Lane? Make a deal with me and we can limit some of the collateral damage.'

Frieda looked up at her, meeting her eyes through the cold camera lens. 'But remain silent? And I bring hell down on them all.'

Chapter 43

500 miles

The steady rhythm of the train should've lulled him to sleep, but Jason was wide awake.

He couldn't shake the image of that smart-mouth girl from his head, the teenager willing to go toe-to-toe with Amy Lane over some ridiculous geocache. Did she remind Amy of herself? Pushing at all the boundaries and willing to go to any lengths for her independence? Independence now shattered by one blow.

Jason had picked up a knife in Glasgow. It wasn't difficult to find, following the decline of the streets until he found the rough heart of the city. They charged him tourist prices, of course, but he felt safer with some protection. His mam would kill him if she found out he was carrying again.

He hadn't heard anything from Cerys, and Amy hadn't answered her phone. She had texted him a couple of minutes later, just as he was about to place a 999 call – she was fine, Cerys was on her way, don't worry. At least, that's what he thought it said. He was getting better at deciphering Amy's texts, but he could never be sure.

The Glasgow geocache had been easy to solve, in the end. He'd sat through hours of classical music before the final bow, slipping unobtrusively down to Row B of the Front Circle to seek out Seat 58. On the underside of the seat, a small black oval was stuck in the centre, difficult to distinguish unless you knew what you were about. And Jason had been briefed by Amy Lane – he knew what he was looking for.

He'd pulled out his phone and scanned the raised spot, which yielded a short alphanumeric code. The cache was his.

Sending the code back to Amy Lane, she'd replied with a short acknowledgement text – *ty @*. Jason tried not to be offended that he'd only warranted three letters in response to the greatest solved mystery of his admittedly short career.

But the taste of victory had soon faded, leaving him to think about Corelia, about Amy, about the thief and murderer who was desperate to solve these puzzles. For Jason, it was a game, but for the killer, it was worth taking a knife to a teenager.

They were missing something. But what?

His phone rang with his boss' song, 'Someday I'll Be Saturday Night' by Bon Jovi disturbing the quiet of the sleeper train. He fumbled to answer it with fatigue-induced clumsiness. 'Amy?'

'Frieda Haas was here. At our house.'

Jason's mouth went dry. 'Looking for me?'

Amy paused, before a soft sigh came down the line. 'No. She was looking for me.'

With all the horror of a ticking time bomb reaching zero, the past few days slid into focus with absolute clarity. She hadn't been hunting Jason at all. She had used him to get to Amy.

'This is about … computers?' he said vaguely, looking about him for eavesdroppers even as his mind reeled away from him. Frieda had used him.

'I have something to tell you,' Amy said. 'It's about my parents.'

Despite the circumstances, Jason felt his heart quicken in anticipation. He'd gleaned bits and pieces about Amy's mysterious past, but never enough to weave a cohesive whole. A small part of him wished she could've told him without being forced, but it was too late for that now and he hadn't the energy to dwell on it when so much was at stake.

'When I was first … ill, Lizzie was at boarding school. Our parents went travelling and left us with our grandmother. She was … her memory was poor. She couldn't do the things she needed to anymore. She went into hospital and never came home. Lizzie and I needed to get out. We needed to hide from Social Services, because I was underage and I was ill and they would take me away.'

Jason could hear Amy labouring with her speech, the tale tumbling out of her in a hurricane of words.

'Breathe. I'm not going anywhere.'

She took a breath. 'I stole from them. I stole from my parents. I hacked into their main bank account and I emptied it. I … I left them just enough for the flight home, to come back for us, but … they never did. They got insurance, or used their savings, I don't know – I don't care. I used it to buy our house and make new identities, to send Lizzie to university and then to Australia. That's why Frieda's investigating me.'

Jason closed his eyes. He'd always been suspicious about Amy's unlimited funds, especially in light of her estranged parents and a spat he'd witnessed between Amy and Lizzie over them. But to know it was stolen? From her own family? That was hard to swallow.

'How much money are we talking?'

'Five million pounds. Not that they missed it. My father always invested wisely.'

Fuck, that wasn't a handful of petty cash. A theft like that made Jason and Lewis' planned gold exchange heist look like a raid on piggy banks.

'Say something,' Amy pleaded.

Jason realised he'd been silent for a couple of minutes. But what the hell could he say to that? 'What are you going to do?'

'I've called my lawyer.'

Jason was well acquainted with Joseph Treves, who had defended him during his most recent run-in with the law. Jason didn't know how Joseph had come to work for Amy, but he knew his stuff when it came to mounting a defence.

'Why hasn't she arrested you?' Jason wondered aloud, before realising that was a question more likely to rile Amy than soothe her.

Yet she answered calmly. 'I don't think Frieda has hard evidence. If she gets access to AEON and the basement server files, she'll be able to find the proof she needs. I can erase as much data as I can, but it always leaves a trail. My hacking skills weren't up to much in 2003, so it's a pretty obvious one.'

'Will she get access?'

'She needs a warrant. If she could get one, she would have one by now. She's waiting for me to fuck up.'

Jason knew the perfect way for them all to fuck up and they were right in the middle of it. 'Amy, these geocaches—'

'We owe this to Corelia,' she said, immediately, voice hard like iron. 'I'm seeing it through to the end.'

'If it gives Frieda the proof she needs, we're sunk.'

'I will worry about Frieda,' Amy said, adding the NCA agent to a long list of anxieties that Jason had watched her buckle under for months. But not break, never break. He never wanted to see that.

'And me? What can I do, Amy?'

'Come home,' she said.

Chapter 44

Twist the knife

With the National Crime Agency holed up in the detectives' office and his best detectives in a little unit of their own, Bryn was at a loss. Until poor Leah Martinez was stabbed at Cardiff Central Station.

The scene itself was a write-off, already trampled before someone had thought to put up a cordon, and he sent his one remaining ally – Cerys Carr – with a uniformed copper to fetch the girl's personal effects and clothing, for Indira to go over.

He should be sending Cerys back to college, away from this mess, keeping things official. But he needed someone on his side right now and if she was all he'd got, he would take her over a hundred uniforms who might have loyalties elsewhere. At least, with Cerys, he knew her loyalties lay in several opposing directions and he could wager that she felt as bad as he did about the whole bloody mess.

But when she returned from the hospital, she dumped the evidence with Indira and scarpered. Bryn made his way down to the forensics lab immediately, despite the clock ticking over to midnight, sensing that this hadn't been some random stabbing. Leah was mixed up in the bigger picture somehow.

Indira had laid out the clothes on a tabletop in the shape of Leah's body, two large monitors in the corner showing radiological images in cross section.

'The hospital sent over their CT scans,' she said, waving at the screens behind her. 'It will allow us to reconstruct events without access to the original wounds.'

Bryn prayed they would never get that access. 'Cerys left in a hurry.'

Indira wordlessly gestured at the small pile of personal effects, not yet relevant enough to the investigation to consider processing for fingerprints, DNA or trace.

Bryn donned a pair of gloves and inspected the items. The plane ticket stubs immediately caught his eye and his heart sank. Return tickets to Belfast? What would a Cardiff school-girl be doing in Belfast, and why would that information have Cerys vanishing into the night?

This had Amy Lane written all over it.

'Very shallow wound,' Indira said, calling Bryn's attention back to the room.

She had altered the CT image so that it displayed a close-up of a spinal bone, pointing at the screen with a plastic probe.

'The tissues have collapsed back where the assailant removed the weapon, but you can see by the mark on the ver-tebral process that the blade must've reached the spine.' Indira moved the image on several layers. 'Yet there's no correspond-ing mark on the superior vertebra.'

'Which means…?'

'Which means the knife was asymmetrical. A shallow, asym-metrical knife. Where have we seen one of those recently?'

Bryn inhaled sharply. 'When the thief took the picture from the frame.'

'It would all be conjecture at this point, were it not for the clothes.'

Indira returned to the table, spreading out the back of Leah's jumper. The material had been hastily cut down the front and was flaking dried blood, but the tear just to the right of centre was still obvious.

'Pass me a swab.'

Bryn handed over a thin plastic-handled swab. Indira ges-tured for him to hold the material taut, as she ran the swab over the edges of the entry point. She held up the end for inspection and, among the rust-coloured bloodstains, little flecks of lilacs and green sparkled in the light.

'I don't think that's your ordinary DIY emulsion. I think this will be a proof-positive match to a certain Renoir painting.'

'So the murders are linked,' Bryn said, his suspicions confirmed.

'The attacks are linked,' Indira corrected gently. 'Leah Mar-tinez is still alive.'

Bryn coloured. 'Of course, that's what I meant.' He had worked too many homicides recently for a small-town cop. 'Anything else you can tell me?'

'Count the ticket stubs.'

Bryn returned to the tray – four stubs, two out and two back. 'She was with someone.'

'I'd check the hospital, if I were you. I think you've got an eyewitness.'

Trying to find an anonymous mail server was like following a breadcrumb trail after the birds had feasted on it.

After several dead ends and ghost routes, Amy tried to look for other sites accessed via the same route, a technique that had previously landed her a backup server in Poland. However, it seemed the thief only used anonymous email and not an IP spoofer. Which meant the rest of the trails were all out there somewhere, unencrypted and waiting – except Amy had no idea where to start.

She examined the raw traffic data for the UK Treasure Hunt website, narrowing down the index of search to Cardiff – if the perpetrator could make it to Cardiff Central with less than an hour's warning, they had to be local. She saved the previous month's data to a database and set AEON to match up public and not-so-public information with the IP addresses. They might be able to narrow down the list by the known demographics of the assailant.

Not that there were many. An approximate height was all they knew for certain, and that could easily be altered by footwear. Amy could only hope something would stick out when she had the list completed.

The last geocaching clue was the only thing left to work on. She hadn't looked at the lines of poetry since Corelia's call. Amy veered her mind away from thoughts of Corelia and tried to focus on the task in hand.

She brought up the lines of poetry alongside the original poems' titles.

Yesterday was St Valentine: 'Valentine – To Lizzie Siddal'
Water, for anguish of the solstice: – nay: 'For A Venetian Pastoral'

Oh! May sits crowned with hawthorn-flower: 'Fior Di Maggio'
And day and night yield one delight once more?: 'Sudden Light'

Something weakly stirred in the recesses of her memory, an association between the titles and something important to the case. But what exactly it was escaped her tired, sluggish brain. Why couldn't she think?

Amy looked at the poems again. The first poem was a comic tale for Valentine's Day, about how much Rossetti missed his lover. The second was a sonnet inspired by a painting, as the full title explained – 'For A Venetian Pastoral, by Giorgione (in the Louvre)'. The painting was still in the Louvre, though it had now been attributed to Giorgione's collaborator and successor, Titian. Not that Amy could find any connection between artists and their particular case – neither artist had work currently displayed in the National Museum Cardiff.

The third poem was a short, four-line effort. Not Rossetti's best work, in Amy's uncultured opinion. The fourth was beautiful, however, a poem of adoration likely directed at his muse – Elizabeth Siddal. But what the hell did they mean? Why those four poems, and why those four lines?

To Amy's mind, a cipher was unlikely. The lines were rendered as originally composed – to find four lines of poetry, even in Rossetti's prolific body of work, that exactly matched the coded message Paul wished to send? It was not impossible, but it was vanishingly improbable. Therefore, the secret must be hidden in the broad brushstrokes. Something about the words or the poems as a whole must solve the puzzle.

The doorbell rang. Amy froze with a convulsive jerk, hardly daring to look at the monitor. Was Frieda back with a warrant? Had the killer come for her?

But it was Cerys' face which stared back at her and Amy let her in, relief sinking deep into her stiff muscles. She needed a hot bath, a glass of wine, and for this hideous case to be over. Before she fucked it up. Again.

The elevator doors closed and Amy spun her chair to greet her. Cerys stood in the doorway to the living room, tense and dripping rainwater from her soaked uniform. Her blonde hair had flattened into a dark bronze mat, trickling water across her neck, though she didn't flinch as it hit her skin.

She looked angry. And dangerous.

With a quiet horror that crept up her spine, Amy remembered that Cerys wasn't a good girl, had run with drug dealers and hard men, had set fire to public property and revelled in it. Cerys wasn't a good girl and she was angry with Amy.

'Well?' Cerys breathed, like a dragon prepared to flame and burn everything in sight. 'What have you got to say for yourself?'

Amy moved her mouth but no words came out.

Cerys' laugh was cold as a tiled floor in winter.

'You sent her into danger. You let her just walk right in and you don't give a shit, do you?' Cerys paced as she raged. 'Is that what you do to my brother? Is that how his bones get broken and gangsters come after him and how Owain almost fucking died?'

Amy braced herself against the onslaught, hands gripping the arms of her chair. She had to keep breathing. Just keep breathing and it would go away.

But Cerys wasn't going anywhere.

'Do you have any idea of the consequences of what you do? The fucking terrible positions you put people in? No, you just sit here in your ivory bloody tower and let other people fall into shit.'

Amy wanted to remind Cerys that she too had been hurt, had faced danger with Jason, but it would only fan the flames. And Cerys was beyond reason.

'That girl trusted you. I trusted you, because Jason said you were a genius and you knew what you were doing. You haven't got a bloody clue, have you? You're just stumbling around in the dark, while other people get hurt.'

Cerys raised herself to her full height, glaring down at Amy.

'I've had enough. Owain is well shot of you, and so am I. You tell my brother – you tell him that if he wants to be part of this family, he'll come home. Our mam's had enough sleepless nights because of you.'

She left, leaving only embers and ashes in her wake, and Amy quietly shaking in her computer chair. She was losing what little control she had and, with an ultimatum like that on the table, how could she make Jason choose?

It was time for this to end.

Chapter 45

Hopeful and brave

Bryn found her at the hospital, hunched over in one of those garish plastic chairs that were made to torture. He'd spent too long in one when Owain was in surgery, and saw the weight of a similar burden on that young girl's shoulders.

'Miss? I'm Detective Inspector Bryn Hesketh – might I have a word?'

The girl looked up at him, startled, revealing the rust stains across the front of her V-neck pullover, stiffening her long, gaping sleeves.

'Am I in trouble?'

Her thick native Welsh accent was coloured with panic, and Bryn hastily shook his head as he sat down beside her. 'No, you're not in trouble. What's your name?'

'Heddwen. Are you going to tell my parents I was here? They think I'm staying over at a friend's.'

Bryn judged her age at about fifteen, sixteen, and decided to barrel on. 'Not if you don't want me to. Though I'm guessing you were meant to be in school today.'

Heddwen nodded. 'We were meant to get back in time for Double Art. But I ... I couldn't leave her.'

She looked down the corridor, as if expecting her friend to walk through the doors at any moment.

'Do you know anyone who might want to harm Leah?'

'Corelia.'

'I'm sorry?'

'She likes to be called Corelia. And I guess it's about what we did for Ada.'

The name triggered something in the back of Bryn's brain. Ada Lovelace – his hacker's heroine, and her favourite alias. Still, he asked the child: 'Who's Ada?'

Heddwen shifted uncomfortably. 'She's working with Corelia on this geocaching thing.' She glanced up to check she hadn't lost him. 'She paid for us to go to Belfast to find a clue there. In exchange, she's going to tell us the Welsh geocache, when she solves it.'

'How long have you been into geocaching?' Bryn asked, careful to pronounce the word correctly to avoid alienating her.

'Not long,' she said, with a small smile. 'Corelia loves it though. It was all she could talk about, this competition. She'd been trying to find the clue at the museum for weeks, she said. Every day she went up there but she couldn't find it. She even asked one of the museum staff to give her this private tutorial so she could get behind-the-scenes access. But then that guard died and she couldn't get in anymore.'

She fell silent, almost exhausted, as if she hadn't spoken that many words together for a long time.

'She was so excited,' she added, finally. 'We didn't know it was dangerous. It was just a game.'

The early morning train rolled into Cardiff at the end of the Friday morning rush. Jason fought his way through the crowd of commuters, spilling someone's expensive coffee as he barged through. Part of the tunnel between platforms was still cordoned off and Jason could see the dark stain on the floor to mark where Corelia had fallen.

Past the ticket barriers, he contemplated the buses for half a second before joining the taxi queue. He needed to get home and grab some shuteye before Amy lurched into another minefield.

He didn't know what had gotten into her lately. He was usually the trouble magnet in this partnership, the risk-taker and the marauder. Amy was the sensible, cautious one, always ready with a warning tone and a hundred reasons for him to stay at home.

But now she was making deals with a blackmailer, thief and murderer, sending teenagers out on missions to Belfast and attracting the attention of the National Crime Agency. All his illusions about his anxious, risk-averse boss were being shattered by these revelations.

And damn it, if that didn't make him love her just that little bit more.

Jason stopped dead in the middle of the pavement. Love her? Where the hell had that come from?

No, that was wrong. She was his boss and his best friend and that was all. He liked her, of course he liked her. He maybe even *like*-liked her a little bit, because he was a man with eyes, but love?

Someone barged past him to take his place in the taxi queue, and Jason came back to earth. He was sleep-deprived, that was all. He needed to get home and get this bloody case over with before it ruined the last of his good sense.

The taxi ride passed in a blur as he fiddled with the strap on his backpack and tried not to think too hard. His bike – that was a safe topic. He needed to get his bike from Dylan's. Except thinking about the bike meant thinking about Frieda, the conniving bitch, which led to thinking about the kiss in Bangor. Which returned his thoughts to Amy's green eyes, flecked with a hundred thousand little bits of brown in just the right light.

Fucking hell, he was in trouble.

He stumbled out of the cab, tipped too much and made his way to the front door. He talked at the box, the voice software opening the door for him. He went up one level to Amy's floor, planning to check in before he ran for his bed. He wanted to see her and he didn't. He was furious with her and he felt something else for her, which left him feeling ropey as hell.

She was on the couch, wrapped up in her dressing gown, the ghostly pale skin of her arms exposed. Her head lolled against the arm of the sofa, neck extended to reveal more stark white flesh.

A vivid memory flashed into his mind, a crime scene photograph, and Amy's confident assertion that the human neck couldn't sustain such-and-such an angle and live.

Jason surged forward, hands flying to her neck to check for a pulse.

Amy yelped and smacked him in the face.

'Fuck!' The heel of her palm had caught his cheekbone, sending shooting pain into his eye socket.

'What are you doing?' Amy shrieked.

'M'sorry, m'sorry – got the angle wrong.'

Amy froze, her entire body stiff as a board, before she pulled her dressing gown closer around her. 'The angle for what?'

Jason waved towards her neck with one hand, clutching his cheek with the other. 'Your neck! The angle of your neck.'

Amy self-consciously raised her hand to cover her neck. 'What's wrong with my neck?'

'Nothing! I thought you were dead – you're not dead, it's all good.'

Amy's hands went to her face, rubbing at her cheeks to colour them. 'Shit, do I look that bad?'

Jason went into the kitchen to raid the freezer for peas. 'You look fine, you look great. Your neck looked weird, for a second, because I'm tired. That's it.'

Amy followed him, folded her arms across her chest and leaned against the counter. 'You could have called my name before assuming I was dead.'

'I panicked.' Jason clapped the peas to his cheekbone, their presence in the freezer purely for such a purpose. Neither of them could stand peas, unless they were mushed puree beside a nice bit of cod and chips.

After a moment, he realised what was missing – or, rather, who. 'Where's Cerys?'

Amy folded her arms closer and said nothing.

Jason pushed. 'Where is she?'

'She came. She left.'

Jason could read between the lines. 'You fought.'

'Doesn't matter. You need to sleep.'

'Amy—'

'Tonight we need to make our move.'

'The museum?'

Despite his fatigue, his heart rate picked up and he felt a new surge of energy. The thrill of facing danger never really went away.

'The museum. Tonight, we save "The Blue Lady".'

Chapter 46

With a kiss

After the hospital, Bryn went home and woke his daughters by kissing them in their beds.

'Silly old man,' his eldest said, turning her back to him and snuggling under the duvet.

But he couldn't shake the thought of that small, hunched-over girl at the hospital, waiting for her friend to wake up – if she would ever wake up. Two curious, adventurous girls who had got mixed up with Amy Lane.

He'd already seen the toll that association had taken on Owain, on Jason. He'd seen it in the mirror. The tense hospital nights, the broken bones. Of course, Amy had experienced her fair share of those wounds, but that was her choice. Where she led, they would follow.

Well, not Owain anymore. Owain was dancing to his own tune, one running at a jarring discord to Amy's. How much of that decision had been based on his injuries, his scars, physical and mental? How much blame for losing his partner could he lay at Amy Lane's door – and how much would he have to bear for himself?

He slept badly, a hundred nightmares of his daughters bleeding out in Central Station, sitting tense in a hospital waiting room. Of Owain and Jason, Cerys and Amy, dead and dying. Pain and loss, in myriad permutations and combinations, that all screamed to him *failure*.

He made his way to the office early. The super had delayed the announcement of his promotion until after this case was solved, but he had the keys to his new office. On a floor above everyone else, removed from the work and the buzz of the investigations. Was he happy that this feeling of directionless wandering, this lack of purpose, would replace the heartache and sleepless nights? Or would those never leave him now?

He had made his choice, regardless. Bryn couldn't see the point of dithering over it. They had to get through this investigation, in whatever limited capacity they were allowed to participate, and then he was moving on. He wasn't leaving anyone behind now, no one he was close to in the detectives' paddock. His former colleagues had all left or met their fate.

He walked past the detectives' office out of habit and was surprised to find the door open. Matt and Frieda were deep in conversation around the murder board, while Owain and Catriona sat to one side with a laptop. A few other NCA agents were milling around or completing paperwork. Bryn wasn't sure any of them had gone to bed.

He attempted to slip past, but heard his name and returned to the doorway. Matt beckoned him forward and Bryn stepped into the alien place that had once been his domain, more hours lived in than his own home.

'Deigning to let us paupers through the door?' he said, unable to resist.

Matt didn't rise to it. 'The stabbing yesterday – you didn't inform us it was relevant.'

Bryn had been hoping to keep that under wraps a little longer, do some real detective work before his last bow. Owain hunched further over his laptop and Bryn realised he was responsible for the leak, perhaps monitoring Indira's lab reports for just such an eventuality. He knew he shouldn't expect anything different now, but it still smarted.

'I had reports of a possible connection last night,' Bryn conceded. 'I was waiting on the forensic evidence to be sure.'

'The paint on the clothes is a match,' Matt said. 'Dr Bharani logged her findings this morning.'

'Where do you think a schoolgirl got the money to buy two return flights to Belfast?' Frieda said suddenly. 'Unless she didn't buy the tickets. Also note the plural – who was with this girl, this underage girl? Perhaps a case of grooming?'

Bryn didn't like what they were implying one bit, but he also didn't want to give away what he'd learned from Heddwen without a fight. This was still his investigation.

'We'll need to track down the source of the tickets.'

'We've done it,' Catriona said. 'Disposable credit card, no registered address. It will take time to gain access to the airline's IP address data.'

'Of course, we don't need any of that, do we?' Frieda smiled, all ice and sharp edges. 'We know exactly who's responsible for this. So, why don't we all just stop dancing around the issue?'

Bryn said nothing, his notebook burning a hole in his jacket pocket. The only admissible evidence that confirmed Amy's involvement was in that notebook, Heddwen's statement pretty damning as to her involvement. Bryn wasn't exactly sure what charges could be brought against her for engineering that trip, but Frieda was angling for child abuse. She could definitely pick up counts of fraud and perhaps endangering the life of a minor, if they could make a case that she had foreseen the risks.

Given that she had knowingly collaborated with a thief and a murderer, it might not be all that difficult for the prosecution to make that leap and have the jury swallow it. Especially given that Amy's character witnesses were an ex-con and coppers she'd fallen out with.

'Amy Lane,' Frieda said, finally, when it was obvious no one else would say it.

Bryn saw Owain flinch, but still said nothing.

Frieda continued, addressing her words directly to Bryn. 'Amy Lane – or, as we now know her to be, Amy Loach. Born 15th September 1988 to Ralph and Marie Loach with one older sister Elizabeth, ordinarily resident in Brisbane, Australia.'

Bryn felt a heavy feeling of dread suspend over him. This wasn't some light background research – Frieda Haas knew Amy's life inside out, including the pieces she had kept buried from even those closest to her.

Frieda went on. 'Attended a private primary school and then fell off the educational radar. Fell off the radar entirely, in fact, until Amy Lane appears at age 15. A completely new identity, one which gained five million pounds virtually overnight. Which, coincidentally, was exactly how much her parents lost when their bank account was raided by hackers.'

Shit. Bryn understood now why Frieda was telling them this, why she was sharing the details of what must be a high-security investigation at the NCA.

They were implicated, all of them. Aiding and abetting a bank robber, even if only through maintaining a 'don't ask, don't tell' policy when it came to Amy's money. Bryn had assumed it was an inheritance – he just hadn't realised she'd got it while her parents were still alive.

'What happens next? This thief and con artist insinuates her way into multiple police investigations, including serial murder and breaking a drugs ring. Cases which are now all tainted by her criminality.'

The last of the blood drained from Bryn's face. All those convictions, all the bad people they'd put away – how many would get off now? He remembered the aftermath of the crooked cops discovered in their department, how many criminals had walked as a result of that furore. How many more would go free because he had run to Amy to solve his problems?

'Finally, this little sociopath's reckless behaviour ends up with a teenage girl getting stabbed, fighting for her life in hospital.' Frieda's eyes pierced him, hollowed him out and exposed him. 'And you still want to protect her?'

He had a split second to decide, to give himself one last chance at redemption, to save his career and maybe that of the boy cowering in the corner.

But did he trust Frieda Haas? She had lied to them from the start, sent Jason into danger, and was relishing every moment of their humiliation. His gut revolted against her. Did he really want to get in bed with the NCA to save his own arse?

He said nothing, and the moment was gone.

'This is the last nail in her coffin, Mr Hesketh. Do you really want to be buried with her?'

'Talia Yeltsova,' Bryn said suddenly, finally finding his voice. 'How does she fit into this?'

Frieda visibly withdrew, not expecting to be questioned. 'That is none—'

'You were seen talking to one of the key players in a murder investigation. As long as we're being honest, Ms Haas…'

'She was helping me with my inquiries,' Frieda said, shortly.

'Talia doesn't know Amy,' Bryn countered.

The silence lingered. Even Matt was looking at her curiously, her supposed colleague also in the dark.

Bryn had all day to wait.

Finally, Frieda relented. 'I approached Talia, using her visa difficulties for a local contact. She thought Mr Roberts could make a connection to Amy Lane, perhaps through the geocaching group. In vain, as it turns out.'

Bryn felt bilious fury rise in his throat. 'You knew! From the beginning, you knew about the geocaching and you said nothing?'

'It wasn't relevant!'

'It sure as hell is now!'

'How about we don't throw stones and bring the whole house down?' Matt interjected, his calm voice grating on Bryn's last nerve.

'The house is already all over the fucking floor – can't you see that?'

Matt gave him a look of pity. 'Your house, perhaps.'

It was over. For all his worries this morning, about trading apathy for a good night's sleep, he would never have to worry about that again. He had time enough to find something new to do with his life.

'Owain?'

He looked up at Frieda's voice and Bryn saw that it hadn't clicked for him yet. The implication of that cold bitch's words had yet to sink him. He was still her puppy dog, if slightly more subdued.

She walked over to him with the calm, cool confidence of a woman who knew she was desired, and bent down to kiss his cheek.

'I'm sorry.'

Bryn watched from a distance as Owain's world collapsed in on itself and he understood, truly understood what had happened. He had turned away from his friends for this woman, for his career, and now it was in tatters.

Their eyes met across the room and Bryn wanted to tell him it would be all right, they would survive this. But he could no longer be Owain's anchor in a storm.

He looked away, breaking the last tenuous thread between them.

Chapter 47

The grass beyond the door

As Jason slept, Amy stared at four lines of poetry and willed herself to see the connection.

She had an advantage – she knew the identity of LizzieSiddal, had access to Paul Roberts' previous caches, and anything left on the museum servers. But if Paul had made any notes, they were locked inside his laptop, beyond her reach.

Reviewing previous caches, she was struck by the frequency with which he used lines of poetry. AEON's analysis confirmed they were mostly from Rossetti and Siddal but also other members of the Pre-Raphaelite Brotherhood.

She reviewed a couple of the forum posts for LizzieSiddal caches, studying the comments of solvers for patterns in how he had worked his magic.

One seemed straightforward enough:

For all the voices from the trees

And the ferns that cling about my knees

It led to a small copse full of ferns and an old computer speaker lodged in a tree hollow. The community had not rated that cache particularly highly.

A more recent effort was far more oblique and seemed to have bemused the local geocaching community for a couple of weeks. The line was 'Take thou thy shadow from my path,' from the bitter rant that was Siddal's 'Love and Hate'. Amy hoped she would someday love someone so strongly as to despise them so thoroughly.

At first, the forum's denizens had thought it was a UV-marked cache, best seen at night with a modified torch. They had traipsed all over the spot and drawn a complete blank, returning to the car cold and as bitter as Siddal had ever been.

But then Corelia, that child prodigy, had looked beyond the line of poetry, to the work as a whole, and found the line 'And thou art like the poisonous tree'. Corelia had noted a tree with bright yellow flowers and tentatively identified it as the poisonous laburnum. Her gleeful chatter on the forum brought to mind her excited messages after she solved the Belfast cache, and the wide-grin selfie she'd posted alongside it.

Amy shook her head, shook off the image, and returned to the Welsh cache. What if there was a similar situation here, where some of these lines referenced the wider poem and not the individual words or even titles?

Of course, that widened the field of options considerably but there were only so many words that could match locations in the museum. And the easiest way to mark a location in the museum would obviously be to reference...

Amy stopped. She brought the four poems up in four windows, spread across all three monitors with her notes and the quoted lines alongside them. Her eyes scanned the poems and titles in line with her suspicions and it all fell into place before her eyes.

Of course. How had they not seen this before?

She leapt from her chair, flinging her arms over her head and shouting for joy.

'What the hell's got into you?'

She turned to Jason, who had snuck up on her, the scent of the shower still lingering on his skin.

'I've solved it,' she breathed, blood surging through her body at a rate of knots.

Jason said something but she wasn't listening, too busy moving on to the next thing.

'We have to get into the galleries ourselves, undetected. I can't manipulate the security settings from here – it's on a separate system, because they apparently have the sense not to network that. We'll need help to get in and then I can divert them.'

She looked up from her computer. Jason was smiling at her.

'What? Why are you smiling like that?'

'You look better,' he said simply.

She felt it too, a renewed sense of vitality, a sense of purpose. She tried to hold on to it, savour it. She would need it for what they had to do tonight, to get her past the fear of stepping outside the front door.

But the future that lingered was bleak and terrifying and, most important of all, lonely. She knew it was only a matter of time before Frieda returned, before she made good on her threat to ruin Amy's life and those of everyone she cared about.

She could no longer protect Bryn and Owain, her former friends far beyond her reach, but she could still do something for Jason. With her last bit of borrowed time, she could fashion him a new identity and send him away.

He would have to leave his family, leave Cardiff for a time, but he wouldn't go to prison again. She would set AEON to self-destruct and she would wait for Frieda like a lamb meek at the slaughter. She could not save herself, but she could save Jason.

Which was only fair, really, given how he had saved her, every day since he had walked into her life. She wished she could be brave enough to tell him, but she feared he would rebel, demand to stay, act like the danger-seeking fool that he was.

No, she would enlist Dylan's help in spiking his drink and sending him on a train, with his new life and a brief note explaining that he couldn't go home until after the trial. Gwen would be angry with her, but she would understand. Cerys would know why she'd done it and it might go some way to repairing things between them. Not that it would matter.

'Penny for 'em?' Jason asked, bringing her back to the room.

'You're trying to sell me back my own pennies,' Amy joked, dodging him. 'I don't pay you enough to waste them like that.'

'I was thinking, though,' he said, 'that I might have a way into the museum. A way that's not entirely illegal.'

Amy forced a smile, snatching at her former job even as it ebbed away from her with the last of the day's sunlight.

'I'm all ears.'

With the Scottish cache attributed to her name, only one obstacle remained: the cache in the museum. The clock ticked down to the demise of 'The Blue Lady', but Truth was entirely focussed on the last cache. It was almost over.

Once she had the money, she would be free. Free from her past, her obligations. She would buy the life-giving organ her mother needed, become a true daughter – a success – and then she would vanish. She would run far away and start again, somewhere where the stain of blood wouldn't spread, taint. She could forget, perhaps, what she had done for duty.

And, failing that, she could fall on her sword.

Her email buzzed with a new message.

Tonight it's over.

Truth felt a strange sensation coiling in her belly, anticipation and fear. The last cache would finally be delivered into her hands, and she would be able to claim the prize fund. Pay the smugglers, buy another kidney, escape.

Unless this creature betrayed her.

What if they used the Welsh cache to complete the game themselves? What if they stole the prize from her, humiliating her, causing her to fall without a shred of dignity remaining? It would all be for nothing, nothing at all.

She had to protect herself. She had to protect her reputation, as a daughter. If the cache was being solved tonight, she knew exactly where her enemy would be. She would have all she needed to ensure her future, out from under her mother's withering stare – a success, at last.

She might have needed help to reach the finish line, but she would be the one to cross it. There were no middle men, no one brokering her fate and her mother's. Only her, standing alone, sword in hand. Ready.

She would wait and watch, and then she would act. She had done it before, after all. What was one more fallen? She had already paved her road to hell.

Truth had trusted in fate before, to her peril. This time, she would leave nothing to chance.

Chapter 48

Step one

The first step was always the hardest.

When she'd taken that first lurch out into fresh air, she'd been fuelled by desperation. Jason, on the verge of losing his life to a madman, had proven to be sufficient motivation to risk her heart beating out of her chest.

The second time round, she'd had no choice at all. Flee from her former sanctuary or take a bullet. The handful of benzodiazepines she'd swallowed had numbed the fear – for a little while. Adrenaline was a powerful drug, the best she'd tasted yet, and she'd leapt from a burning building while in its grip. Once she was pushed beyond the door, she'd found she could run.

But every time since, she'd chosen to cross the threshold. Not because someone's life was in danger, but because she wanted to be free. Free from fear, and good enough for Jason. Good enough to keep him close, to prove she was worth the investment of his time.

Tonight, she had to take that step once more. Except this step was a deliberate foray into danger. She could stay at home, stay safe, and screw the bloody painting. She could watch movies with Jason and eat ice cream and not take the chance that her heart would beat out of her chest, that her weaknesses would lead to their failure.

But Corelia was in hospital because of her. This was a mess of her own making and she had to be brave. She had to swallow down her medicine, her fear, and take the first step beyond.

'You okay?'

She laughed nervously, unable to articulate how far from okay she was. Jason had watched her swallow the tablets nervously, checking the dose before he even gave them to her, making sure she was on the level. That she wouldn't freak out, or pass out, or let him down. How little he knew about how badly she'd already let him down, and her barest of plans to save him.

She called the lift, clutching her tablet to her chest like a life preserver. Jason hovered beside her, like a shadow, and his warm hand settled on her shoulder. Silently there for her. Always there for her. What would she do when he wasn't?

She couldn't think on that now. She had to concentrate on tonight. Get in, find it, get out. All without getting arrested. How hard could it be?

The lift arrived and she stepped inside, the walls threatening to close in, but she held them at bay with the sheer force of her will. *I will not panic. I will not panic. I will not panic.*

The floor sank, silently conveying them to the ground floor, to the door. The archway into hell itself. She was voluntarily throwing herself unto the breach, going into battle with herself, with only one man at her side. The only man she would ever need – if only he could stay.

The lift door opened and Jason stepped past her to hold open the front door, like a gentleman does for a lady. As if she was worth that, as if she was something more than a little girl playing dress up, pretending to be a grown woman and hoping he would never notice how uncertain she was inside.

'After you,' he said.

She breathed in. Breathed out.

And stepped out into the world.

They waited outside the museum in the Micra, parked around the corner at the front of the Main Building of Cardiff University, where Jason had first spied Frieda.

Of course, now he knew that she'd wanted to be seen, had reeled him in to get to Amy. And he had let her, intrigued by her strange mixture of flattery and derision, playing hard to get so he would push harder.

What a fucking mess he'd made, thinking with his dick.

He'd fetched the Micra from outside Dylan's garage, not venturing inside, not ready to face his mate's questions about his trip with Frieda. He would've preferred to have the Harley, but Dylan might not have caught all of Frieda's damage and Amy would never consent to ride pillion. He had a hard enough time persuading her outdoors, let alone onto the back of a vintage motorcycle.

Her fingers drummed on her tablet case, a bass line that was vaguely familiar to him, her eyes darting from shadow to shadow through the windscreen.

'All right?' he asked, for what must be the hundredth time.

She nodded once, her neck so tense it looked like it might snap at the action.

'It's okay if you're not,' he added.

She took a deep breath and let it out with control. 'I want to be at home in my bed with a cup of tea.'

'As soon as we're done,' he promised.

His phone rang once and stopped.

'That's the signal.'

They exited the car, Amy taking a moment to get her legs under her. She was wrapped up in an old hoodie of her sister's, still not possessing a coat of her own that wasn't over ten years old. She'd resisted any attempt on his part to suggest she buy one, as if owning a coat meant she was now a person who went outside.

They rounded the back of the museum and ducked the barrier into the car park. Crossing the dark, empty space, they descended down to the loading bay for the museum.

Silhouetted in the doorway, a figure waited for them.

'The night guard is patrolling the ground floor. We don't have long.'

Talia held the door wide and beckoned them inside. They followed her up a back staircase and into a gallery, objects in shadow forming menacing shapes in the half-dark. She led them to the security office without a word, the door ajar.

Amy slipped past her and bent to insert a USB stick into the terminal that was connected to the rotating images on screen. A mess of code scrolled across the screen for a few moments, before a new screen showed the computer logging Amy in as an administrator. She brought up a code box and typed fast as lightning, swearing under her breath every time she had to backspace due to clumsy fingers.

Talia moved away from him and Jason caught her arm. 'Where are you—?'

'I've played my part,' she shrugged. 'Make sure you get her back.'

Jason held on to her, unsure whether he could truly trust her. But she misread him, leaning in to plant a soft kiss against his lips.

'Maybe in another life,' she said, and vanished into the dark.

Jason looked back to Amy, just in time to see her look away from his reflection in a blank monitor. Shit, she had seen.

'Amy—'

'I've replaced the feeds,' she said quickly. 'We have blank corridors for the next hour.'

'That was—'

'I'm tired and I want to go home. Let's get this over with.'

She removed the USB stick and uncovered her tablet, the live camera feeds now streaming directly to her.

'I'll be in the lab,' she said and made her way down the corridor alone.

He adjusted his Bluetooth headset to hear her breathing in his ear, anxious about letting her wander off on her own like that. But what could possibly happen to her in a deserted museum?

He made his way upstairs along the agreed route – the one with the most cameras, contrary to his instinct. But Amy needed to see him and she could warn him of any impending discovery.

Jason entered the main gallery from the back. But this time he walked away from the entrance to the adjacent gallery, where they had found Paul Roberts and what remained of 'The Blue Lady'.

Instead, he flashed the light from his phone onto a scuff mark on the floor, one that had yet to be cleaned away from the last time it had been made. From there, he angled the torch up and took in the beauty of *Venice at Dusk*, the spectre that had drawn Paul Roberts here night after night.

Of course he would choose his favourite painting for this most important of caches. And beholding it for the first time in the paint, Jason could understand the thrall of Monet's *San Giorgio Maggiore at Twilight*.

But he could not linger. Tearing his eyes away from the painting, Jason started his search.

Chapter 49

Outside looking in

They were here to learn their lesson, nothing more.

When Frieda had called him at midnight, Bryn had anticipated a gloating call – 'We've captured your friend and the evidence is ours entirely.' But instead, it seemed Frieda wanted him to witness the humiliation in person.

Together with Owain, he sat in the back of Matt's car and waited for events to unfold. Matt had looked uncomfortable at their presence, but he was clearly playing second fiddle to Frieda's bombastic tune. Bryn almost felt sorry for him.

Owain had said nothing the entire time, and the silence was worse than any harsh words exchanged between them. Bryn wanted to reach out, to comfort, but he knew that was far from his place now.

His phone rang in his pocket and he pulled it out, Indira's name on the screen.

'Hello?'

'I was looking at the trace analysis and I found something strange.'

'Indira, now isn't a good time.'

Matt glanced in the rear-view mirror and Owain looked up at the pathologist's name. Bryn fought the urge to turn his shoulder, give the illusion of privacy out of spite.

'Because you're outside the museum, waiting to catch Jason and Amy breaking and entering?'

Bryn glanced up at Matt's eyes in the mirror. 'How the hell do you know that?'

'You think you can keep a bust that big on the down-low in this station?'

Bryn conceded she had a point. 'Then you know it's out of my hands.'

'You think I'm gonna call *them*? Bryn, this is important. The paint we found on Leah's jumper is a match to *La Parisienne*.'

'I know. Frieda rubbed my face in it this morning.'

Matt coughed and shifted in the driver's seat. Bryn ignored him.

'Yeah, sorry about that. Can't get out of the habit of filing. Anyway, I thought that the killer might've trailed the paint through the museum, if the flakes showered when he cut it. So I checked the elimination samples and I found them.'

'Where?'

Bryn flicked the phone to speakerphone and held it between him and Owain, a peace offering of sorts. And if Matt heard, what would he do? They were already all for the guillotine, Indira included – what was one more crime?

'The fine art lab.'

Bryn deflated. 'Of course they'd be there. They've been working on the painting.'

'But not until after we took this sample. Of course, there could be a painting with similar composition that happened to shed a few flakes of pigment there. So I looked at the rest of the sample – and there's sand, Bryn. Beach sand in the lab.'

'I thought you said it was a contaminant?'

'I did, but—'

'How much sand?' Owain said, suddenly.

'Lots,' Indira said gleefully. 'Far, far more than was in the gallery, more than in any other location. I think whoever treaded that sand into the gallery spent hours, maybe days walking in that lab. Which means—'

'They worked there,' Bryn and Owain said as one.

'Bryn, how did Frieda know Jason and Amy were at the museum?' Indira prompted.

'I don't know,' Bryn said, confused at the sudden change in subject.

Matt turned in his seat. 'Turn it off. Hang up now.'

Owain grabbed at his sleeve. 'She'd need an inside source. One she's used before.'

The answer slid alarmingly into focus. 'Talia.'

Bryn watched Matt's face fall, making the slow connection that he couldn't trust his own agent, because her source was compromised. Now he knew how it felt, that betrayal lodged hard in the gut, festering like an infected wound.

'We need to tell Frieda,' Matt said.

'She won't listen,' Bryn said. 'She reckons she has this all sewn up, doesn't she?'

'Then what are we going to do?' Owain asked.

Owain's door suddenly flew open, the angry face of Cerys Carr looming from the darkness.

'Where is my brother?'

Bryn looked to Owain, who shrugged helplessly.

'We think he's inside,' Bryn said.

'That is confidential—' Matt started.

'Bryn,' Indira's voice piped up from the phone, 'if Talia tipped off Frieda, she must have concrete information. And the only way to know for certain would be if she was inside the museum.'

'You mean Jason and Amy are inside the museum with a murderer?'

'What?' Cerys' pale face flushed red with anger. 'We have to warn them!'

'We have no idea what's going on inside,' Bryn tried to reason. 'There's an armed response unit backing up the NCA on this.'

'Well, I'm not leaving him there!'

Before Bryn could protest, Cerys was running into the dark towards the museum.

'Cerys!' Owain bolted from the car and chased her down.

Bryn closed his eyes for a moment. He was getting too old for this.

'Don't even think about it,' Matt said.

But his eyes were panicked. No point in bluffing when you barely knew what cards were in your own hand, each one of them likely to turn on you at any moment.

'I'm not sorry,' Bryn said. He climbed out of the car, prepared to summon the last of his energy to run after the young lovers, loyalty both uniting and dividing them.

A hand gripped his arm.

'If you go in there, it's over. Your career, everything.' Matt's poker face was back in play, his expression earnest.

Bryn pulled his arm free. 'If I don't, I can't live with what that makes me. Can you?'

Matt said nothing, did nothing. His hand lifted to his radio – and then fell away.

Bryn turned and ran.

Chapter 50

En garde

Amy opened the door to the fine art lab and turned on the lights.

The room was dominated by the empty frame that formerly held 'The Blue Lady'. Amy couldn't resist a closer look, examining the fine layering of the oil paints first-hand. It was much more impressive in real life than through AEON's monitor, despite the fine resolution.

She sat down at the nearest desk and propped up the tablet. Jason had arrived in front of *San Giorgio Maggiore at Twilight*, which was indisputably the answer to Paul's riddle.

Once she'd realised the larger poems were the key, the Italian word for saint had leapt out at her, and the turning of day to night, of course, referred to the dusk setting of the work. Child's play. She would have to tell Corelia—

Except she wouldn't be telling Corelia much of anything until she was out of hospital, her condition in the nebulous 'stable' range, which ranged from climbing the walls to merely breathing. And, once she was out, what could she say to her? 'Sorry' didn't seem sufficient for a dagger in the back.

The corridors were clear on the approach to the galleries, the night guard clearly patrolling elsewhere. Amy was uneasy about Talia leaving but she preferred that to her flirting with Jason right in front of her. What was with that man? He attracted both women and danger with equally disastrous consequences.

With the corridors empty of threats for now, Amy turned her attention to the rest of the laboratory. Three distinct workstations were marked out, the one she'd claimed belonging to someone of East Asian descent. The small trinkets on the desk were definitely Asian in style, and an empty scabbard decorated the wall above the workspace. However, it didn't look like a katana in shape and Amy itched to Google ancient warrior swords.

At the back of the room a large rectangular crate stretched along the work desk. It was marked up for courier collection but several days earlier. Amy frowned and picked a hammer up from where it was protruding from under a cloth on the work surface, prying open the nailed-down top.

A few flakes of rust fell from the hammer onto her hand and she wiped them on her jeans as she peered inside. A large cylinder took up most of the space, cushioned with bubble wrap at the edges, and with a thin semi-transparent paper over the surface. Amy folded back the edge.

The lilacs, greens and blues were instantly recognisable to her, and the deepest, purest blue caressed her fingertips. Amy released it in shock, stepping back.

'The Blue Lady' was lying in a box inside the museum.

Amy stared at her fingers and the hammer on the workbench. The flakes weren't rust, but dried blood and bone. She was holding the murder weapon. Paul Roberts had been killed by someone who worked in this laboratory.

Something cold pricked against the back of her neck, parting her hair to touch metal to skin.

'Do not move. Or I will kill you where you stand.'

It took less than a minute for him to find it.

The chip was barely visible, a small black raised square on the bottom left corner of the frame. Jason had no idea how Paul had stuck it on there without activating the alarm, or maybe he had just let it blare out, knowing he could switch it off in a few minutes.

Jason scanned the chip, the alphanumeric code appearing on his phone. Mission accomplished.

'Amy? I've got the code.'

But something was wrong. He could no longer hear Amy's faint breathing over the line, the connection between them completely silent. He checked his phone, but the call was still connected.

'Amy?'

'She's here.'

He turned and his whole body seized in horror.

Amy was standing in the gallery with a sword across her throat.

The person behind her was pressed close, holding the blade against Amy's skin, dressed in the all-black outfit that the killer had worn when he'd stolen 'The Blue Lady'.

'Let her go,' he heard his voice say, surprisingly steady.

'Give me the code.'

It was a woman's voice, he realised, and one he recognised. He racked his brains for where he had heard it before. What was that accent?

'Let Amy go and I'll hand it over,' Jason insisted.

Amy cried out as the sword bit into her skin, a thin trickle of blood running over her pale skin.

'No!'

Jason stepped forward, but the killer stepped back, dragging Amy with her and pressing the sword in close once more. He held up his hands, terrified by what could happen next.

'She's bleeding. You have to stop the bleeding.'

'The code. You must give it to me. I have to be first!'

Jason struggled for some composure, 'Is it worth it? Is it worth killing over a game?'

'This is not a game!' the woman cried out, her brown eyes wide beyond the mask. 'It is life and death!'

'Tell us,' Jason persisted. 'We … we can help.'

'You can't,' she said, her voice choked with emotion. 'I asked for help once. Never again.'

It was then that Jason recognised her, the tear-filled words stirring his memory.

'Soo-jin?'

The killer tensed, pulling Amy into her. 'You … you know!'

Jason took a step closer, his hands still raised.

'I know you don't want to kill her,' he said, trying to keep his voice level. 'I saw how upset you were, after Paul died. I'll give you the code, but you have to give me Amy.'

'Is that a fair trade – a life for a life? My mother for your girlfriend?'

Jason didn't think now was the time to argue semantics, seizing on the nugget she'd given him. 'The money's for your mother?'

The mask crumpled as the face beneath contorted in misery. 'She needs a kidney.'

The image flashed before him, the memory as vivid as the real thing.

'The kidney … it was for your mother. You were going to trade with the gangs.'

'She promised they would take it!' Soo-jin screamed, choking Amy with the flat of the blade. 'She promised me my mother would not die!'

'She?' Jason seized on that. 'Who is "she"?'

'The one willing to obtain this painting at any price. Where is it, Soo-jin?' Talia Yeltsova stepped into the light, an antique crossbow in her hand.

Soo-jin wheeled, her blade flashing as she moved, bringing the sword up to face off against Talia.

Amy staggered, her frantic eyes meeting Jason's as she clutched at her neck. Her lips formed one word though there was no sound: *Jason.*

The first trickle of blood flowed over her fingers and she collapsed to the gallery floor.

Chapter 51

The price too high

The gallery floor was cold beneath her chest, her forehead grateful for the cool marble.

But the respite was not for long, her body turned and dragged up into warm arms.

'Amy? Open your eyes!'

She hadn't realised they were shut, but she obeyed anyway, Jason's face clouded with worry and an edge of panic.

He pulled at her hands and she let go of her neck, feeling warm liquid turning sticky on her skin.

'It's not deep,' he said, relief infusing the words. 'You'll live.'

He shrugged off his T-shirt and pressed it over the wound, the hairs on his bare arms rising in the chill of the midnight gallery. It was only the two of them, for those few seconds, before the scrape of metal against metal intruded.

'I have killed! I will kill again!'

'Attacked a man from behind? Stabbed an innocent teenager?' Talia's tone was mocking, taunting. 'Did you get a taste for killing, after the first time?'

'She saw me! She was here, asking about the painting. She had to go. Like you will go.'

'If you wanted to kill me, you would've done it days ago. Instead of sending me little notes in the post. Did you think that would frighten me?'

Amy pushed herself up, grounding her hand on Jason's thigh, as she watched the two women circling each other.

'I did what you asked, and still my mother lies dying. And now you come here, to ruin my last chance.'

Talia laughed. 'Do you think the police will let you walk out of here and collect your money? They are watching your stupid little game. They will know that the winner is the killer and you will rot in prison, as your mother dies.'

'I will not fail!'

Soo-jin lunged, striking the sword against the crossbow's body and causing sparks to fly. Talia jumped away, circling her once more, her eyes cold and pitying.

'You have already failed. I wanted you to scout around the painting, not cut it. You couldn't even get that right. You still think you can trade? Those men would eat you alive without me. Give me the painting, Soo-jin.'

'I tried your way!' Soo-jin shouted. 'They never came for the painting and there is no kidney. You lied!'

'Ask him why your mother has no kidney.'

Talia's gaze landed on Jason, and Amy felt his body tense behind her.

Soo-jin looked, her anger diverted momentarily.

Talia aimed the crossbow at her back.

'NO!'

A large vase crashed down over Talia's head, fragments of ancient pottery showering the gallery floor. Her eyes rolled back into her head and she slid to the floor, Cerys standing over her.

But the disturbance did not distract Soo-jin, who barrelled forward as if she'd been fired from a cannon, sword outstretched as she lunged towards Jason.

Amy raised her hands to deflect the blow, but Jason shielded her with his body, a flash of metal in his hand.

The short knife lodged in Soo-jin's arm, her hand opening reflexively and dropping the sword with a clatter. Bryn and Owain appeared behind Soo-jin, grabbing hold of her and placing her in handcuffs.

'She lied, she lied … *omoni*, she lied…' the girl moaned, sinking down to the floor.

Jason twisted, Soo-jin forgotten as he reached down to Amy.

'Are you all right? Are you hurt?'

Amy laughed, then winced as the movement aggravated her neck.

'Apart from that,' Jason corrected.

Cerys crossed the room before she could answer, giving them a quick once-over before nodding her satisfaction that neither of them were dying.

'How did you know we were here?' Jason asked.

'Owain texted me,' Cerys said. 'Frieda brought them here. For you.'

It was now or never, Amy realised, her stomach sinking through the floor. The pain in her neck paled in comparison to that of her heart.

'Cerys,' she said, trying to hide the tremble. 'I need your help.'

Jason never wanted to let Amy go, despite the fact she was a deranged moron with a death wish. Who tried to grab a sword with their bare hands?

Bryn was reading Soo-jin her rights as Owain tentatively approached the unconscious Talia with another set of handcuffs. Jason held his T-shirt against Amy's neck. The blood hadn't soaked through the material, so she was probably going to be okay. She had better be okay, or Soo-jin would meet with more than trouble when she got to prison.

He wanted to get Amy to A&E and then take her home for a cup of tea and as many biscuits as she could eat. And then they were going to sit down and he would tell her that she wasn't to put herself in danger again, because he couldn't bear to lose her. Because he hadn't been just sleep-deprived as he got off the train from Glasgow, and he hadn't been wrong.

Because she was everything that mattered to him, and she needed to hear it.

But when Amy asked Cerys for help, his heart stopped. Something was wrong. Something was very, very wrong.

'What did she do to you?'

Amy ignored him and spoke directly to Cerys. 'I'm making this right. I can make a distraction but you have to get him out.'

She was talking about him, he realised numbly. Amy was talking about him getting out, while she … what? Threw herself to the wolves?

'Whatever the fuck is going on, I want to know about it.'

Amy stood up, out of his embrace, leaning on Cerys' shoulder. She looked fragile, empty, as if the world around her was falling into the sea.

'This is for you.'

She didn't meet his eyes as she handed him the plain brown envelope from inside her hoodie. But he wouldn't look at it, not until she stopped this shit.

'Amy, what is going on?'

'They're going to arrest me,' she said, as if she were describing the weather. 'And if you walk out that door, they will arrest you too. I'm not letting that happen.'

Jason wanted to throw the envelope in her face, rant and shout and scream that he would never abandon her, that he would go to prison again if it meant staying with her just a few moments longer.

But he said nothing, the resolution clear in her beautiful eyes. He was suddenly certain that she would lie, beg and steal to keep him out of prison, to keep him safe. And that to go against her careful preparations for his safety would actually be the biggest betrayal of all.

He looked down into the envelope, crisp notes and the maroon edge of a passport inside, wrapped in a thin strip of ripped paper.

'You have to get to her before they do,' Amy was saying, trying to capture his gaze. 'Do you understand me?'

'I don't want to do this,' he said.

'I know. But someone needs to visit me in jail.'

A sound rose in his throat, half-laugh half-choke, and before he knew it, Amy had surged forward and pressed a dry kiss to his cheek.

'Good luck,' she said and moved away, reaching for Soo-jin's discarded sword and running out of the gallery.

He changed his mind in an instant, moving to follow, but Cerys hauled him back.

'Don't let this be for nothing,' she said, shaking him. 'Let her go and live your new life. You're no use to her in jail for the next ten years.'

Jason did not resist, as his sister led him away, his eyes stinging at his traitor's heart dying in his chest. *Goodbye.*

Chapter 52

Armed and dangerous

She ran as fast as her legs could carry her because if she stopped for even a moment, she feared she would retreat and fall into Jason's arms.

Amy hesitated in the museum's main hall, the bloodstained sword in her hand. She could've run away with him, but she would always be looking over her shoulder. If Jason escaped without her, she didn't think Frieda would pursue him, not so hard and swift that he could not outrun their meagre resources.

She would not let Jason go back to prison. She would do anything to keep him free from harm.

Amy pushed open the front door of the museum, alarms blaring behind her, and she ran down the steps with the sword outstretched.

Suddenly, the air was thick with voices, dark figures shining high-powered torches at her, blinding her, the beams reflecting off the metal of their guns.

'Police! Drop it!'

'Drop the weapon!'

'Lay down on the ground. On the ground!'

The chorus was deafening, a cacophony of sound and light. She felt dizzy and frozen, unable to move or speak in the spotlight and the storm of shouts.

But she had to stall them. She had to kill time for Jason to escape. She had no hostages to provoke a negotiation – except one.

Amy held the sword to her own neck.

The shouts died away, the men shifting uncomfortably, their guns suddenly uneasy in their hands. Her eyes grew accustomed to the glare and she made out nine figures, arranged in a rough semicircle about one or two metres away from her.

Beyond them, the shapes of several cars lurked at the bottom of the steps, a huddle of people blocking their headlights.

'I want … I want to speak to Frieda Haas. Only her.'

One of the men reached for his radio and relayed the stark information. And then they all waited in the cold September night, Amy shivering despite her hoodie. The sword blade irritated her wound through the T-shirt glued to her neck with her blood, throbbing in time to her slow, steady heartbeat.

For once, she wasn't anxious. She was outside and she was surrounded by men with guns but the worst had already happened. She had lost Jason.

Or she had lost so much blood that her veins were now mostly full of diazepam and her heart couldn't beat faster if it tried.

After a few long minutes, Frieda came up the steps, flanked by a man in a suit that Amy vaguely recognised from the footage on the night Jason had handed over a kidney. A kidney meant for Soo-jin's mother.

'Stop this, Miss Lane,' Frieda said, as if she were scolding a schoolgirl. 'You can't hope to gain anything by this.'

'Gain?' Anger rose in her, surprising her with the strength of feeling that could still be torn from her chest. 'You've taken everything from me! You've as good as killed me!'

Suddenly, the sword at her throat felt powerful, like more than just a distraction. Like a choice. Amy closed her eyes and, for a moment, it seemed like the only way to quell the anger, the hole in her chest.

But when she closed her eyes, she saw Jason. Jason's warm, patient eyes. It was enough. For now, it was enough.

She opened her eyes again, to see a crack in Frieda's façade. Amy was pleased to see she looked strained, off-kilter. This night had veered so far away from her plans that if she wasn't delirious with pain, Amy would laugh in the icy bitch's face.

The man stepped forward – Matt, was it? He looked appropriately concerned, empathetic towards the trembling woman holding a sword to her neck on the marble steps of a museum.

'Miss Lane – Amy – we need to get you back to the police station, sort this out. Is there someone we can call for you?'

A burst of hysterical laughter bubbled up in her chest. 'Who? I've lost all my friends because of you. And you know my family. What they've done.'

They didn't know what to do, she could see that. They wanted to lock her away somewhere where they wouldn't have to look at her, deal with her. They wanted this to be someone else's problem.

'I solved the case, by the way,' she said, for something to say, for time to drain away, for the sword to look less like an option. 'It was Soo-jin who killed Paul, stabbed Corelia – Leah – but it was Talia who goaded her on. She orchestrated the whole thing. Were you in on it too?'

The way Frieda flinched was satisfying, in its way, and Amy had precious little to amuse her right now. She swayed a little on her feet, saw the guns flicker as if they thought she was about to eviscerate one or more of them. She would be filled with a hundred rounds before she gave them a scratch. She could think of worse ways to die.

'You're bleeding. You need a doctor.'

The way Frieda said the words, Amy could tell she had a very specific doctor in mind and not one who would offer a few stitches and a bandage. A psychiatrist. She shuddered at the thought, a hundred bad memories flooding forward all at once, the panic rising in her chest once more.

She was very far from fucking calm now.

Her heart leapt in her chest, proving it could still race like the wind. But her body had been through too much, had lost too much blood, was running only on benzos and coffee from hours before, and she collapsed as suddenly as a winter sunset.

As the back of her head thudded against the steps, she was suddenly, swiftly grateful that she hadn't been shot. That she still had a chance to fix this.

'She needs an ambulance. Get a blanket and some tea.'

As darkness swept over her eyes, Amy wanted to cry, to laugh. Maybe a cup of tea really could solve everything, but could it put Amy Lane back together again?

Chapter 53

End of an AEON

Every step he took away from the museum felt like another stone in his pocket, weighing him down until he was forced to sink to his knees in defeat.

But Cerys didn't have time for that. She'd snatched the Micra keys from him and driven them away just as a riot of sound and light came from round the corner of the museum.

'That's Amy,' he said distantly.

'That's a distraction,' Cerys countered.

Jason wasn't sure if she meant to enable them to get away or to distract him from his task of running as far away as he possibly could.

As she drove up North Road, away from the city centre and back towards Amy's house – their house – he looked inside the envelope again. He counted £1,500 in assorted notes and an additional €500, because Amy clearly thought running away involved the Channel Tunnel. The passport and driving licence were in the name Bradley Thompson, with an address somewhere in Newport that could feasibly fit his accent. The photograph had been lifted from an arrest mugshot from his late teens, when he had a little more muscle and a lot more hair.

The strip of paper wound around the cash and passport had a long code of numbers and letters, which were completely meaningless to him.

'What is it?' Cerys asked, leaning over his shoulder when she was meant to be looking at the road.

'I don't know,' he said.

But then Amy's parting words returned to him. He had to deal with AEON.

He realised almost too late that Cerys wasn't driving him to their house.

'Where are you taking me?'

'Airport,' she said. 'You have a passport, don't you?'

'I need to go home first.'

'Are you insane? There'll be cops all over that place!'

'I have to do something. It'll only take a minute.'

Thankfully, the street was deserted, all the cops in Cardiff attending Frieda's party at Park Place, with Amy the guest of honour. Thinking about her hurt, so Jason tried to stop, but that only made it worse. She couldn't be surgically amputated – it would be like losing a limb.

Jason considered a clandestine route, breaking in through Amy's grandmother's old house or hopping the back gate. In the end, he decided that time was more important than stealth, entering through the front door and straight into the elevator.

He shook AEON awake with minimal fuss and entered the long code where it asked for a password. However, instead of logging him in, a black box with white writing appeared in the centre of the screen:

CONFIRM SELF-DESTRUCT? Y/N

Jason hesitated, his hand hovering over the keyboard. Erasing AEON, wiping the server that housed her identity, was like killing a part of Amy. Yet leaving it here would sign Amy's life away, damning her with the evidence housed within AEON's dark spaces.

In the distance, he heard sirens. He had no idea if they were coming for him, if this was the end, but he had to make a decision. He couldn't let Amy's battle charge be in vain.

He hit Y.

AEON didn't start a countdown, no possibility of reprieve. Just a long empty bar that slowly filled with white. Jason couldn't wait for the final flatline, switching off the monitor and walking away. He stopped only to drop his phone on the sofa, leaving behind anything traceable.

They would live to fight another day. But right now, Jason would give anything to see Amy at home, with him, cup of tea in hand. But there was no tea and no happy endings.

Jason closed the front door and walked out to the car, the rain falling on his bare head like a baptism.

Amy woke in A&E, handcuffed to the gurney like a five-star criminal who might bolt at any moment.

She had drips in both arms, one clear and one red with rich blood, effectively pinning her down even without the cuffs. Not that she was sure she could even stand up right now. And where would she run? She had nowhere to go, no safe spaces anymore.

In two days she would be twenty-six. She had hoped this year would be different, that she wouldn't have to spend another year alone in the dark. But wishes were horses, cantering off into the distance, out of her reach.

The lone cop at the end of her bed had fallen asleep, his head nodding with every snore, a wisp of cotton from his jacket fluttering with every breath. She envied his rest.

Beyond the hastily drawn curtain, she could hear voices, including a couple she recognised.

'Prints are a match to the Oxford millennium heist,' Matt said. 'Yeltsova is up to her eyes in this. She used that poor girl's desperation to steal a priceless painting. Aiding and abetting doesn't even cover it.'

One small victory. Bryn had been right, and Frieda would not escape with her reputation unsullied. If Amy was going down, she was taking the NCA agent with her. Of course, she would rather remain vaguely afloat, treading water until the storm passed. If that was an option, even if it meant Frieda walking away without a blemish, she would be okay with that. Anything to bring her closer to going home.

Unseen, Frieda's voice was clipped and taut. 'We can deal with her later. Search it again. He must be inside.'

Amy grimaced, the action pulling at her face muscles and stiffening the bandage around her neck. They'd given her painkillers, she realised, dark liquid joy that numbed the pain from her wound. But not yet her heart.

Jason was gone. Far, far away from Frieda's clutches.

'We have all units on the museum, except for the retrieval unit.'

'Concentrate on the server. We need it in custody to compile the charges.'

Her supposition had been correct – Frieda had enough for a warrant, more than enough to hang her for Corelia's misadventure, but didn't have everything to condemn her for the bank robbery. Amy had a chance, a slim chance, but a chance nonetheless that she might escape jail time. That she could call Jason home and they could be partners again.

Equal partners this time, as they should've been from the beginning. An understanding that they needed each other, like breathing.

Maybe she'd had a few too many painkillers. Or maybe the truth hurt and they had merely numbed it, allowed her to taste it.

A nerve-jangling ringtone, all discordant strings and too much bass, carried through the curtain and was cut off mid-screech.

'Hello? What do you mean it's silent? Maybe it's hibernating or something. Find the on switch!'

They were in her house now. Looking for the key to unlock AEON, her server. But if Jason had understood her message, if he'd performed one last task for her before slipping off into the night…

'What the fuck do you mean it won't work?'

And Amy smiled, a leisurely smile that brought a corresponding leap to her heart. Jason had killed AEON and now he was gone. Waiting for her to get better, get stronger, start again.

They would start again. As long as Jason was out there, dodging the cops and keeping out of trouble, she could get through this. She could get them both through this.

The curtain was pulled aside, the copper starting to his feet and Amy clutching at the bedclothes. But it was not Frieda or any other officer who greeted her, but a tall East Asian doctor wearing a peculiar three-piece suit. Unusual attire for A&E at three in the morning.

'You're the shrink,' she said, and he made a self-deprecating gesture.

'You can call me Doctor Chin,' he said and sat down across from her.

She could lie, of course, tell him everything was fine, she was fine, nothing to see here, move along. But part of her was sick of hiding, cowering in the dark, afraid of her own shadow as soon as she stepped beyond the door.

She wanted to be better. If they were all getting a second chance, she wanted to do this right. She wanted there to be something other than a wreck for Jason to come home to.

'Do you need anything before I ask you a few questions?'

Amy let out a breath, flattening her faintly trembling palms on the bed. It would be all right. *Time to confess, Amy Lane.*

'Cup of tea would be nice.'

About the author

Rosie Claverton is a screenwriter and novelist. She grew up in Devon, daughter to a Sri Lankan father and a Norfolk mother, surrounded by folk mythology and surly sheep. She moved to Cardiff to study medicine and adopted Wales as her home, where she lives with her journalist husband and pet hedgehog.

Also by Crime Scene Books

Inspector Truchaud series by R.M. Cartmel:

The Richebourg Affair (2014)
The Charlemagne Connection (2015)
The Romanée Vintage (2016)

'A well-crafted treasure of unforgettable characters.' **Jeffrey Siger**

'A very complex mystery with lots of different elements. R.M. Cartmel was born to write.' **Sharon Powell**

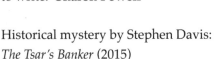

Historical mystery by Stephen Davis:

The Tsar's Banker (2015)

'A thrilling novel painted in glorious period and geographic detail with the real life conspiracy theory of Dan Brown and the glamour of Ian Fleming at his best. It compels you to turn the pages to find out how Philip Cummings and the British Empire are embroiled in the destiny of Tsarist Russia. I loved it.' **Caspar Berry – Poker Advisor on Casino Royale**

Thriller by Michael Cayzer:

50 Miles from Anywhere (2015)

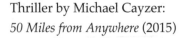

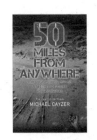

'Michael Cayzer doesn't shy away from a truth that is sometimes unpalatable, but he still managed to show that even in the most awful of circumstances there remains a relative good side to people.' **Candy Jeffries**